The Mislaid Magician

or

TEN YEARS AFTER

Patricia C. Wrede
and Caroline Stevermer

The Mislaid

BEING THE PRIVATE
CORRESPONDENCE BETWEEN
TWO PROMINENT FAMILIES
REGARDING A SCANDAL
TOUCHING THE HIGHEST LEVELS
OF GOVERNMENT AND THE
SECURITY OF THE REALM

Magician

or

Ten Years After

Harcourt, Inc.

Orlando   Austin   New York   San Diego   Toronto   London

www.HarcourtBooks.com

Library of Congress Cataloging-in-Publication Data
Wrede, Patricia C., 1953–
The mislaid magician or ten years after: being the private correspondence
between two prominent families regarding a scandal touching the highest levels
of government and the security of the realm/Patricia C. Wrede and
Caroline Stevermer.
p.   cm.
Summary: In 1828, English cousins Cecelia and Kate and their husbands
search for a missing German railway engineer and with the help of their
wizardry skills, uncover a plot that could endanger the unity of England.
[1. Supernatural—Fiction.   2. Letters—Fiction.   3. Europe—Social life
and customs—19th century—Fiction.]   I. Title: Mislaid magician.
II. Title: Ten years after.   III. Stevermer, Caroline.   IV. Title.
PZ7.W915Mis   2006
[Fic]—dc22   2005036011
ISBN-13: 978-0-15-205548-6   ISBN-10: 0-15-205548-7

Text set in Simoncini Garamond
Designed by Lydia D'moch

First edition
A C E G H F D B

Printed in the United States of America

The
Mislaid
Magician

~

or

TEN YEARS AFTER

February

24 FEBRUARY 1828
TANGLEFORD HALL, KENT

Dearest Kate,

It was splendid to see you and Thomas and your boys again this fortnight past. (And I still think that Baby Laurence is the image of his papa, even if he is still quite bald. In deference to Thomas's feelings, however, I shall not mention the resemblance again until little Laurence is old enough to have grown some hair.) My only regret is that we could not stay longer at Skeynes. You have turned it into such a comfortable home that I do not wonder at your reluctance to go up to London, though I do hope James and I can coax you all to visit Tangleford next summer, so that we may return your hospitality.

Two weeks was hardly enough time to catch up on all your doings of the past few months. I know James was as sorry to leave as I, and as for the children—well, you saw how Baby Alexander cried when we left, and Diana and the twins all sulked for two days straight. (I had expected it of

Diana, who is only four, after all, but I had hoped that at the age of nine, the twins would have grown out of such tricks. Apparently it takes longer than that.)

Speaking of the twins, I am afraid Arthur has confessed that he and Eleanor sneaked into Thomas's study on the last day of our visit. Eleanor has been suffering from a trifling ailment since we left—no more than a bad cold, but Arthur was convinced that it must be the result of some dreadful magical protection they had triggered, and so he poured out the whole story to James and me the night after we arrived home. I do not know where he can have come by such a notion, but he was so earnest in his concern that both James and I had difficulty in keeping a sober expression. I promise you that we did so, however, as neither of us wishes to encourage him to undertake any similar adventures in the future. Poking about in a wizard's study is serious business.

The reason I mention it is that Thomas may need to readjust his warding spells. (I am still not entirely sure how Arthur got past them; please do let me know, if you should discover it.) And I wish you would advise me whether Thomas maintains a continuous scrying spell on the gazing ball in his study. Arthur claims to have seen things in it, and if he is neither making up tales nor using an existing spell, I may need to find him a magic tutor who can oversee more advanced work than his present teacher.

James is going up to London to consult with the Duke of Wellington. (I suppose I ought now to say with the prime minister, but I am not yet accustomed to thinking of him so.)

Though I am not sure what the duke has in mind this time, I am quite pleased for him by this turn of events. James becomes bored and most unhappy when he does not have enough to do, which is a habit I am sure he picked up on the Peninsula when he was aide-de-camp to Lord Wellington. And whatever the duke needs, I doubt it will be boring!

At first, I had hoped to go to London along with James, but both Baby Alexander and Diana show signs of coming down with Eleanor's cold, and I really cannot leave Nurse to manage them all alone, most especially if Arthur is going to remain in good health. For he is sure to get into some scrape while her back is turned, and she has a decided partiality for him that sometimes persuades her to be less firm with him than she ought.

Indeed, I am feeling nearly as sulky as the children, for I had been looking forward to seeing Aunt Elizabeth and Mr. Wrexton again. What with Mr. Wrexton's work at the Royal College of Wizards, they are so firmly settled in London now that it is nearly impossible to induce them to visit outside the city. (I *cannot* bring myself to call Mr. Wrexton "Uncle Michael," though he and Aunt Elizabeth have been married these ten years. I suppose I have never quite got out of the habit of thinking of him as my magic tutor.) I especially wanted Mr. Wrexton's opinion of the discursive-chain cantrips Thomas and I had that disagreement about.

I had also hoped to order a few gowns in advance of the Season, and to review the redecorating of our town house (for you know that now the duke is become prime minister, we shall have all kinds of distinguished persons visiting, so it is most important that everything be properly done).

Now it must all be left to the last minute, for James is quite hopeless at such things. I daresay he would not notice even if the drapers put crimson drapes in the blue salon. It is most provoking, and of course I cannot complain of it to James. So I write to you instead.

Love,
Cecy

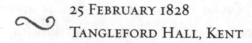

25 FEBRUARY 1828
TANGLEFORD HALL, KENT

My dear Thomas,

The eldest of my young hellions has confessed to sneaking into your study near the end of our visit. The offense has already met with suitable punishment, but I trust you will let me know of any damage or disruption that he has not seen fit to mention. He has not provided any reason for the excursion other than a desire "to see a real wizard's study." Sometimes I think he takes after my dear Cecelia a little too much.

I am off to London as soon as may be. Wellington's summons was waiting for me when we arrived home. I am not yet entirely sure what the business is about, which will tell you a good deal right there. Unless he has good reason, Old Hookey has always been clear about his orders; I infer that the matter is serious. I need not tell you to be discreet.

Cecelia stays here with the children. I shall write when I know more, and tell you what I can.

Yours,
James

$\backsim$ 27 FEBRUARY 1828
SKEYNES

Dear Cecy,

I do hope full health has been restored to the Tarleton household by the time you read this. To be honest, it is but a faint hope, for things here at Skeynes are just as disease-ridden, all sniffles and coughing, hot bricks and red flannel. Nothing serious, thank God. This, too, shall pass, and you'll have your chance at London before you know it. It will be lovely to see the Wrextons again. I agree that it would be vastly preferable to have a bit of extra time with the dress-makers and the drapers for once, but I'm sure that you will work your customary wiles upon them, and that no one would ever suspect you accomplished so much in so very little time.

The same mail coach that brought your letter has brought us another visitor: Georgy! She arrived with only one maid, can you believe it? and we had not a word of warning she intended to come. Hardly the distinguished behavior one looks for from Her Grace, the Duchess of Waltham, you'll agree. "More to this than meets the eye," says Thomas darkly, "so I'll leave you to get to the bottom of it," and off he gallops to Waycross. Thomas claims he needs to see if the damage from the flooding is as bad as the man of affairs there says it is. Provoking man! He knows I know floods are a matter of utter indifference to him (until they intersect with his comfort, that is), so why not just stay here while I get on with interrogating Georgy? One might have wondered if there were a warrant out for his arrest, he set off with such speed. Anyone would think that a journey to Waycross in this weather was a high treat.

Come to think of it, given the sniffles and the coughing, it might have been a bit of a relief to the poor man to get away from the sound of sick babies crying. Not that he's subjected to much of that, thanks to blessed Nurse Carstairs. Without her, Cecy, I shudder to think what life would be like. Something akin to that big painting at the Royal Academy, you remember the one, with Thomas in a long white beard as Ossian, and the children and me as his faithful followers, huddled at his feet, wearing nothing but plaid blankets. Laurence would do very well swaddled in a plaid blanket, but I shudder to think how dirty Edward's feet would get. They are quite dirty enough now, with half the staff reminding him to put his shoes back on.

Enough of that. I can't tell you anything about sick babies you don't know from experience. All this vaporing is by way of explanation of why I haven't yet told Thomas about the incident of Arthur and Eleanor and Thomas's study. He was off before I'd even opened your letter. When he comes home, I will be sure to tell him.

I cannot help but admire the persistence the children showed, for that door is not often unlocked. You know your children best, of course, but I would not wonder if we learned that Arthur made the enterprise sound as if it were all his idea in order to protect his dear sister. Eleanor, when in health, seems far more likely to have had the idea originally. If I have heard her ask Thomas once to show her a spell please, I am sure I have heard her ask him a hundred times. She asks very nicely, of course, and there is no question that Thomas is the softest touch going when it comes to indulging a small girl's taste for such amusements. I don't fault her in the least for her interest. I merely point out that Arthur may have had a bit of help in entering the study.

From the piercing cries that just began to emanate from the nursery, I should judge that someone has spilt boiling water on a lion, or Edward has frightened one of the maids, or Laurence has awakened from his nap. The only thing that rules out the possibility of all three is the happy circumstance that we do not own a lion. My appearance on the scene will only intensify the din, but if I don't demonstrate a proper degree of concern, Edward will keep finding ingenious new ways of frightening the maids, and that will never do.

So I leave you, Cecy, precisely as you last saw me, halfway to distraction, but still your devoted,

Kate

March

Dearest Kate,

Georgy arrived on a mail coach? With only one maid? Of all the utter goosecaps! Depend upon it, the news will be all over the Ton within a week, and all the gossips will be saying that she has run away from her husband. (I don't suppose that *is* what she has done? If she has, it would be the first piece of good sense she's shown in years—and coming straight to you would be the second. The gossips cannot make a mysterious elopement out of it if Georgy is known to be staying with her sister, after all.)

I hope she does not keep you guessing as to her purposes for too long. The Season will be starting soon, and once it does, her behavior is certain to be the primary topic of conversation. Fortunately, it will probably not be long before some new scandal arises, but in the meantime, I should like to be prepared with whatever story the pair of you decide to set about. Or, more likely, with whatever story you and I decide to set about, as Georgy is seldom of any help in such matters. It is *just* like Thomas to abscond at such a moment.

As regards Thomas's study, I am quite certain that Eleanor was up to her pigtails in the matter, right along with Arthur, but even I would not venture to guess which of them was more responsible to begin with. Had I been able to interrogate them both immediately after Arthur's revelation, I might perhaps have discovered more, but Eleanor was too ill at the time, and now it is much too late. Arthur may take after me (as James often asserts), but I think Eleanor is more like you (which may have something to do with Thomas's susceptibility to her wiles)—at least as regards concocting plausible tales.

On rereading my letter, I see that it sounds rather snappish. Do believe that I am not out-of-reason cross with Georgy; she has always been a pea-goose, and I suppose she always will be. I am simply out of sorts this morning. James has been gone since Monday; the children are all absolutely *full* of colds (except for Arthur) and running Nurse ragged; and Arthur has been running *me* ragged.

I expect I had best tell you the whole, but you are *not* to worry. Last night, I was sitting up rather late over my books (what with the children's illnesses, it was the first opportunity I had had to look over the copy of Gregorius's *Arcana* that Thomas so kindly loaned me). It was well past eleven when there was a soft rap on the study door, and a moment later, Arthur slipped in.

I was at first inclined to read him a lecture, for though I do not keep so complex a magical laboratory as Thomas's, I try not to neglect my Arts, and the children all know that they are not allowed to interrupt when James or I are in the study. But Arthur was plainly much agitated; his eyes were wide and he was as tense as one of the strings in your pianoforte.

"Mama," he said before I could speak, "I am very sorry, but there is somebody outside in the garden, and I think he is trying to get in."

"Is there indeed," I said. I marked my place and set the book aside, then rose in a leisurely fashion, for I have found that a show of great calm is very reassuring to agitated children. I was not nearly so sanguine as I appeared, however. Arthur is a *creative* child, but not generally an over*imaginative* one, and so I had every dependence on the accuracy of his statement. "You did very well to come to me first, instead of alarming the servants," I told him as I snuffed the candle. "Now, show me."

We went down the hallway and across to the back of the house. There is a small, oddly shaped room there that is used mainly for storage. The window bows out over the back of the house, and moonlight was streaming in. Arthur scrambled into the window seat and pointed.

At first, I did not see anything. Then the bushes below the scullery window shook, and wobbled, and the dark figure of a man emerged. All I could determine with certainty was that he was of medium height, for he wore a workman's cap and a jacket that seemed to be several sizes too large for him. He brushed himself off and started toward the next window.

I was not much concerned, for he must have tried several of the rear windows before he reached the scullery, and the wards were holding. I was therefore tolerably sure that he was no magician. I whispered to Arthur to be very quiet and not move, and then I cast the Greater Cessation. Fortunately, it is not a long spell, if one already has solid wards in place to use as a base.

Arthur was, surprisingly, a model of decorum. I finished the spell and looked down, expecting the prowler to be frozen in place. Instead, I saw him continue to move, though very slowly, as if someone had attached lead weights to his arms and legs. His head turned, and then he began to— well, *run* is not precisely the right word, as even Baby Alexander could have caught up with him easily. Still, it was clear that he was *trying* to run, and he did succeed in moving. And the farther away from the house he got, the faster he went.

I shook off my surprise and turned to Arthur, who was staring, wide-eyed. "Go and fetch Mr. Hennesy," I told him. He barely took time to nod before he bolted for the door.

Needless to say, I did not sleep for the rest of the night. First I set Hennesy and the footmen to scouring the grounds. Though I had very little hope that they would find anything, I thought that the evident activity would discourage any further attempts at intrusion.

Then I took Arthur around the house to review the wards with me. He is not, of course, advanced enough in his studies to cast the wards himself, and while I could certainly attune them to him (as they are already tuned to James and myself), I had no intention of doing so. But by the time I finished explaining matters to Hennesy, it had become quite clear that Arthur was far more thrilled than frightened, and that for the promise of a farthing two years' hence, he would have happily joined in the search. I wished to give his thoughts another direction, as I do not want to have to roust out the entire household again *tomorrow* night to look for Arthur.

So I impressed upon him the importance of the house warding spells, and told him that, as he is responsible for his sisters and Baby Alexander while James is in London, I would show him how to read them tomorrow. I am about to go fulfill my promise. He is quite far enough advanced to learn the simplest of the warding cantrips, and I hope that it will keep his mind safely occupied. I expect, however, that for the next several days, at least, I will be informed of every thin spot in the warding spell almost as soon as it develops.

Hennesy and his fellows found no trace of our prowler. As soon as I finish with Arthur, I intend to set a lesser ward about the grounds near the house—nothing strong enough to be noticeable, just a sort of alarm bell to let me know of any unanticipated visitors. It is all very well to say that I would have known immediately if he had somehow managed to get through the house wards, but I find that I would very much rather know of his presence *before* the house wards were breached.

The consensus in the lower hall is that the prowler was some itinerant hoping to steal food or perhaps a little money. This seems plausible, as anyone who knew Tangleford Hall would know that there is a magician in residence and would therefore have anticipated the house wards. The only flaw in this argument is the peculiar way in which the prowler evaded the holding spell I cast. I have not pointed this out to anyone; the servants are quite upset enough as it is.

Since I have not heard from James, I expect he will be home in another day, or perhaps two. He is very good about keeping me informed when he is away, but he is far more casual when he knows he will return soon. For once, I shall have news as interesting as his to tell him!

Your exhausted,
Cecy

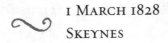

1 MARCH 1828
SKEYNES

Dear Cecy,

I hope this letter finds you and the children well. I congratulate you on having dealt exceedingly well with your prowler. Indeed, you have almost convinced me not to be alarmed on your behalf. But only almost! Do take care, Cecy!

Forgive me. I know you do.

Thomas is not yet home from his venture to Waycross.

Thus, I have yet to tell him of the intrusion into his study. Nor has Thomas yet seen the letter James wrote him, for it arrived in the post after he departed. I do hope it contains nothing of vital importance.

Thomas has also missed his mother's latest letter. Lady Sylvia is in her usual fine health and spirits, busy as ever providing good counsel to the league of her old friends—most recently, the proprietor of Ragueneau's pastry shop in the Rue St. Honoré.

Lady Sylvia helped Ragueneau rid his kitchens of a spell that soured the milk and turned butter rancid the moment it arrived in the place. Ragueneau had suspected a competitor of casting the spell to ruin his business, but no such thing. Ragueneau's son, Lady Sylvia discovered, had devised a spell to keep pastry cream from ever curdling. This spell, as so many seem to, had unexpected consequences. After a few false starts, Lady Sylvia was able to refine the pastry-cream spell to prevent any further ill effects. Even Ragueneau concedes the resulting pastries surpass all previous efforts. His gratitude to Lady Sylvia has been expressed in chocolate éclairs.

I am sorry to report I have made no progress at all in fathoming the mystery of Georgy's visit to us. For all her sudden professions of fondness for the simple country life, from the moment of her debut, she has been happiest in London. Of all times to choose to rusticate herself, the beginning of the London Season is about the least likely.

To think I used to fault Georgy for being a watering pot. I

would give a good deal for her to go off on one of her tearful flights just now, for when she cried, I could nearly always get her to tell me what was troubling her. These days, unless she is being disagreeable to the servants, she is as stoic as a soldier.

Georgy being Georgy, she is in her very best looks. Pale silence has always suited her best, I fear. The only time she smiles is when she is talking with Edward. Indeed, when she is talking with Edward there are moments when Georgy looks only a little more than six years old herself.

Perhaps I refine too much upon Georgy's abrupt arrival. Perhaps there is no mystery about it. Perhaps it is only that she had a whim to see Thomas and me, precisely as Georgy insists.

Yet, consider. Georgy refuses all social engagements, neither paying calls nor receiving any. She waits for the post with such fidelity, I could set the clock by her, yet she seems relieved rather than disappointed when she receives no letters. Strangest of all, she devotes hours to reading the scandal sheets and even the newspapers. It is most unlike her.

What of Georgy's husband, you ask? I wish I could tell you. His name has not crossed her lips. No message has come to her from him, nor (to the best of my knowledge) has she posted even a line of correspondence to him. The only assurance I could wrest from Georgy (and only after I reminded her at some length that it is the duty of sisters to protect one another) is that he has not mistreated her in any way. Georgy is not afraid of him, I swear, but she is afraid of something. I think she's hiding here, Cecy.

Georgy has made me promise to keep her presence here

in strictest confidence. Of course I will do so, but I made her grant me an exception in your case. I cannot imagine that anyone would ask you Georgy's whereabouts, but you will be in London soon, and you may well encounter some unlooked-for social circumstance there. So please do bear it in mind that Georgy is not really here at all. I know you will handle matters far more adroitly than I would, so we trust you with this secret.

Believe that I will write the moment I learn anything else pertinent to the matter. Or indeed, the moment I learn any-thing pertinent to *anything*. Writing to you is the one spot of civilization in a daily routine dominated by wailing children, muddy shoes, and wet dogs.

With all the usual best wishes and even more affection,

Kate

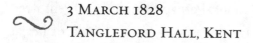 3 MARCH 1828
TANGLEFORD HALL, KENT

Dearest Kate,

The children are much better, by some measures, which is to say that they have reached the stage in their recovery at which no persuasion, no bribery, and no force can keep them abed. I shall be *exceedingly* glad when James returns. I had a note from him this morning, at long last, saying that he had expected to be back yesterday, but needed to remain in London a few more days. He includes no further details, save that he anticipates returning by the end of the week.

I find this rather odd, for it is most unlike the Duke of

Wellington to call James urgently to town merely to chat, and then send him home again. I do hope that James is not staying to have the blue salon redone as a surprise for me, or anything similar. He is occasionally taken with such notions, and it does not *do*. But one really cannot lecture one's husband on the suitability of the surprises he chooses, and after all, it is quite pleasant that he still thinks to do such things at all, even after ten years of matrimony.

Georgy is an utter goose, but if she wishes her whereabouts to remain unknown to anyone, I shall oblige her. I suppose I can simply look down my nose like Aunt Charlotte and inform people sternly that I do not wish to discuss the Duchess of Waltham, when they ask, but that may very well add fuel to the gossip, once it begins. If Georgy wishes to remain undiscovered *and* undiscussed, it would be better to have some tale to set about. Perhaps a sudden, urgent need for the latest in French pelisses? No one will look for her at Skeynes if we set it about that she has gone to Paris to shop.

There has been no sign of our prowler about the house or the nearby grounds, but yesterday I took Arthur out riding to work off some of his energy, and we found quite a mess out by the gazebo on the far side of the hill, near the ancient earthworks. It looked almost as if some amateur had been attempting to cast a spell, or perhaps cook a peculiar sort of dinner—there were chicken feathers and onion skins all over, a couple of broken sticks with charred ends, and random lines drawn in chalk here and there. I would have suspected the children had they not been laid up all week.

Arthur's surprise was evident . . . as was his desire to investigate everything at once. I made quite certain that there was no magical residue and then let him collect feathers. He found a shiny silver button in one corner, quite flat and polished to a mirror finish. If it belonged to the would-be magician, then he is no vagrant. I plan to test it tonight, after Arthur is safely in bed.

I do wish James would come home. I have no particular concern about the prowler himself, of course, but I am growing more concerned about Arthur's fascination with the notion of discovering him. I spent considerable time and effort, very early this morning, placing yet another ward around the house—to detect anyone attempting to sneak *out* late at night. I could almost wish that Arthur would catch the cold like the rest of them, but he remains disgustingly healthy.

Yours,
Cecy

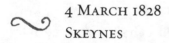

4 March 1828
Skeynes

Dear James,

In London, are you? Bored rigid yet?

Sincere apologies for my tardiness in replying to your letter. Rest assured that your young hellion has not damaged anything. I think I can promise that he won't be able to duplicate the feat.

The fact that Arthur contrived to do it even once interests me. I look forward to my next interview with him, as I have it on excellent authority (my member of the league of holy matrimony had it from your member of the league) that the lad claims to have seen things in my big paperweight. A truly reliable gazing ball would come in very useful, so if he has found a way to create one, I owe Arthur a debt of gratitude. I can promise you that if I had a truly reliable gazing ball, I would never again return to my home weary from the hardships of the road to find my sister-at-law still visiting. Certainly not when the visitor seems to labor under the impression that she is hiding from a mysterious organization that plots her demise. (Not that I don't occasionally sympathize with the urge to plot her demise.)

No, if I had a truly reliable gazing ball, you would find me putting up at a quiet and comfortable inn, playing shove ha'penny, sampling the ale, and doing no harm to anyone. Instead, I return to find domestic chaos, and Kate, Edward, and the infant afflicted with streaming colds, whilst I, sadly neglected, am left to my own devices.

I may come to London myself. There are some fates worse than boredom. Put in a word for me with Old Hookey if you think I can be of the slightest use.

Kate sends her love to you, to Cecy, and to the rest of your merry band,

Sincerely,
Thomas

6 MARCH 1828
TANGLEFORD HALL, KENT

My dear Thomas,

No, I won't invite you up to London. Find your own excuse to avoid your domestic disasters. Not that I blame you for wanting to avoid Her Grace, the Duchess of Waltham — or have you suddenly acquired some other sister-at-law whom you wish to avoid?

In any case, as you observe, I am no longer in London, nor do I anticipate returning soon. Our new prime minister found some letters that had been sitting unopened in the "Secret" packet since October, if you please! Some Prussian railway surveyor has gone missing in the north. It ought to have been looked into at once, but Lord Wellington has had his hands full with the royal family since he became PM last month. King George has never seen eye to eye with his brothers on political matters, and he and the Duke of Cumberland have had another row over the succession. Something about the Duchess of Kent and her daughter, I believe. It was all Old Hookey could do to keep it out of the papers.

But that business has blown over, for the time being at least, and now Cecelia and I are off to Leeds to see what we can find out. It will take us a few days to pack and make arrangements, but Wellington wished to keep additional delay to a minimum. I will send you our direction as soon as I know it.

Meanwhile, if you can forward me any information on the theoretical interactions between magic and railway lines or steam engines, I'd appreciate it.

Yours,
James

6 MARCH 1828
TANGLEFORD HALL, KENT

Dearest Kate,

James is back, and I am utterly distracted. Our esteemed prime minister, His Grace, the Duke of Wellington, may be the greatest general in the history of England, but I doubt he has ever had to deal with uprooting a household of children on a moment's notice. I expect I will have a few things to say on the subject when next I see him.

For that is what I must do. His Grace wishes James and me to travel north to Leeds—I will explain it all another time, or perhaps James will write to Thomas and you can learn of it from that. I cannot take the children, for though they are much recovered they are not yet in their usual robust health (always excepting Arthur), and such a long trip would risk a relapse, or perhaps some more-serious infection. And I cannot simply leave them here with Nurse, not with mysterious prowlers and peculiarly nonmagical messes in the gazebo and so on (and *especially* not without someone to keep Arthur from charging off to discover whatever he can, regardless of possible peril).

Dearest Kate—I know that you are already dealing with Georgy, and that Thomas will dislike it excessively, but *could* I prevail on you to take in my four rapscallions (and Nurse, of course) for a few weeks? If you cannot manage, I shall have to write to Aunt Elizabeth, which will take some time, and James is eager to be gone. Please let me know as soon as you can.

> Your distracted and importunate,
> *Cecy*

8 MARCH 1828
SKEYNES

Dearest Cecy,

Of course the children must come at once.

Thomas will meet you at the Bull and Mouth in Aldersgate Street. Such is his delight at finding a legitimate reason to leave for London, he intends to set off as soon as possible. With any luck, by the time you read this letter, he will be waiting there to collect the children from you and drinking beer and playing shove ha'penny, no doubt.

I will keep my consternation to myself for the moment, as you have quite enough to deal with for now. But do be careful!

Georgy may well benefit by this circumstance, for she adores the children, and their presence may help to turn her thoughts from whatever troubles her. She still won't confide in me.

Just between us, Cecy, I doubt Georgy spares a thought for what the Ton says of her. She is afraid of something—if only I knew what—and that fear trumps all rational concerns. I'm sure you are right that putting it about that she has gone to Paris is much the best course of action. I only wish I could persuade her to *talk* to me. I can bear the curiosity, but I hate worrying about her. Edward and Laurence seem to take up all my customary fretting.

Even more between the two of us, Cecy, I simply cannot contain myself a moment longer. In his haste to leave Skeynes for London, thus neatly avoiding Georgy and all her sighs, Thomas has convinced himself that he is being clever. He (he and Ripley, the coachman, to be exact) will drive to London and back, enjoying himself thoroughly the while. In his view, the mere matter of transporting a number of small children and their nurse adds nothing to the complexity of this endeavor. To you and you alone, Cecy, I must say ha! Ha! And again ha!

There. I feel much better now. When Thomas returns with your children safe and sound, I will be the soul of sympathy as I listen to his heartrending account of the experience. Indeed, I am sure he will deserve my sympathy by then, and I am just as certain that his account will be as entertaining as it is plaintive. But while Thomas is preparing so happily for his latest escape from domestic bliss, I simply had to express my true feelings, and I can trust only you.

You know you can trust us with the children. They will be perfectly safe here, come what may. I know you will do what you must to aid His Grace, but rest assured you may do it with a clear mind where the children are concerned.

Love,

Kate

P.S. Do not, on any account, permit Thomas so much as a glance at this letter. I am already suffused with guilt at having found amusement in the trials he is about to endure. —*K.*

8 MARCH 1828
SKEYNES

Dear James,

Make up your mind. Railway lines or steam engines? The current state of opinion on theoretical interactions varies considerably with whom you ask. As usual.

Given sufficient time, I'll warrant I can find you any argument you please: Steam engines are the work of the devil, a providential opportunity to improve the condition of all mankind, or an explosive death trap waiting to be sprung. Railway lines contain too much iron to be of reliable use in a magical interaction. Conversely, they invite magical interactions by nature of the similarity of their engineering to the engineering of Roman roads. There is also a school of thought that finds they constitute a hopeless blot on the landscape. Take your pick.

If you care to hear my theory, although God knows you have seldom paid the slightest attention before, I think the steam engine is certain to lend itself to some exceedingly useful interactions. Nothing so thoroughly comprised of the elements of earth, water, air, and fire could fail to do so.

I am of two minds on the question of railway lines. On the face of it, the lines show great promise as a way to link two (or even more!) points with a durable physical connection. Are you by any chance familiar with the work of Hans Christian Oersted? I haven't yet met him, but I have obtained a recent essay of his on magnetism. He has succeeded in producing magnetism at will. The procedure requires a central element, say a rod of iron, wrapped about with wire. Most intriguing stuff. I'll bring the essay with me. One never knows. There may be the (purely theoretical!) possibility of a similar application on a grand scale. Rods of iron aplenty involved in a railway line.

Yet, because railway tracks are made of many bits of metal placed end to end, considered as a staging point for a spell, it would be like running the Derby in installments. The enterprise might eventually work, but one would need a dashed good reason to take the trouble.

I plan to be in town before you, to have a look through the library at the Society and to gather any other references that might be of use to us. It won't hurt young Marrable to run up and down those ladders a few dozen times on our behalf. Trust my discretion. I won't tell him what I want to know or why I want to know it. No, honestly. After all, I don't know myself.

The Bull and Mouth is far from elegant, but I suspect your children will love the bustle of the place. For once they will behold chaos they did not create themselves. I'll meet you there.

Sincerely,
Thomas

12 MARCH 1828
THE BULL AND MOUTH, LONDON

Dearest Kate,

We have arrived in London and are ensconced at Thomas's inn. I am not sure what he was thinking to have chosen it. It may do very well for a lone gentleman of a certain style, but it is really not the place for a family with young children. Particularly not when the children in question are my older three (Baby Alexander is thankfully not yet mobile enough to go out in search of adventures).

There were no additional anomalies about the grounds at Tangleford once James arrived home (much to my relief and Arthur's frustration). James and I rode the boundaries together the day before our departure, he looking for suspicious physical evidence, I searching for more arcane manifestations. We found nothing, so I hope that our nocturnal visitor either was driven off by all the activity attendant on our preparations for departure or simply departed on his own.

London is, as usual, a hotbed of gossip. Lord Kernsbury has gambled away the last of his fortune and has been forced to fly the country to escape his debtors. Lady Prothmire's daughter has broken her engagement to old Lord Heppelwith, and her mother has hauled her back to the country in disgrace. And the Duchess of Kent snubbed the Duke of Cumberland most pointedly in the park last week. Rumor has it that they are on the outs over her daughter Alexandrina, who some (including, of course, the duchess) think should stand next in line for the throne after her uncle William. The duke naturally thinks that as one of the old king's sons, *he* should be king after his two elder brothers, while the duchess contends that since her late husband was older than the Duke of Cumberland, her daughter is the rightful heir.

The royal dispute is supposed to be private, but everyone knows of it. Even Aunt Charlotte has heard, though she has not visited London in weeks. I had a letter from her deploring the duchess's actions and accusing her of pushing her daughter's interests more than is seemly (which makes me think the Duchess of Kent must be quite an agreeable person after all). That is all the news I have been able to garner, but of course the Season has not yet properly begun.

James has gone to call on the Duke of Wellington, to see if he has anything more to add before we depart for the north, and Thomas is off at the Royal College. I am taking the opportunity to write you while I can, and to thank you and Thomas from the bottom of my heart for taking in my family. I would express a pious wish that they will be well-behaved for you, but I know it for a forlorn hope, at best.

I fully enter into your sentiments regarding Thomas's probable response to two days' travel with the four topmost shoots on the Tarleton family tree. Indeed, I could hardly help but do so, having just spent a day and a half getting them to London. (Diana was severely carriage-sick, which necessitated an unscheduled stop on the way; normally it is only a one-day ride, even with the children in tow.)

Arthur has conceived a passion for things mechanical, which I hope will be short-lived. He spent much of the carriage ride plotting with his twin to induce his godfather to take him to see some steam-works or other when we arrive in London. (He already tried to persuade James, without success; I believe that if the Duke of Wellington also fails him, he intends to try Thomas. I am torn; on the one hand, I would be quite pleased for the duke to get a taste of the difficulties he has made for us, but on the other, it would be just as satisfying, and somewhat more likely, for Thomas to have the honor. And if it is Thomas, then I shall no doubt have an account of the affair from you, while if the duke takes Arthur, I shall have to use my imagination.)

Later:

I was interrupted at that point in my letter by a summons from the innkeeper. With some trepidation, I followed him to the common room, to find a large ostler in a homespun cap and rather muddy boots glaring at Arthur and another boy. I noted with resignation that Arthur's jacket was torn, his breeches muddied, and his left eye already beginning to swell. (I expect it will have come out in rainbow colors by the time he arrives at Skeynes.)

It was instantly clear that Arthur and the other boy had got into a row. The ostler's part was soon explained—the row had been in the handling yard (how Arthur came there and what he thought he was doing have yet to be determined)—and they had disturbed some of the carriage horses, very nearly to the point of causing a runaway. Or so the ostler said. I thanked him very kindly for saving my son from the dangerous uproar, which threw him quite off his prepared speech, and saw him and the other boy off without further ado. I suspected he had intended to ask for compensation of some kind, and I was not prepared to commit to any such thing without first determining the facts of the case.

As soon as I had Arthur to myself, I took him to the private parlor that James had bespoke, then asked for his version of events. (It is best, with Arthur, to do this as soon as possible, without an audience, and most especially before he has had a chance to consult with Eleanor. Arthur has an unfortunate habit of adapting his story to the expressions of whatever adults happen to be within hearing, and he is very good at reading faces.)

"It was the burglar, Mama!" he burst out. "I saw him out the door when I came down to see if—when I came down. And I ran after him, and he ran between the horses, and I ran into Bill, and he said who did I think I was shoving, and I said don't let him get away, and he said that's it, then, and he knocked me down, so I got up and knocked him down, and the horse reared and the ostler shouted at both of us and called us bad names. And he got away."

I gave him a stern look. "Setting aside, for the moment, whatever reason you saw fit to wander about the inn alone when I *distinctly* recall telling you to remain in the rooms until your father returns, I should like to know what possessed you to go running out into a strange place, after a person who may well be dangerous, without informing anyone of your whereabouts."

"I could have *caught* him, Mama!" Arthur said.

"And what would you have done with him then?" I said. "Even if it is the same man, he is much larger than you are. It seems clear that you require some practice with fisticuffs before you can successfully deal with an opponent of your own size and weight. It therefore seems highly unlikely that you would have succeeded in apprehending the villain."

Arthur looked chagrined at this reminder of his poor showing against the stableboy, and I continued, "More likely, *if* it was the same person, he would have captured *you,* which would have greatly distressed your sisters and your father."

"Not you?" Arthur asked.

"I should have thought that being kidnapped and fed only bread and butter in an underground dungeon was just what you deserved for so serious a lapse in judgment," I said mendaciously. "As it is, you are fortunate to have come away with only a colored eye."

Arthur grinned. Then he looked thoughtful. "I see. Next time, I will be more careful."

I was not sure what to make of this ambiguous promise, but fortunately James and Thomas arrived at that moment, having met up at the Royal College of Wizards. At first they were inclined to be amused by what they took to be a schoolboy prank (Thomas even offered to teach Arthur to box properly). When they heard that Arthur thought he had recognized our prowler, however, they began querying him intently as to exactly how he had known the man and what the fellow might have been doing.

I slipped away to make arrangements with the innkeeper to pay the disgruntled ostler. If the prowler has indeed followed us to London, I am more than ever glad that the children are to come to you, though I think it most likely that Arthur is a victim of his own overeager imagination, and perhaps some similarity of headgear. Even quite a long look at someone is not enough to identify him positively when the look has been had in the dark at a distance of thirty yards or more.

We depart London tomorrow, in our several directions. James intends to put up at the King's Head when we arrive in Leeds. I shall try to write you something more coherent as soon as things are more settled.

Yours,
Cecy

14 MARCH 1828
SKEYNES

Dear Cecy,

May this letter find you and James safely at the King's Head in Leeds. Thomas returned with your children a few hours ago. Everyone seems much as usual. No, let me amend that. Upon reflection, I believe that Georgy has been smiling ever since the children came. Distracting they may be, but it is the very best sort of distraction.

I am sure your Nurse Langley will write to you of Thomas's methods where Diana and her carriage sickness are concerned. She objects to them.

Let me put your mind at rest. Diana has suffered no ill effects, and indeed asks at regular intervals when she might go driving with Thomas again. Driving is putting it a bit high, I think. Thomas told me that Diana, wedged securely on the seat between him and Ripley, fell asleep in her cocoon of blankets after the first ten miles. No further need for a basin, I am happy to report.

I am just as sure that when they write to you, Arthur and Eleanor will protest their treatment on the journey. Eleanor blames Thomas's refusal to spring the horses entirely on Diana. "My sister is a very poor traveler," she told me, with such an air of utter world-weariness that anyone would think they had just arrived here from Samarkand.

Arthur pronounced the whole journey sadly flat. "Nothing to what Papa would have done." They are united in allotting Thomas the blame for the brutal way he condemned them to sit inside with Nurse Langley, when either of them would have been much better help driving than Diana was.

As far as your journey to Leeds is concerned, I hope that you and James made swift work of it indeed. That was why Thomas chose the Bull and Mouth, of course, to permit you to arrange with Mr. Sherman's firm to use his post-horses for the changes on the road north, and to put you on that road in the shortest possible time. If comfort were of the essence, rather than time, naturally he would have stayed at the house in Mayfair instead.

This reminds me of another of Thomas's crimes. He has refused Arthur his steam-works. You will hear about this at length, I am sure. Heartless as ever, dear Thomas is. In his defense, Thomas says, given Arthur's burglar, he could not in good conscience risk the safety of the children in London a moment longer than necessary.

I thought that might make you smile. As if Thomas has ever possessed anything remotely resembling a conscience, good, bad, or indifferent. You and I know the sorry truth of it, of course. Thomas does not wish to play bear leader to Arthur unless it is for something Thomas himself has a keen interest in. If Arthur had conceived a passion for magnetism, Thomas would have taken him straight to Mr. Faraday's laboratory and let any question of conscience go hang.

Upon reflection, I must admit things could be worse. Thomas and Arthur could share a keen interest in pugilism.

Come to think of it, I will refrain from jests on the topic, for Arthur has not yet forgotten the rash promise Thomas made to teach him how to box. I can only imagine Edward's wrath if he is left out of the proceedings. A keen interest in pugilism is all too likely to sweep the nursery. I will keep silent, lest I provoke it.

You may wonder about the keen interest in the study of magic Thomas shares with Arthur and Eleanor. That would be the reason Thomas kept the twins amused at the inn by teaching them to scry in a dish of India ink. The nurse may well include the resulting stains in her list of objections against Thomas. I am very sorry for any inconvenience the ink may have caused, but I feel I must take at least part of the blame. His time with me has given Thomas a fine indifference to stains of all kinds. It is not a disregard shared by Nurse Langley.

I think the day and a half it took you to make the short journey to London put the fear of the Lord into Thomas. That's why he was so brutal with the children.

Why he was brutal with the nurse as well is quite beyond me. Anyone would think he was a perfect Turk from the way Nurse Langley carries on. Happily, she has formed a pact of mutual support with Nurse Carstairs, who has the highest opinion of Thomas, so I hope she will be won over eventually.

Meanwhile it is quite diverting to watch the two women vie to show the babies to best advantage. It is clear that each privately feels her own charge to be the most beautiful and gifted. The older children are slightly less enchanting to them and thus are sometimes privileged to go for hours at a time without comparative assessment.

Still, it is fortunate that both Alexander and Laurence are too young to understand the boasts put forth on their behalf, or they would be insufferably pleased with themselves. (As it is, Laurence stands to inherit that quality from his father. Certainly Edward has done so. No matter what, Edward's good opinion of himself is quite invincible.)

I am quite sure everyone will be in much better spirits in the morning. The rigors of travel take a toll on the sturdiest of us. I suspect Thomas is dealing with his fatigue most efficiently. He has locked himself in his study. Now that relative peace has descended, the children having ascended to the nursery at last, I will go and seek him in his lair. I look forward to the full version of his side of the story. She who laughs last may not invariably laugh best, but she does laugh. The nice thing about Thomas is that he will probably laugh quite a lot, too.

Good night and best wishes to you and James on your enterprise.

Love,
Kate

18 MARCH 1828
THE KING'S HEAD, LEEDS

Dearest Kate,

If I had any fear that you would be taken in by my brood's outrageous claims, I should be very worried. As it is,

I trust you to provide all proper sympathy, without in fact allowing Eleanor to spring Thomas's horses or encouraging Arthur to sulk over a dearth of steam-works.

I am somewhat more concerned over Thomas's impromptu magic lesson with the twins. Not that I have any doubts of his skills as a tutor, you understand (and certainly not a concern over ink stains); it is more that I am not sure he took sufficient account of the twins' natural creativity and curiosity. To be quite plain, if Thomas has taught the twins to scry, you had best put wards against scrying about your bedrooms . . . and anything else you hope to keep private. And it would not be at all amiss to lock up the ink, as well, if only to slow them down a little.

As for us, we have, as you see, arrived in Leeds. The trip was uneventful, though hurried. James spent his evenings poring over several tomes on railways that Thomas supplied him with in London, though he would not say what he was looking for. (I expect that Arthur will find them fascinating once we return, particularly if I tell him they are too difficult for him. In fact, had I thought of it, I should have done so while we were still in London. If anyone could ferret out useful information from such dull books, it would be Arthur.)

James's sudden interest in railways stems from the reason behind our sudden venture into the north. We are in search of a Prussian railway surveyor-magician who has been missing since last autumn. I think it safe to assume that such details as I know are not a matter for secrecy, or James would have mentioned it. The situation is as follows:

Herr Magus Franz Wilhelm Schellen arrived in London last September as scheduled and made his way north along the same route James and I took. (James made inquiries at the posting houses, and several remembered the gentle-man—"Very polite, he was, and freehanded for a foreigner" was the general consensus. It is fortunate that he was so generous; had he been stingy, I doubt his memory would have remained green long enough for us to discover his traces.) He was to review the railway that runs between Stockton and Darlington, and then proceed to Manchester, to assist with the surveying of the proposed new steam railway between that city and Liverpool. He never arrived; indeed, there has been no word of him since he set out for the north. So we are to look for him.

You will perceive at once that there are a number of questions raised by this sketchy history. It is no surprise that the railway construction companies were unable to find a British surveyor-magician to aid them and had to send to the Germanies for one. The professional combination of surveyor and magician is hardly a common one. It is, however, altogether unclear why they required a surveyor-magician in the first place. Furthermore, if his intention was to survey a route between Liverpool and Manchester in the west, why would he need to look at the Stockton line in the northeast? No explanation has been given.

We are thus reduced to the crudest of methods, simply asking around in hopes of discovering the gentleman's whereabouts. Having established that he did not take rooms at the

King's Head, James has gone to investigate the other local inns, leaving me time to write and—

Later:

I had got so far, when James returned with two extraordinary pieces of news. First his search for Herr Schellen has borne a peculiar sort of fruit. Though the gentleman himself remains missing, James has turned up a letter intended for the surveyor-magician. It was waiting at a small inn near the edge of town. Herr Schellen evidently stayed there for a week when he arrived and, when he left, asked that they hold any letters against his eventual return, warning that he might be delayed. The innkeeper faithfully did as he had been asked, only providing the letter after some persuasion.

Unfortunately, the letter is writ in German. I have never studied that tongue, and James's knowledge of it is limited to what he refers to as "soldier's phrases," which I take to mean a combination of military commands and vulgar language. James is sending it to the Duke of Wellington for translation; I hope it may contain something more useful. Tomorrow, we will drive out to the railway, to see whether we can trace Herr Schellen's movements any further.

The other news was that on his way back to the inn, James ran into your brother-at-law! What His Grace, the Duke of Waltham, can have been doing in Leeds is beyond me—there is little here in the way of the Society he loves, and I do not believe there are any notable gaming hells, either. James said that he seemed quite distracted and did not so much as mention Georgy. (And it should go without saying that James did not mention her, or her whereabouts, either—but I know Georgy, and I am sure she will ask, so pray reassure her on that head.)

His Grace is evidently settled in the area for some little time, as we are invited to dine with him next week. (We were invited to dine tomorrow, but James begged off on the grounds of our expedition to Darlington to see the railway.) I am in hopes that he will unbend after a few glasses of port and allow James some idea of what is amiss between him and Georgy. (Do not mention this to Georgy if you think it will overset her.)

That is all my news for the moment; give my best love to the children, and keep a share for yourself and Georgy.

Yours,
Cecy

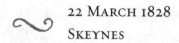

22 MARCH 1828
SKEYNES

Dear Cecy,

I am on tenterhooks to hear the result of your investigations. What a pity the letter was in German. I can offer no useful advice. You must be content with my admiration for James's thoroughness.

Under separate cover, for Thomas is very generous with his franks, you will find letters from your children. Do not believe everything they tell you. The part about the snake is true enough, but I assure you there are no basilisks in Thomas's study. I would have noticed.

I mentioned your advice about a shield for the scrying spell to Thomas. Judging by his countenance, I promise you that steps will be taken immediately. Thank you very much for the suggestion.

For the moment, thank goodness, the twins show no sign of using the scrying spell for anything but their own entertainment. They play hide-and-seek. One twin hides, and the other uses the scrying spell to find the hiding place. This makes the game far more quiet than when we played it, but I now know that quiet is not always to be preferred. The result of this refinement to the game is that they have been seeking darker and darker hiding places, the better to foil the scryer.

When you and I played rainy-day games with Georgy and Oliver, we spent most of our time in the attic or the box room. (Remember how Georgy invariably hid in the library window seat? I must remind myself she has always been a creature of habit.) It seems strange to me that the twins tend to neglect the attics here. (Too near the nursery to prove of interest, perhaps.) On particularly dreary days, I am tempted to explore them myself.

Last time I did so, I found the box with Thomas's lead soldiers. There is a motley assortment of regiments represented, and some look quite old. I suppose they came into Thomas's possession after his brother Edward outgrew them. With Thomas's permission, I gave our Edward command of the troops. He fell upon them with cries of joy. It touches me to the heart to think of Thomas playing with those same soldiers when he was Edward's age and years later going off to be a soldier himself. Should Edward ever join the military, I have perfect confidence in his ability to forage.

There are also some excellent box rooms on the premises. (Certainly they met with everyone's full approval on previous visits.) Yet these promising hunting grounds are disdained in favor of the cellars, the cupboard under the back stairs, or (on one memorable occasion) inside one of the stable grain bins. I live in fear that one of them will hide in a chest that can't be opened from the inside.

This means that the entire staff has been charged to keep a sharp eye (sharper even than usual, I mean) on the children. Edward seems to find the focus on his cousins inspiring. He has shown great ingenuity in finding new items of scientific interest to bring to the nursery. I would have thought it quite early in the season for snakes, but he has made a more thorough study of the subject than I.

I told Georgy of your encounter with her husband, partly to assure her that you would never betray her whereabouts and partly to assess her response to the mention of his name. She did not seem particularly alarmed. I judge she was relieved to learn that her stay here is to be held in confidence.

Really, I am consumed with curiosity. What could possibly have stirred Georgy to bury herself here in the country, with no entertainment but that provided by the children, and to utter scarcely a word of complaint over the change in her circumstances—and then to *stay* here.

I have every confidence in your skill at interrogation and in Daniel's complacency. The man's sublime interest in himself is only matched by his serene assumption that the rest of the world shares it. With luck, Daniel will never even notice he's been questioned.

Good luck with every enterprise.

Love,
Kate

22 MARCH 1828
THE KING'S HEAD, LEEDS

My dear Thomas,

Still no sign of our missing German. It seems he spent a few days observing the local terrain, made an excursion aboard the Stockton and Darlington Railway, then packed up bag and baggage and removed to Stockton. At least that is what he told his landlord he was doing, as near as the landlord could make out. Due to the unfortunate combination of accents—moderately intelligible Yorkshire, in the case of the landlord, and vilely thick German (according to the landlord) on the part of Herr Schellen—communication seems to have encountered some difficulties.

The references you provided in London have been

instructive, though I have as yet had little opportunity to put their information to any practical use. I shall reserve for light reading the books you included on magnetism, once I have completed the task Old Hookey set me. For the time being, railways and steam engines must be my focus.

I remain uncertain of the Herr Magus's reason for insisting on a personal visit to examine the railway here. Cecelia and I spent a day replicating Herr Schellen's railway ride from Darlington to Stockton and back. I am of two minds regarding the likelihood of such a mode of travel ever catching on. On the one hand, the trip was both fast and cheap; no pauses were needed to rest and water the horses, for there were none, and the entire journey cost us but a shilling apiece. On the other hand, the experience was disconcerting enough to discourage anyone of a nervous temperament. Once one has taken a seat in the wagon, one cannot see the engine, and there is no means to communicate with the driver should the need arise. Then there are the coal wagons—twenty of them, all filled to overflowing on the outward journey, and most of them following the passengers' wagon, so that the slightest accident must squash it like a nut in a nutcracker. Perhaps something might be done with separate trains, one for passengers and one for haulage, but I doubt there will be enough call for such transport to justify the expense.

In any event, we made our journey without incident, in both directions. Cecelia informs me that she sensed nothing magical about the engine or the route. Had anyone else told me, I don't think I would have believed it. It ought to be quite impossible for men to travel at such astonishing speeds (fifteen miles an hour at times, or so the engineer informed me) without magical aid, but she was quite certain of her observations.

I anticipate further investigations in Stockton, but they must wait upon the social niceties. We dine with your brother-at-law on the twenty-fourth; I all but ran him down in the street the other day, and the resulting invitation was unavoidable. Do not ask me what he is doing in Leeds. I have even less interest in the doings of the Duke of Waltham than you, if that were possible. I intend to leave for Stockton on the day following the dinner. In the meantime, I would appreciate it if you could learn something of Herr Schellen's movements in London, and perhaps the proposed Liverpool-Manchester line as well. If Herr Schellen's disappearance was due to foul play, someone might have feared what a surveyor-magician would find out once he began his work there. If you can discover who proposed hiring him, and why, and whether anyone objected, it could prove very useful. You will not need to stir from home; common gossip is all I want at this point, of the sort that can be had in correspondence. I'd write the letters myself, except that it might give someone the wind up to receive such a missive from me, posted from Leeds.

Yours,
James

25 MARCH 1828
THE KING'S HEAD, LEEDS

Dearest Kate,

I do hope you will not be troubled any further with un-
seasonable livestock, but you must admit that snakes in the
nursery are better than basilisks in the study would be. For
you can order the children to relinquish the snakes, but
Thomas would be most unlikely to give up so magical a
creature as a basilisk until he was quite finished investigating it. And perhaps searching for more snakes will distract
the twins from their scrying.

I considered writing Arthur and Eleanor a stern parental
lecture regarding their studies of magic, in hopes that if they
could be induced to view their scrying as obligatory practice
instead of as a fascinating new game, they might neglect it.
Upon consideration, however, I do not think it will serve. If
they have been playing hide-and-seek with the scrying spell
for a week or more, no parental injunctions will have the
least effect. You might, perhaps, redirect Arthur with steam-
works, if you happen to have any handy, but I fear that
Eleanor will not be so easily diverted. I trust you have laid in
a good supply of ink.

Our excursion on the railway line would have been just
the thing to distract Arthur. The steam engine was a perfectly enormous cylinder on wheels, with a huge black pipe
at the front, trailing a plume of coal smoke, and a shorter

pipe at the rear, to vent the steam. Behind it came the train of wagons. (I regret to say that our train was only twenty wagons long; the gentleman from whom we purchased our tickets in Darlington informed us that some of the steam engines haul as many as twenty-four wagons, fully loaded!) Most of the wagons were hauling coal from the mines to the west, but two had been fitted out with chairs for passengers.

We boarded the wagons when the train stopped in Darlington, and rode from there to Stockton in three hours, coal and all. It was a mad ride, like a normal carriage journey turned inside out, for the steam engine works properly only when it moves on smooth, nearly flat ground, so wherever there was a hill, the railway builders had to cut a great rift through it to keep the tracks level, and where the land dipped, they had to build it up. One felt as if one were in a valley whenever the train passed through one of the cuts in a hill, and as if one were on a mountain whenever the land was low!

We spent several hours careering madly between hills and along the river to Stockton, with damp clouds of steam-scented smoke from the engine engulfing us from time to time and the noise of the wheels pounding away far more rhythmically than in any ordinary carriage. What was most impressive, however, was the speed, and the fact that it took us very little longer to return, though much of the way was uphill. The ride itself produced no useful information— I sensed nothing unusual that might have attracted Herr

Schellen—but during our brief time in Stockton, James discovered the name of the lodgings to which Herr Schellen removed when he left Leeds.

We had planned to transfer to Stockton ourselves today, but matters have taken an unexpected turn, thanks to Georgy's husband, of all people. We dined with him last night in a private parlor at the Footman's Chase. If I was surprised to learn that Daniel was spending time in so unfashionable a place as Leeds, I was even more astonished to find him putting up at an inn that at its very best could only be described as "respectable," whose patrons (those we passed on our way into the parlor, at any rate) had a distinct air of the shop about them. *Not* what one expects of His Grace, the Duke of Waltham!

When we reached the parlor, Daniel greeted us and introduced us to his other guests, a couple who had arrived before us. I hid both my surprise and my disappointment (I had expected a quiet meal *en famille,* during which I had hoped to cross-question him at length). Daniel's choice of companions was as unusual as his situation. Mr. Ramsey Webb and his sister Adella were both impeccably turned out, from the Italian lace edging on Miss Webb's cap (for she was a spinster of at least thirty) to the champagne polish of Mr. Webb's boots. Nonetheless, there was something slightly *off* about them. You may say that this is only to be expected of His Grace's cronies, but rackety as they may be, you must admit that they are all persons of the first consideration. Ramsey and Adella Webb are the sort that Aunt

Charlotte would refer to as "encroaching mushrooms"—and I am not entirely certain her judgment, in this case, would be unfair.

James and Daniel were immediately occupied by Mr. Webb. This left me with Miss Webb, or, rather, with Adella (as she immediately insisted I call her).

"His Grace was so very kind to invite my brother and me tonight," she began. "But then, he is always so very kind. Unlike many others of high position."

I made a noncommittal noise. "Kind" is not a quality I usually associate with Daniel. Of course, he is not particularly *unkind,* either; the word that comes to my mind is *self-absorbed.* "To be sure," I said vaguely when I saw that Adella expected more. "How are you acquainted with His Grace?"

"My brother made his acquaintance in course of some business dealings," Adella replied readily enough. "He is a connection of yours, is he not?"

"He is married to my cousin Georgina," I said. "I am afraid we do not see them often."

Adella frowned slightly. "I thought His Grace spent most of his time in London. What with Parliament and the Season . . ."

I had to suppress a snort. The idea of Daniel actually attending Parliament is even more absurd than that of Thomas doing so. For I am sure that if the Duke of Wellington asked it of him, or if there were some bill that seemed likely to affect his interests, Thomas would exert himself.

Daniel took up his seat in the House of Lords in the first place only because he wanted an excuse to spend time in London, and he has not attended a single session of Parliament since.

"His Grace is certainly in London a good deal," I said instead. "Georgy—Her Grace, that is—enjoys the Season enormously. I suppose she is there now, preparing for it." (Of course, I know very well from your letters that it is no such thing, but I thought it best not to give a hint, even in such an out-of-the-way place, that I thought differently. Who knows what correspondents Adella Webb might have?)

Adella gave me a sharp look. "Are you sure? It seems very odd to me for her to go off to London without her husband."

I smiled, though I was beginning to dislike Miss Webb. "Georgina does not live in her husband's pocket. And she prefers London to the country at any season. Why, she and Daniel seldom visit even her sister, though she lives quite close to London."

"Her sister?" Adella said.

"My cousin Kate," I said. "The Marchioness of Schofield."

"The Marchioness of Schofield!" Adella looked impressed. "Your cousins both married very well indeed! Is her husband, the Marquis, in Parliament as well?"

My dislike of Adella Webb was growing rapidly. "Thomas has a seat in the House of Lords, of course, like every peer," I said. "But he is not much involved in politics. His interests run more to magic. And magnetism, at the moment."

"Magic!" Adella frowned. "He is a magician, then?"

"A wizard," I corrected her. "And a full member of the Royal College of Wizards. You disapprove? But I think membership in the Royal College of Wizards ought to make one at least as respectable as the Order of the Garter. The Royal College is the older association, after all."

"Yes," Adella said. She sounded oddly disappointed. "Still, one never knows about wizards. There are all sorts of spells they could be doing in private!"

I smiled to myself and replied with great certainty, "Well, whatever Thomas is doing, it isn't basilisks."

"Basilisks?" Adella looked thoroughly taken aback. Clearly, that was not what she had been expecting.

"No," I said. "And I must say, I am glad of it. Arthur would undoubtedly wish to investigate, and I am sure the results would be catastrophic."

"Arthur?" Adella was more and more at sea.

"My eldest son," I said. "He and the other children are staying at Skeynes while James and I are in the north. He is such an enterprising child . . ." And I launched into a thoroughly misleading description of my children, full of glowing praise for their dubious virtues, such as must have made me appear a doting mama of the most boring sort. I took positive pleasure in forcing Adella to stay and listen until dinner was served at last.

The conversation around the table was unexceptionable. I kept an eye on Daniel, who seemed unusually ill at ease. He kept glancing at James, then at Mr. Webb, and then applying himself to his plate (and I assure you, the food was nothing that deserved such attention).

Near the end of the meal, Mr. Webb asked James how long we intended to stay in Leeds.

"We leave tomorrow," James answered. "I have found some property near Stockton that I wish to look over, and it will be more convenient for the business if we are nearby."

"Stockton?" Mr. Webb said. "How convenient! You must stay with us."

Daniel looked up with an expression of horrified indecision on his face. "I, ah, er, is that really . . . I mean, Stockton? Not even a watering hole. Bath would be better. For anything."

"My great-uncle left me an old guard tower near Stockton," Mr. Webb continued as if Daniel had not spoken. "It's a relic of the Civil Wars, I believe. There's plenty of room, and it's near the main road."

"Sure to be drafty," Daniel said.

"Not at all." Mr. Webb frowned at him. "I've spent some effort on repairs, and it's quite a cozy retreat now." He smiled suddenly. "Come and see for yourself. I'm having some other friends to stay, quite respectable; we'll make it a house party."

"I, ah—" Daniel looked trapped, as indeed we all were. There being now no way to decline the invitation without appearing to slight Mr. Webb's accommodations, his veracity, or both, we perforce accepted.

So Mr. Webb and his sister go to Haliwar Tower today

to have the Holland covers off and make preparations to receive us, and James and I and Daniel travel there later in the week. James is quite put out, as he thinks this will make his investigations more difficult. I am less annoyed, as I hope it will facilitate mine—surely Daniel cannot avoid us entirely during a weeklong house party!

Yours,
Cecy

30 MARCH 1828
SKEYNES

Dear Cecy,

I write to you at the address of Mr. Webb's cozy retreat. May your stay in the wilderness be comfortable. If it is not, at least we have the petty consolation of knowing that Daniel suffers along with you. But sometimes the most unlikely combination of people can result in a pleasant house party. I hope it may be so in this case. Perhaps the Webbs will be more congenial at their home.

Do you think Adella Webb would be more put off or less if she learned the true nature of Thomas's past research? It disgusts the casual inquirer, I've found. On the whole, I think you were wise to reassure her with basilisks and leave it at that. From your description of her, it seems unlikely that she would see the merit in his work. More probably, it would have put her off her meal entirely.

Not that Thomas's work is as easy as a brief description

makes it sound. Insects must go somewhere, after all. Banish lice and fleas throughout Skeynes, and one must be prepared to deal with the consequences visited upon the neighbors. Lord knows the Cramptons have made their opinion of the result perfectly clear on more than one occasion. It's a miracle they still speak to us.

I have high hopes for Thomas's study of magnetism. Magnetism may be of less immediate use, but I trust unsuccessful experiments will also be less disruptive to the household.

Georgy has heard extracts from your letter. I selected them with care and watched her with great attention as I read aloud to her. She seemed reassured by what she heard, although whether by your account of her husband's demeanor or by the knowledge that he is safely at the other end of the country, I cannot tell.

This morning I asked her again to tell me what is wrong. She ignored me and devoted herself to the *Gazette*. One might almost think she were trying to commit the scandal sheets she reads to memory.

To Georgy, we owe the news that the king is to attend Cheltenham races this season, though his colt Teazle is far from the favorite. You may imagine the consequences to the local social calendar. There is no excuse too flimsy to serve as justification to be in Cheltenham at the proper time. I trust Aunt Charlotte will have a few withering remarks to make upon this subject when next she writes.

Arthur and Eleanor have taken to spending most of

their time in the gardens. I asked them, not without some trepidation, if they shared Edward's interest in foraging for wildlife. (I thought it well to be prepared in case we find imports of additional livestock.)

"Snakes," said Eleanor, as if the word tasted bad. "Certainly not. *We're* explorers."

"Natural history is all very well in its way," Arthur conceded handsomely, "but we're making a detailed and accurate map of the grounds." On occasion, Arthur sounds so like his father, I must struggle to keep my countenance.

"Grounds?" I repeated blankly. "What grounds?"

"These grounds." Eleanor took pity on me. "Skeynes."

"Not the whole estate," Arthur assured me. "Ripley says we'd be riding for miles and miles, hundreds and hundreds of acres. We don't have paper enough for that. But we shall map all the gardens, and the whole park, and the home wood, all the way to the common."

I told the twins I thought making a detailed and accurate map of the grounds was an excellent idea and promised to provide whatever they needed in the way of supplies. For a moment, I feared my approval might put them off the whole idea, but instead they clamored to visit the mock-ruined hermitage, the better to map that end of the gardens.

I have warned the servants not to permit the children to stray too far afield in pursuit of their enterprise. I confess I find making maps a pastime far preferable to the perils of hide-and-seek by scrying.

Diana and Alexander are in bounding good health, as

are Edward and Laurence. Nurse Carstairs and Nurse Langley continue to deal extremely, praise be to a merciful providence.

Thomas has been in town for the past few days, but I expect him to return by Tuesday, Wednesday at the latest. His letters assure me that he devotes himself only to the most pressing of his business affairs, and that nothing on earth would induce him to remain away from home a moment longer than necessary. (Nothing on earth, I surmise, but good company, a well-stocked wine cellar, or a library he hasn't had a chance to examine in detail.)

When you and James have unraveled your mystery, when Georgy has come to her senses, and when we are all back in town for the Season, you and I must indulge ourselves with similar irresponsibilities. I long for a leisurely chat with you over a nice cup of tea. A new bonnet would not come amiss, either.

Love to you and James,
Kate

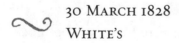 30 MARCH 1828
WHITE'S

Dear James,

I hold you responsible. Were it not for you and your infernal Herr Magus Schellen, I would be comfortably at home at this very moment. At home, and in perfect health. Come to think of it, I would most probably be in church,

virtuously reading the lesson to a lot of sheep-faced hyp-
ocrites. Believe me when I tell you I would prefer that fate
to the head I have on me this morning, a head that is all your
fault.

"Common gossip is all I want," you said. You know as
well as I do, for gossip, there's nowhere better than the club.
So to the club I duly took myself, despite the trouble, the inconvenience, and, worst of all, the silent look of reproach
Kate administered as I announced my plans. Thus, common
gossip have I pursued for much of the past week. I cannot
vouch for its accuracy, but I have collected some choice *on-
dits*. I will spare you those titbits unsuitable for a respectably
married man and concentrate on the questions you set me.

Still, you asked for gossip. Not my gossip in particular,
but you didn't exclude the possibility, so there it is.

Item One: Shares in the Stockton to Darlington railway
enterprise have fallen alarmingly of late. Accidents have
dogged the line from the start. The casual investors are cut-
ting their losses before things grow worse.

There is at least one other proposed railway route in the
vicinity, this one on the southern bank of the River Tees. The
investment fever inspired by Liverpool-Manchester, and indeed the Stockton-Darlington in happier days, has spread
rapidly. I expect there are a number of similar schemes by
now.

Item Two: Who hired your Herr Magus Schellen? What
was he hired to do? This is the cause of my hangover, and
you owe me, James. I spent hours with Fremantle last

night—no, curse it!—this morning. Hours! I don't know why the man was so closemouthed, but I assume it is all part of his general policy. He knows everything and must be seen by the world as discretion itself. Fortunately, discretion itself has a taste for cognac.

According to Fremantle, Mr. Pease, of the Stockton-Darlington line, hired Schellen to do the official survey of the railway line. Pease wanted him because he'd be uninterested in the petty rivalries involved. You can't get anyone more neutral than Herr Magus Schellen, and neutrality was the whole point.

So that's what Fremantle says, and if it turns out to be a waste of good cognac, you can make it up to me the next time we have a drink together. In about fifty years, the way I feel at the moment.

I leave for Skeynes in the morning. If I'm not home for Easter, Kate will worry. Bad enough as it is. If I had been home to read the lesson, I think this morning's verses would have been the plague of frogs, and I was rather looking forward to the impression that would make on your hellions. And mine, of course.

Sincerely,
Thomas

April

2 APRIL 1828
LEEDS

My dear Thomas,

Thank heavens you wrote to the inn at Leeds. Cecelia and I have removed to Haliwar Tower, and the post there is being opened. The Webbs, who got up this miserable house party, stick to us like cockleburs—Ramsey Webb to me, and his sister to Cecelia. He accompanied me even on this purported business visit to Leeds; I barely managed to give him the slip long enough to retrieve your note. You had best direct further correspondence to Haliwar, but take precautions. Warn Kate, as well. There have been several disturbing developments; I shall send you a full account at the earliest opportunity, using the cipher you worked out when we were on the Peninsula.

Yours,
James

2 APRIL 1828
HALIWAR TOWER

Dearest Kate,

We arrived at Haliwar Tower last Thursday, and Mr.
Webb was not prevaricating when he described his im-
provements to the place. It is quite as comfortable as a London town house, which seems a little odd as it is so very far
from town Society. The Webbs have kindly insisted that we
remain with them for as long as we stay near Stockton, so we
are well settled for some time. James returned to Leeds
today on some business or other, but I expect him back tomorrow morning. It is very tiresome to have him forever
talking of this property and that. I will be glad when he
makes his decision.

I hope the children are behaving well. More than ever, I
wish I could have brought them. There is a large pond just
east of the tower, where Mr. Webb and James fish in the
mornings. Arthur would adore it, though upon reflection,
perhaps it is just as well he is not here. I shudder to think of
the effect his muddy boots would have on Miss Webb's
carpets.

I enclose a shawl I have been knitting for Diana. I was
trying to duplicate the pattern that Lady Sylvia showed us
when we were on our wedding journey, but I fear there are
mistakes. I trust you remember what she showed us better
than I, and can correct my errors. I should like to knit a set

for all the girls, but I will not attempt it until you confirm that I have the stitches right.

Yours,
Cecy

(Translation of coded shawl sent from Haliwar Tower, 2 April 1828)

Dearest Kate,

I trust you understood my hint, and still remember the knitting code Lady Sylvia taught us so many years ago. At first, I wasn't certain I would remember the meanings of all the stitches myself. Your letter arrived yesterday; James brought it up to our rooms and handed it to me with a frown. "Someone is tampering with the post," he said, and showed me where the seal had been lifted and then carefully replaced.

I was outraged, the more so when James pointed out that we must assume that any letters we send you are being treated in similar fashion. I was ready to give the Webbs a dressing-down in Aunt Elizabeth's best manner, but James pointed out that we cannot lay this at their door with any certainty. The post sits in the main hall after its arrival, where anyone might get hold of it—Daniel, the other guests, one of the servants. And since two of the guests are elected members of Parliament, and one sits on the Opposition bench, James thinks it likely that the snooping is politically motivated. It is no secret that he is a great friend of Lord Wellington's. Confronting the Webbs would merely put everyone on notice that we know what is going on. It will be much better to try to catch them in the act, or perhaps to mislead them by writing letters full of false information. (Hence the mention of James's tiresome interest in property in the accompanying note. It would not do for someone to discover that he is here at the Duke of Wellington's request.)

I hope you can make sense of this, as it is the quickest safe method of informing you of the situation. I mean to invent some magical alternative soon, as knitting is cumbersome and it will undoubtedly raise suspicions if I send too many parcels. For now, though, it will have to do.

I have still not been able to corner Daniel alone. The closest I came was a brief encounter with Daniel in the hall last night after dinner. He started, glanced around quickly, and realized we were alone. "Mrs. Tarleton!" he said in a loud whisper. "I must speak to your husband!"

"Tell me whatever you want to say, quickly, and I will tell him," I replied.

It ought to have been obvious even to Daniel that it would be near-impossible for James to escape from Mr. Webb, and that this was his best chance to say anything, but he hesitated. Naturally, Adella Webb came out of the room at just that moment, and the chance was lost. I shall do my best to find another as soon as I possibly can.

I had best close now, as otherwise this shawl will be

three sizes too large for any child and someone will surely become suspicious.

Yours,
Cecy

3 APRIL 1828
HALIWAR TOWER

(in cipher)

My dear Thomas,

Herewith the account I promised you. A week ago last Monday, Cecelia and I attended one of those semi-obligatory social events you weasel out of with such regularity—a dinner, given by the Duke of Waltham, in course of which we were inveigled into attending a house party. We arrived here on the twenty-eighth, and it was immediately clear that our hosts, Mr. and Miss Webb, had something more in mind than the usual house party.

There are three other couples in attendance. Two of the gentlemen are local MPs, one from our side and one from the Opposition. I fully expect the political arguments over the after-dinner port to end in a brawl some evening, despite my best efforts. A formerly-impecunious baron completes the party. Not content with his wife's fortune, he seems to be looking to increase his holdings in any way possible. Not the most congenial of company.

At least Ramsey Webb's reason for putting together this

peculiar group have become plain. He is railway mad. He's up to his neck in a scheme to found a new railway corporation. To do so, he will have to get a bill of incorporation passed in Parliament, hence the local MPs. The baron and Waltham are here both for their possible votes in the Lords and as prospective investors.

And what are Cecelia and I doing in this carefully chosen company? It is all Waltham's fault. He told Webb that if anyone could persuade you to vote in favor of his incorporation bill, I could. Yes, you may laugh. His sister has already tried twice to sound Cecelia out on the matter. Cecelia routed her with blather about the children and basilisks and who knows what other nonsense. I have no such plausible recourse. If you learn that I have murdered His Grace, you will understand why.

To top things off, our mail is being opened; the seal on Kate's latest letter had been lifted and reapplied, with more than amateur skill. I suspect the Opposition MP; Cecelia began by suspecting the Webbs, but now seems more inclined to think Waltham must be the culprit.

Nonetheless, we remain at Haliwar Tower. Why, you ask? In part it is because this railway matter begins to look more serious than I had thought. Two weeks ago, on 19 March, one of the steam locomotives exploded in Stockton, killing an engineer and injuring several other people. One would expect such an event to have been a nine days' wonder in the area. Even if it had not been the talk of the town, one would have assumed that Cecelia and I would have heard some mention of it when we took our railway ride the following day. Yet we did not; I heard of it only by accident, yesterday in Leeds (one of the ostlers at the King's Head is cousin to one of the injured men and happened to be discussing it with a companion when I stopped there to retrieve your letter).

The clear conclusion is that someone has suppressed, to an extreme extent, general knowledge and talk of the accident. You know what gossip is like in small towns; it would take great authority, strong magic, or both together, to keep so sensational an incident from discussion.

A similar silence surrounds my missing surveyor. Once out of Leeds, away from the inn where he stayed, no one seems to have seen or heard of him. Yet it is clear, from the innkeeper's remarks, that Herr Magus Schellen behaved much as Cecelia and I have done—on his arrival, he made some investigation of the Darlington end of the railway, then paid his shilling to ride to Stockton and return. Someone ought to remember him, but no one does.

The question is, why? The whole affair smells of old cheese. I am sorry to have brought Cecelia along, but unless you could persuade Kate to concoct some serious illness on the part of one of the children, there would be no getting her to leave now. (As such a deception would be quickly uncovered, with results I do not like to consider, I will not ask it of you.) Remaining at Haliwar Tower seems the lesser of two evils. It also seems the most likely means of discovering what they are about, not to mention finding out who is opening our mail, and why.

One matter, at least, shows progress. You recall the letter that was waiting at the inn for my missing German? Wellington's people have at last provided a translation. It arrived in Leeds just after we removed to Haliwar, and was waiting for me along with your note when I returned. It seems to have been written by a fellow magician and close friend of Herr Schellen's, one Heinrich Kruger. Much of the letter was of a personal nature, but there were several relevant paragraphs, which I copy for you below:

> I have searched the archives as you requested. The maps of England are woefully out of date, as you might expect, and several of the translations are very bad. Nonetheless, I can find neither mark nor mention of a ley line running along the Tees river, though at least one crosses it near Stockton-on-Tees. Not even the English could miss a segment of such density as you describe; it must have been left off the maps deliberately. Your theory that it is a new line is absurd; I pray you will not mention it to anyone else, as the damage it would do your professional reputation would be considerable. The fundamental stability of ley lines is one of their most predominant characteristics; they do not appear and disappear like images in a mirror.
>
> The area between Liverpool and Manchester has been more thoroughly surveyed. There are several ley lines in that region, but none that run along,

or parallel to, any of the routes you asked about. I cannot, of course, vouch for any lines which may have been deliberately left off the maps. If you have English sources, I would suggest you check them, as only the most overzealous of British authorities would remove information from their *own* maps.

I can find no observations on the effect of running a steam locomotive in the vicinity of a ley line. The stationary steam engines used in mines have, to date, not been located near enough to ley points for any difficulties to become apparent, if difficulties there are. I found, however, any number of papers regarding the tapping of ley energies. Most of them warn of inadvisable methods of attempting it, or deal with the catastrophic results of applying such techniques. The few successful methodologies are complex, and require diagrams of immense proportions, anchored by elemental energies. I will copy out the procedures, if you request it, but I am reluctant to spend so much time on the mere chance that they might be of interest.

I am still uncertain as to what brought Herr Schellen to Stockton, when he was hired to survey the Liverpool-Manchester line, but I begin to have a glimmer of a notion — his curiosity regarding ley lines and steam locomotion is suggestive, you will agree, especially when taken in conjunction with the explosion of the railway engine two weeks ago.

I intend to devote my immediate investigations—if I can ever escape from Webb to make any—to discovering whether there were other, earlier accidents on the Stockton-Darlington railway that might have drawn the Herr Magus's attention in this direction. Meanwhile, I shall ask my dear Cecelia to see what can be ascertained about the ley line the letter implies is nearby. If she complains of the headache, even Miss Webb cannot deny her a quiet afternoon alone, and I doubt it will take her an entire afternoon to work the basic series of detection spells.

Yours,
James

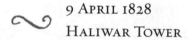

9 APRIL 1828
HALIWAR TOWER

Dearest Kate,

I am so happy that I cannot resist writing at once. (And besides, I think it possible that you are having difficulty reading the shawl I sent, or more likely with composing one in response. I intend to try a new enchantment on this letter, which will make it appear yet another compilation of complaints and queries about the children to any eyes but yours. Ignore the symbols along the edges; they are part of the enchantment.)

I am happy because my dear Walker has finally returned from her French holiday. No other maid has her hand with a curling iron, nor her thoroughness in pressing a seam. (She frowned darkly and said something in French when she saw the state my gowns are in after three weeks of travel, but I expect she will have things well in hand shortly.) She reports that things are quiet at Tangleford Hall.

She has also proven to be a useful ear in the servants' quarters—not that I ever doubted her ability (which she has proved repeatedly, as you well know), but I had expected that the circumstance of her being French, combined with the Yorkshire accent (which all of the servants possess to some extent, and which is, in a few, entirely impenetrable even to James), would make it difficult for her to play her usual role.

Happily, I was quite out in this regard. According to Walker, the combination of her English surname and obvious French origins elicits all sorts of questions, which serve to open a conversation. Several of the maids find her story excessively romantic—the French girl who married a young English officer, only to be cast out, penniless, when he died. In return, they regale her with similar romantic titbits from the Webbs' family history.

The most interesting bit of knowledge that she has so far unearthed is that the Webbs are descended from nobility. Haliwar Tower is all that remains of their splendid past. No one seems quite certain how or when the title was given up, though its loss is apparently something of a sore point for the Webbs. No one was willing to admit *which* nobleman was responsible (though I am certain they all must know; "old family secrets" of this sort are always common currency among the servants, no matter *how* long ago the events occurred).

Why should this be at all interesting (apart from the usual fascination that salacious gossip holds)? Well, because there is something very odd indeed about Haliwar Tower—but I must tell you this part in order, or I fear it will be utterly incomprehensible.

Last week, James received a translation of that German letter we have all been wondering about. It implied, quite strongly, that our missing Herr Magus was interested in a ley line that passed near the railway—quite a strong one, from the sound of it. (Has Thomas set you to studying ley lines yet? They are natural flows of magical energy, rather like rivers, though quite straight. A sufficiently hardy wizard can tap them to perform powerful magics. The longer the ley line, the more power it contains. And because a ley line is a natural phenomenon, one cannot simply *feel* it as one does an ordinary spell; not unless one has been sensitized by casting the proper spells of discernment. It was only about two hundred and fifty years ago that Ferranolo developed the detection spell that proved their existence, though it turns out they are quite common. There is a small one at Tangleford, and probably several near Skeynes.)

Naturally, James asked me to verify the presence of the line. It took me nearly a full day to surreptitiously assemble the materials for the spell (such things will be *vastly* easier now that Walker is here, as she can excuse all manner of peculiar ingredients as being part of her secret receipt for face cream), and another half day to detach myself from Adella Webb long enough to perform the detection spells (fortunately, I had a long letter from Papa that morning; I had only to show it to her to convince her that it would take me an entire morning of private endeavor to decipher it). Then I cast them all twice, just to be certain I had done everything right.

The spells, you see, are meant to give a clear "yes" or "no" answer to the question of whether there is a ley line in the neighborhood (and Haliwar Tower is quite close enough to Stockton and the railway for me to have detected whatever was there). If one has a map, one can even draw them in place. The answer I got was a muddle—there was *something* nearby, quite strong, but it did not have the crisp edges, clear path, and sense of flow that a ley line does. It felt more like a stagnant pond than a river of magic.

James was quite disappointed, though he assured me he did not think my skills were at fault. I was more disgruntled. The detection spells are really quite simple, once one knows them, and ought not to be susceptible to ambiguous reading unless the caster is extremely unskilled. (It is times like this, Kate, when I feel my lack of formal training. It is all very well to *say* that there is little real difference between a magician and a fully educated and accredited wizard, but you and I both know that it is no such thing.)

To coax me out of the dismals, James persuaded the Webbs that an afternoon ride was in order. (And it was indeed a splendid day for it—the morning drizzle had passed off, and the sky was only dotted with clouds, not smothered by them.) I fear that I was not at first in such good spirits as he had hoped—the Webbs' stable is merely adequate—but the opportunity to avoid yet another game of cards was irresistible. Two of the other couples decided to join us on the ride, and we set off with a minimum of fuss.

As soon as we passed the outer gate of Haliwar Tower, I felt the ley line (for the effects of the discernment spell do not fade for several hours). It was practically under my feet, running straight toward the river, and quite as strong as the German letter had implied.

Naturally, I gave no indication that anything was at all out of the common way. Fortunately, just at that point, Mr. Webb asked if we had any preference as to the direction of our ride.

"Is it far to the river?" I asked, looking east as if I thought that was the proper direction (when I knew perfectly well it runs west of Haliwar).

Mr. Webb frowned, as if he found something odd about my request, but before he could say anything, Adella leaned forward. "Oh, that will be perfect!" she said. "It is one of my favorite rides."

"It is just as like as not to rain before we get back," Mr. Webb said, frowning even more furiously.

"Then perhaps we should ride toward Stockton," I said a little too casually. "If rain comes on, we can take shelter there."

"An excellent notion," James put in promptly.

Mr. Webb's eyes narrowed slightly. Just as he was about to speak, one of the other ladies said, "Pish-posh! A little rain will not melt anyone."

"I bow to the ladies," Mr. Webb said. "Adella, as it is your favorite, will you lead?"

It took about an hour to reach the river at the slow pace Adella set, pausing occasionally when she saw a vista of particularly fine composition, and we crossed and recrossed the ley line as we wound our way along the lanes. As we came over a rise, I could feel the ley line even more strongly than before. Near the bank of the river, I could see one of the steam trains coming up the railway line.

Adella pulled her horse to a stop at the crest of the hill. "Is it not charming?" she said, waving at the river.

As I began to answer, the steam engine reached the point just opposite us, and the ley line began to tremble. The engine slowed, as if a sudden weight had been added to its load—and it had, Kate, for I could feel the steam train actually pulling the ley line sideways, like the string of a bow as it is being drawn. The horses felt it as well and began moving restlessly.

"What on earth—?" said one of the gentlemen as he tried to control his mount.

"The animals dislike the train," Mr. Webb said. "It makes them nervous."

Just then the steam engine blew a long whistle—James told me later that it is a way of letting off the pressure when the steam becomes too hot—and the ley line snapped back into place, vibrating. The horses all spooked; mine tried to rear, and I was very nearly unseated. The train picked up speed once more and disappeared among the hills, though a long, white plume of smoke continued to mark its position.

The other ladies were rather shaken, and I pretended to be, so we made our way back to Haliwar Tower at once. Mr. Webb was ungentlemanly enough to remark that if we had not insisted on visiting the river (and, perforce, the railway), we should not have been discomfited, but he did not make a great point of it. And as we returned through the gate, I felt the same blurring of my sense of the ley line, though by then the detection spell was fading rapidly.

So there is something about Haliwar Tower that dampens magic, or ley lines, or both together. It has the feel of something long-established, I think, though it is not easy to determine from inside. Still, it makes it unlikely that either of the Webbs is a magician, for they could not have failed to notice the problem, just as I have, and I am sure they would not have stayed here without attempting to do something about it.

There is also the matter of the ley line, which ought to run right under Haliwar (or rather, Haliwar was built directly atop it). So James has written to London to discover whatever old records there may be of the history and ownership of the tower. Meanwhile, I have dropped a hint that a visit to Stockton for purposes of shopping would not come amiss. (Which indeed it would not—I am in need of curl papers and yellow embroidery silk—but I am hoping to find a local history, or at least a volume on ley lines, at a bookstore or circulating library. Ley lines are a rather specialized area of study, even for full wizards, and I of course am familiar only with what is common knowledge among magicians.)

I trust the children are well and have created no permanent disasters, nor continued to populate your guest rooms with reptiles or other livestock. I do not, however, depend upon it. Give them my love.

Yours,
Cecy

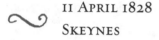

11 APRIL 1828
SKEYNES

Dear Cecy,

Heaven knows when I shall be able to send you this letter, for Thomas will have to enchant it for me. After ten years of study, I can dependably do the two spells Thomas taught me (finding him and calling him) and the spell Lady Sylvia showed me to keep my hair up, but I'm afraid that the fine points of magical cipher and anticipher will always be beyond me. I know Thomas despairs of me as a student. I cannot bear the cacophony of most spells, and I wonder at anyone who can.

The Webbs sound on a par with snakes and frogs. You have all my sympathies. On top of all that, Daniel seems an even greater social burden than usual. It is outside of

enough. There are some duties no one should have to perform, and in my view, gracious behavior under such conditions qualifies.

Forgive my grumpiness. Georgy is burden enough for
me. I am out of all patience with her sulking and her sighs.
This afternoon she shall join us, willy-nilly, for a walk across
the park to the hermitage. It is a lovely day, one of the finest
we have had, and if there is no other way to prise her out of
doors than to bully her into accompanying the children and
me (and the nurses, of course) on a combined mapmaking
expedition and frog hunt, so be it. (There won't be any frogs
at this time of year, of course, a piece of cynicism on my part,
which I freely admit played a primary role in my reasoning
when I agreed to the suggestion.)

I must seem a trifle obsessed with frogs. Do forgive me.
Given the scriptural lessons we hear at this season, the assorted plagues of Egypt have come to be a topic of rich
interest in the nursery. I am only grateful, given the alterna-
tives, that the plague that caught the children's interest was
mere frogs.

Although the quest for amphibian life is doomed to disappointment, we shall be adding to the Map (believe that it
deserves the dignity of a capital letter, for it is a stately creation, all Arthur and Eleanor's own work, constantly revised
and improved) as we negotiate the gardens and groves of
the park on our way to the folly. I trust praise of the twins'
Map will balance the inevitable disappointment at the lack
of frogs.

Of course, even if we find no frogs, there is every possibility Edward will find something just as disgusting. A snake, perhaps. Possibly a hedgehog. If we are really unfortunate, a nest of hornets.

Oh, the joys of family life. No wonder Thomas is taking so long to wander back from London. Who could blame him? When he returns, I will ask him to enchant this letter. At least I need not apologize for the delay, as you won't miss any news of importance.

Cecy,

Your children are safe. We have them (and Laurence, of course) under lock and key and every guarding spell conceivable. I will write the moment I have more news.

ᕫᕤ 12 APRIL

Dear Cecy,

What a dreadful mull I have made of this letter. I must repair my shattered wits and try my best to make sense of it for you. At least I have the comfort of knowing that the moment I conclude, Thomas is waiting to prepare it for me, so that you will read this in decent privacy. To anyone else, it would resemble the longest request for advice on child rearing in recorded history. I wish whoever is spying on you joy of the various receipts for pap.

In the opening (and I trust more lucid) passage of this letter, I made reference to an afternoon jaunt across Skeynes

Park. Ignorance is bliss, Cecy, make no mistake. I was so ignorant, I was quite blissful as we set forth across the grounds.

It was a lovely day. The grass, although damp underfoot, was not slippery. The children ran like colts, shouting with pure animal spirits. I felt a bit like shouting myself.

Georgy seemed as delighted with the beauty of the day as all the rest of us. Arthur and Eleanor led us, the Map held carefully between them, and Edward strolled from our left flank to our right and back, hands in his pockets and eyes on the ground. No snail, no salamander, no toad had a hope of escaping his notice. Diana, the infant Laurence, and Baby Alexander were safely in the keeping of Nurse Carstairs and Nurse Langley, and we had footmen along to carry the vast assortment of impedimenta our expedition required.

Our visit to the hermitage was a great success. After a thorough search of that Gothick ruin, during which Edward turned up a small grass snake, we settled in to enjoy a nice rest. Repose, although pleasant, did not last long. Arthur, Eleanor, and Edward were off again in just under a quarter of an hour. We less hardy souls composed ourselves to wait for their return. It seems a world away, that sleepy interlude during which the great concern on my mind was the possibility of grass stain.

Georgy grew concerned when the children did not return. She rose from her spot on the rug, brushed imaginary dust from her skirts, and challenged me. "Where can they be? Aren't you worried?"

"Don't you remember how tiresome it was to have Aunt Charlotte forever fretting over us?" I countered. "Let them alone. They can have a bit of an adventure for once."

"I'm going to find them," said Georgy. "Come along."

With reluctance, I joined her. We left the nurses doting upon Diana and the babies and walked down the path beyond the hermitage. A few hundred yards beyond, we were deep in woodland. The path continued, the trees thinned, and we found ourselves at the stile that gives on to the road.

Arthur and Eleanor were crouched beside the stile. As Georgy and I approached, they turned to us with gestures enforcing silence. With caution, Georgy and I approached and peered over the stone wall.

Standing in the middle of the road, for all the world as if its owner intended to set up permanent residence there, was a tinker's caravan of the most fascinating kind. There was a well-fed donkey in the traces, but no driver on the box. The body of the cart was freshly painted, with carved ornaments picked out in contrasting colors all around the curved roofline. There were spanking-clean curtains at the little window, and its tiny panes of glass gleamed as if polished by a jeweler.

The gaily painted cart was hung about with pots and pans and harness brass. Even motionless, it clanked faintly as the breeze stirred the pans. The door at the back was ajar and the step beneath was so neatly placed, it begged the onlooker to try for a peek at the snug quarters within.

I do not consider myself a magician, despite Thomas's best efforts to teach me, but I can sometimes detect the presence of magic. The charming sight we beheld convinced me that we were in the presence of strong enchantment. When the driver climbed over the stone wall on the far side of the road, I was sure of it.

I cannot describe the driver to you with any degree of accuracy, for I am certain the appearance I beheld was a disguise. Whoever it was, to me, the driver looked as if she were an elderly woman, stooped with great age, yet strangely nimble.

The driver gazed at us, bright-eyed, and crooked a finger at Georgy. "Glad to see you, missy. I've been waiting for you."

Georgy hasn't been a miss for a good many years now, never mind a missy. All scorn, she looked down her nose at the old woman.

"Your man," the old woman continued in the same goading tone, "is a sad specimen. He spends like he's rich, but the dibs ain't in tune. Who knows that better than you? To set himself to rights, he gave his word he'd help us. You remind him, missy. Remind him what he swore blind he'd do for us. Bring him up to the mark, missy, or something bad will happen, and chance it happens to you."

I felt Georgy stiffen at my side. Before she could reply—lord knows what she could have said to answer such extraordinary words—the old woman had clambered neatly up to the driver's seat, clicked to the donkey, and set off down the road.

We watched, all four of us, in dumbfounded silence as the cart clanked away, all pans rattling. I distinctly remember wondering how the driver had contrived to close the door at the back of the cart. I had not seen her go anywhere near it, yet as the caravan drew away, that door was shut.

With their usual grasp of essentials, Arthur and Eleanor homed in on Georgy. "Who was that, Aunt Georgy? Who was that lady?"

Georgy's indignation was immense. "Lady! Hardly! I've no notion who that creature was. I number no gypsies among my acquaintance."

"That was no gypsy," I put in. "That was someone in disguise. Could it be someone you know? Someone who thought you might recognize her?"

"Don't be ridiculous, Kate. I never saw that foul harridan before in my life. Oh, do let's go back. Just looking at her makes me want to wash my hands."

After our thorough exploration of the hermitage, the old woman had been, if anything, rather cleaner than we were, but I let Georgy's statement go unchallenged as we brought Arthur and Eleanor back to the nurses.

It was there, amid the rugs and picnic things, we discovered disaster had struck. Arthur, Eleanor, Diana, Alexander, and Laurence were all present and accounted for. Edward was nowhere to be seen.

We called him. No response. We called again and again. The footmen went peering through the shrubbery. Nothing.

There was a distinct clutching sensation under my heart. It was difficult to draw a shallow breath, impossible to take a full one. With the faultless intuition of any mother, I knew precisely what Edward had done. That fascinating caravan, its door ajar most temptingly, had lured him in. Edward had gone foraging.

"He's in the caravan." I spoke as I thought, too distraught to govern my words as I should. "He must have climbed inside to look around."

"Oh, no!" Georgy protested. "He couldn't have been so foolish."

"Of course he could. I know he did," I insisted. "I wanted to myself. Didn't you?"

I called the footmen out of the shrubbery. To Nurse Carstairs and Nurse Langley, I said, "Take the children home at once. Stay in the nursery, and don't come out for anything." I sent them back in the keeping of the footmen. I told Georgy to accompany them, but she refused.

"What will *you* do?" Georgy demanded. "Aren't you coming back with us?"

"I have to find Edward," I said. It was foolish to set off on foot, but I could think of nothing but to climb that stile and follow the caravan at once.

Georgy must have read my intention in my face, for she snorted and said, "Don't be absurd. Come back to the house with us."

"I must follow the caravan."

"By all means, but do so in a curricle. It's not as if you don't have dozens of carriages to choose from."

We don't, of course, not dozens, but the reminder that I had more resources than I realized steadied me. "Very well," I said, "but hurry!"

We made our disorganized way back to the house. Never has time passed more slowly. It was agony. I called for a carriage to be brought round. Georgy had a word with the butler, who had a word with the groom, and so forth. By the time I had given Reardon orders to pack a valise for me, Thomas's light curricle was at the door, his best pair in the traces.

Piers was ahead of me, checking the harness. "Shall I drive, my lady?" he asked, for all the world as if Thomas had engaged half a dozen bodyguards for me to choose among.

"Yes, of course. I'll just be a moment." I made sure that all reasonable preparations were in train, all children safely battened down, and then I used the password Thomas had given me to enter his study.

From the first magic lesson Thomas gave me, it has been dinned into my head that just as each of us has a distinct voice, each of us understands our magic in a way distinct from all others. Each of the spells I know well enough to perform fluently hurts my ears. When I set the wards, the world recedes as it should, yet the roar of discord caused by shutting out the world beyond the wards intensifies as I go deeper and deeper into the spell. Many a time I have finished a lesson with Thomas with my ears ringing. It is the way of things, yet I have not grown accustomed to the discomfort.

I cast my calling spell first, and I cast it without a thought of the discord. I meant to call Thomas with all my might. The wards came into place with an ease and speed I have never achieved before. I shut out the world with all my strength, braced myself against the onslaught I knew would come—and marveled at the focus I was able to achieve. I held the notes of my spell (for it has always seemed to me that casting a spell is like singing while accompanying myself on the piano) without half trying. It built in power as I went on, and I hardly noted the rage of crossed tones and mismatched rhythms at the edge of my hearing.

The calling spell seemed to have taken no time at all, once I cast it. I knew that was false. Time was fleeting. Yet I spared no effort in making sure that I closed down the spell properly and disposed of the leavings.

When I had every trace of the calling spell cleared up, I cast my finding spell for Edward. Many times have I used that very spell to locate a missing key or a lost pair of scissors. This time I held the wards in place as easily as if I were playing counterpoint. When I came to the heart of the spell, I cast it with such force that I felt my own heart lurching in time with it, a solid rhythm running under the mismatched thudding and shrieking beyond the wards.

It took great effort to clear up the finding spell properly, for the pulse of it beat so strongly in my veins, it was hard to keep still. I was quite beside myself by the time I had leisure to scrawl you a note to say your children were safe. It occurred to me that I could never post such a note all by itself. Sharing the news with you would have to wait until I could write properly.

I closed Thomas's study, sealed it as carefully as I knew how, and tied the strings of my bonnet uncomfortably tight beneath my chin.

There was no duty left for me to do but put on my heaviest cloak and march out to the curricle. I was free at last to go after Edward. I dreaded what lay before me, but it was quite a relief to turn at last in the only direction I wanted to go, and to know that in a few minutes, Piers would be driving me at top speed, that I would be following the call that beat inside me like deep music.

The hall seemed small and dark. I knew people were there to see me off, but they seemed remote and unimportant compared with the brightness of the light in the direction I needed to go. I said nothing to anyone, just moved with all possible speed toward the curricle.

When I was outdoors, Piers was standing at the horses' heads, and Thomas was there. I thought for a moment I was seeing things, that I had wished for him so hard that I'd turned my brain with longing. But it was Thomas in truth. He was looking rather pale, leaning against the curricle, and rubbing his forehead.

I threw myself at him, and his hat fell off as he gathered me to him. I couldn't speak at first, and when I could, it was to utter pure idiocy. "You've come."

"Of course I have," Thomas said gently. "I was almost here when you called me. Shouting down a rain barrel ain't in it, my darling. You've half deafened me."

"My calling spell worked?"

"Not that it needed to. I was only half a mile away," said Thomas. "It worked a treat. And you've cast a finding spell to match it. If you cast any more spells of that caliber, my head may come clean off."

I could not seem to let Thomas go. I could not seem to steady my voice enough for words, but I buried my face in Thomas's neck, and he soothed me with great efficiency.

"There now, better?" he said, at last.

I looked up at him and nodded. Words were beyond me. He produced a handkerchief, and I made good use of it.

"Good girl," Thomas said, as he helped me up into the curricle. He climbed up beside me and took charge of the whip and reins. "Piers, you're our tiger."

"Yes, my lord!" Piers retrieved Thomas's hat for him, then, nimble as a stableboy, clambered up to take his place behind.

"Hang on," said Thomas, and sprang 'em.

Is anything more noble than a pair of fast horses at a full gallop? All the rocking and lurching of a curricle is worthwhile for the sake of such speed. I would have followed Edward by mule if necessary, but a thousand times over I blessed the curricle and the team and Thomas's skill as we bowled along.

I used the first few miles to compose myself. When I

could speak sensibly again, I put the handkerchief away, then told Thomas, "Edward is in that caravan. He climbed in to explore."

"I know. He was hidden from them at first," said Thomas. "They've found him now."

I stared at him. "How can you know that?"

"Arthur and Eleanor told me they scryed it in the cup Nurse Langley uses to rinse her watercolor brushes," Thomas replied.

"Impressive." I had been so intent upon casting my own simple spells, I never noticed the children casting theirs.

"I agree. Good day's work I put in, teaching them that." Thomas drove on.

The miles spun away behind us. I leaned against Thomas to brace myself against the swaying of the carriage and the pounding inside my heart and head. I could feel Thomas's strength beside me, and I knew that he was using his power to help me use mine.

"Edward's not in the caravan now," I said, after a long uncertain time. "He's so frightened. Oh, Thomas."

"Don't falter, love. Take heart, and he will, too. Hold the link between you steady as you can." Thomas brought the horses down to a trot, intent on husbanding their strength and endurance.

It made it hard to pay attention, focusing all my strength on that inward vision. I lost track of our progress. It seemed we had been traveling forever, rattling along as fast as the horses could safely go.

Our route descended from the gentle hills. My vision seemed to darken slightly at the edges. When our speed slackened further, I realized we had begun to climb out of a valley toward a town on a hillside overlooking a river. With disbelief, I gauged the angle of the sun and found it was hardly midafternoon. "Where are we?" I asked Thomas. I was dismayed at how weak I sounded, how downhearted.

"This is Stroud." Thomas used the whip to show me the crossroads we approached. "Stay on this road?"

"Yes, it's straight on." I was sure of that. "Keep on toward the heart of the town."

"How is Edward?" Thomas sounded a bit strangled, but otherwise quite calm.

I rubbed my eyes, but the darkness I sensed had nothing to do with the sunny afternoon we drove through. "He's somewhere very dark," I said. After another little while, I was able to identify the feeling that tugged at the edge of my awareness. "He's not so frightened now. More . . . interested."

"Lord help us," muttered Thomas.

We drove on. The streets of Stroud tangled around us.

"This is the place," I said. I had not the slightest doubt of it.

We found ourselves before a perfectly ordinary house, namelessly plain, in a street of respectably drab houses. Thomas put out a hand to stop me when I started to rise from my place in the curricle. "Let me."

Thomas descended from the carriage. I stayed where I was, trembling with fatigue and emotion.

With minimal gesticulation yet unmistakable authority, scarcely murmuring a word aloud, Thomas cast what even I could recognize as a spell masterly in its restrained power. Silence followed for a split second, and then a series of clicks sounded, like a thousand crickets gone mad.

"What was that noise?" I asked.

"The tumblers of every lock and the latch on every door in the place," Thomas replied. "It's all open now."

I followed Thomas up the steps into the little foyer. After the bright day outdoors, it was so dim I could hardly see. The house smelled old, a compound of dusty furniture and damp wallpaper.

Thomas said a word under his breath, and I could feel the pulse of power beneath the small sound. Although to the casual observer he may have appeared entirely undisturbed, Thomas was furious.

"Come out," Thomas ordered. Despite his soft voice, the words carried throughout the gloomy house.

No one came out.

We searched together from room to room, from floor to floor, and found no one. I had every confidence in Thomas, but my consternation grew as we went on. The entire house was deserted, no one there for us to curse or question.

As my despair and fear rose, I lost control. The tears began in earnest.

"Wait." Thomas's curt tone was belied by the gentle touch of his hand on mine. "Listen."

From above us on the stair to the attic came a rustle of cloth followed by a soft familiar footstep. We stared up into the gloom.

"Edward?" I whispered.

A blessedly familiar voice said, "Mama!"

Edward descended the rest of the attic stairs in a leap that ended in my arms. One last throb beneath my breastbone and the finding spell faded away. I sat down hard in the dusty passage, cradling Edward as I buried my face in his hair. "Oh, you bad boy! We've been so worried!"

"Me, too," said Edward. His voice was a muted squeak. "Loosen up a bit. I can't breathe."

"You won't need to breathe when I've finished with you, young man," Thomas thundered. "What do you mean, giving your mother such a fright?"

In his inimitably eel-like fashion, Edward freed himself from my embrace and turned to call with lordly pride up the attic stairs, "This is my father."

Thomas helped me to my feet as we gazed in silence. From the top of the shabby staircase descended a girl no older than Eleanor. To judge by her expression, the child was quite unafraid of us. The dignity and grace with which she moved kept her petticoats clear of the dust on the steps. At the foot of the stair she stood, head held high, her back wonderfully straight, and regarded us in silence.

Edward took her hand. He is young for formal introductions, but I was surprised at the instinctive ease with which he made it known to us that the girl was named Drina, and to the girl that we were his mother and father. "Drina took care of me." Edward regarded her with a proprietary air. "May she come home with us?" His tone was exactly what it would have been had he suggested he be permitted to keep some reptile or bird he had found.

Drina said nothing. It seemed a matter of complete indifference to her what we did or didn't do.

"She will want her own home and her own mother and father, I'm sure." I turned to address the child directly. "Or is this your home?"

"Drina doesn't live here. Her people aren't here, either, and I want to go home now." Edward regarded his filthy hands with deep satisfaction. "Could use a wash."

I drew Edward toward the light. "Darling, you're simply covered in soot." Belatedly I realized that I was covered in soot, too. Thoroughly as our son was coated in the stuff, there had been plenty to rub off on me as I embraced him.

Thomas handed me his handkerchief and took up the questioning as I did my best to repair first Edward's appearance and then my own. "Hid up the chimney, did you?"

"They locked me in with Drina." Edward gazed adoringly over the handkerchief at his trim young friend. "She gave me a leg up so I could climb into the chimney."

"Oh, well done." Thomas turned his attention entirely

to Drina. "There's no one else left in the house. If anyone should return, I will deal with it, trust me. There's no need to be afraid."

Drina made no reply, but her chin lifted a fraction of an inch. The tiny movement spoke volumes. Drina feared no one, least of all us.

Thomas asked, "Where do you live?"

Drina looked at him in silence. I put the grimy handkerchief away and dusted my hands briskly. "Thomas, let's go home. If Drina doesn't care to accompany us, she can tell us so."

Thomas seemed at a loss for a moment, but the look we exchanged persuaded him to trust me. "Very well."

I held out my hand to Drina, and after a moment's hesitation, she took it. If she had not clung so tightly, I would have found her entire lack of emotion disquieting. As it was, the minor sign of distress touched me to the heart. Young Drina, whoever she was, had helped Edward in his imprisonment, so she could ask anything of us and I would give it gladly.

I tried to conceal any trace of my curiosity, for to be honest, I found it a trifle vexing that a child of Drina's tender years could outdo me in the matter of sangfroid.

"I would have climbed out the chimney if you hadn't come," Edward informed us. "Even if you hadn't come, I would have escaped."

"Yes, dear. Of course, dear." We left the house and descended to the street, Edward clattering and chattering at our heels, as prosaically as if we were returning from a social call.

Thomas settled Edward and Drina between us in the curricle with his cloak spread over them for warmth. Piers took up his position behind. With all due respect for the exertions the team had endured, we turned for home. I believe that both of the children were sound asleep by the time we reached the Gloucester Road. I dozed a little myself.

We arrived at Skeynes without incident. Edward stirred awake at the hero's welcome he was given. Happy return indeed. He is in perfect health, although prone to fits of irritability when Arthur and Eleanor pester him for details of his captors. I tried to stop them, but Eleanor was reproachful as she pointed out my error. "We would never pester Edward, Aunt Kate. We are just gathering clues."

The child Drina remains mute, although it is plain that she understands every word spoken. At first she was such a stoic, I wondered if she viewed herself as our prisoner. If so, I think she has revised her opinion. Edward alone might not reassure her, but Arthur, Eleanor, Diana, and the babies seem to have done it.

Georgy has locked herself in her room, which I find a curious response to Edward's safe return. More curious still, Georgy helped herself to the last of my best writing paper. I will ask her why when she emerges. Meanwhile, please excuse this paper. It is some the twins were given for their Map.

Thomas is deep in inquiries concerning the house in Stroud.

As soon as Thomas has enchanted this letter so that it can be read by your eyes only, I will post it. Perhaps then I shall lock myself in the nursery. Perhaps I shall stay up there with the children and send down only for meals. When you and James and Thomas have unraveled all these mysteries for us, I may descend. Then again, I may not. It depends on how thoroughly the old nursery tranquility works its spell.

Yours in deepest consternation,
Kate

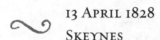

13 APRIL 1828
SKEYNES

Dear James,

This was going to be such a brief letter. I was going to make it look like a dunning notice from your tailor. It then occurred to me that, as in all likelihood you've never made your creditors wait so much as five minutes for payment, you wouldn't recognize such a missive should you receive one.

So instead you have my cipher note containing instructions on how to persuade this letter to permit you to read it, a note which you must have deciphered or you would not be reading this now.

Oh, enough of thinking about things from your point of view. Not only does it slow me down, it may make you doubt this letter's authenticity, and we can't have that.

I owe you, James. Cecy, too, I suppose. I'm very grateful to the pair of you for loaning us your children. Diana and Alexander still seem harmless enough, but Arthur and Eleanor have been an immense help in the past few days.

No, this is not some new kind of code. I am quite sincere.

Kate will have told you (via Cecy) of all the excitement we have had here. They began without me.

Kate's finding spell, cast entirely on her own, with no assistance from me or anyone else—not that there was anyone else qualified to help—was a hell of a finding spell, James, a finding spell that would have worked had Edward been shanghaied and shipped out to the Fiji islands. I am so proud of her, I can hardly contain myself.

Edward has answered our questions readily enough. If he knew precisely what happened to him and why, he would tell us. Unfortunately, he has only a dim idea of where he went and no idea why. Indeed, he seems to delight in confusing us with varied accounts of his adventure.

Luckily, his cousins are superb inquisitors (as you have reason to know), and I trust that soon they will have the whole story out of him in accurate and comprehensible form. Arthur makes a particularly ruthless questioner, for he burns with indignation that his cousin should have had this adventure. In Edward's place, Arthur is sure he would have made a much better thing of it, if only he hadn't behaved with such foolish good sense and restraint.

I applaud Young England's desire for adventure, but I have made a point of thanking Arthur for behaving as a true gentleman should. He looked to the welfare of the ladies before his own. If Edward demonstrates even half as much good sense at Arthur's age, I will be proud of him.

The most unsettling result of this adventure is that we find ourselves in (temporary, I trust) possession of a superfluous child.

I suspect you enter into my sentiments on this matter. That is, after the first half dozen, one child more or less makes little difference to the general chaos, disorder, and stickiness of life. However, I am reliably informed that *this* child (like any other) must possess a name and address, parents, siblings, and a station in life. It is my duty to discover all these things as soon as possible. I would be very happy to oblige, but the child refuses to speak. When I attempt to question her, I soon find myself removed from the room on grounds that I am frightening the child. Believe me when I tell you, that child is not in the least frightened of any of us, least of all me. There is simply no pleasing Kate sometimes.

Still, I have made some progress in this matter. I have made inquiries about the house in Stroud (thoroughly and abruptly abandoned just before our arrival—apparently they felt us coming) where Edward was taken.

I have a name—Adolphus Medway—for the individual who hired the house, but although I have explored the entire street, I can find no two people who agree on his appearance. He has been described to me as entirely common in height and build, extremely tall and thin, and remarkably short and stout. His voice is reedy, deep, and nasal, depending on who it is we talk to. Unless the nefarious Mr. Medway is a committee of some kind, we are dealing with a shape-shifter.

None of the neighbors is able to cast any light on the identity of our surplus child. They never noticed she was there. I can only suppose the versatile Mr. Medway exhausted their powers of observation.

Wrexton has some interesting sources in the ministry. I've shared as much of our puzzle with him as I felt proper. He is well connected at the Royal College of Wizards, so his inquiries may bear fruit.

In the very near future I shall be compelled to interrogate my watering pot of a sister-at-law. Kate has been given every opportunity to coax a confession from Georgy. No result. It's time to take a firm line with the little baggage.

There's really no excuse for these goings on, and I have every reason to expect her husband, dunce that he is, will be found ultimately responsible. How I wish I had yielded to my baser instincts long ago. I should have broken his neck at the wedding, when he took such pleasure in pointing out to me that Georgy would now take social precedence over Kate. Duke he may be, but his behavior has never matched his supposed breeding.

I'll write as soon as I have anything of substance to add. Until then, do try to stay out of trouble. I have my hands full here.

Yours,
Thomas

14 APRIL 1828
HALIWAR TOWER

Dearest Kate,

What a fright you gave me! It is the oddest thing, to be sure, but somehow it is not at all soothing to discover an unanticipated reassurance, however sincere, in the middle of a letter where one had expected nothing more stimulating than an account of how many times one's children had contrived to fall into a creek or pond. I am so very glad that you recovered Edward promptly.

My first reaction to your letter was neither so calm nor so sensible. Indeed, I am afraid that the intensity of my emotions led me to act with uncharacteristic rashness. To be quite plain, as soon as I had read your letter, I thrust it into James's hands and set off in search of Daniel. Most unfortunately, I found him almost immediately, before I had had time for my head to clear. He was in the gun room, examining a set of dueling pistols with two of the other houseguests. I did at least retain enough presence of mind to say in what I thought was a matter-of-fact tone, "I beg your pardon for interrupting, but I have something of a private nature to discuss with my cousin-at-law. Rather urgently."

I must have sounded more decided than I intended, for Daniel went pale and began stammering that there was no need, while the two gentlemen with him immediately bowed and left. I managed to contain myself until the door had closed behind them, and then I said in a low voice, "How *dare* you!"

Daniel backed away, for all the world as if I had pulled a shotgun from one of the wall mounts and threatened him with it. "What? What? How dare I what?"

"I was hoping you would tell me the details, my lord," I said coldly. "I'm sure you have some excellent reason for your actions. Threatening Georgy until she runs away, and then following her and setting gypsies on to kidnap our children—how *dare* you!"

"Georgina?" Daniel blinked, then looked, if possible, even more distressed than before. "Has something happened to her? Lucky said he'd call them off, but that was before . . . Where is she?"

"She's with Kate and Thomas, as you must know, and if you think Thomas will let you get away with this, you are very much mistaken. If there's anyone Thomas cares for as much as Kate, it's Edward. Duke or not, you are going to be very sorry your people laid a finger on that boy."

"What has Edward got to do with Georgina?" Daniel said. Then he frowned slightly, and added, "Or with me, for that matter."

"You know quite well—," I began, and the door behind me opened. I spun around and found James, wearing a puzzled expression and holding your letter.

"Cecy," he said in that long-suffering tone he occasionally uses, "why is it of such enormous urgency for me to read an account of the sniffles that have attacked the nursery crowd at Skeynes, along with several receipts for cough mixtures?"

I stared at him, then realized what must have happened. When Thomas enchanted your letter, he did a thorough job of it—*no one* else could read the real message, not even James. I took a deep breath, arranged my thoughts, and gave him a summary of the relevant portions.

"I see," James said when I finished. "And you rushed out here . . ."

"To find Daniel and drag an explanation out of him," I said, turning as I spoke. "And he—" I stopped. The only sign of Daniel was the half-open French door that led to the garden.

"Come on," said James, and we followed.

We did not find him. We did find the Webbs—or they found us, for they appeared almost the instant we left the gun room. They were perfectly happy to help us search for Daniel, at first, though naturally they refused to split up. They became much less happy as time went on with no sign of my lord duke, and they displayed positive signs of annoyance when news arrived that his mare was missing from the stable. The annoyance was quite clear at tea, when he still had not returned. Mr. Webb said, rather shortly, that he hoped Daniel's horse had not met with an accident, then sent one of the grooms out to look for him (a singularly useless gesture, since no one had seen him leave and therefore no one knew in which direction to look for him).

And that is how the matter stands at present. It is after midnight now, and Daniel has not returned. I do not think he means to. His valet is very dignified and closemouthed, but I believe that is mere show; the man cannot know where Daniel went, nor why, since Daniel left immediately after our conference in the gun room.

Naturally, everyone wanted to know what "personal matters" Daniel and I had been discussing. Fortunately, I had had plenty of time to consider my response by the time they thought to ask. I told them, with a great show of reluctance, and in utmost confidence, that I had just learned that my cousin Georgy had run away from him and was nowhere to be found, and I wished to know why. Whoever read your earlier letter must know that this is sheer fabrication on my part, but they all looked suitably shocked by the revelation. (I place no dependence on their discretion; if the story is not all over London by the end of the week, it will only be because none of them has any social acquaintance there to correspond with. It is most unfortunate, but there really was no other news that would have served.)

Upon reflection, I am not entirely sorry to have lost my temper with Daniel. Now that I have had time to consider all that he said, and your report of the gypsy woman's remarks, it seems to me very likely that it is not actually Daniel who is threatening Georgy. He appeared genuinely concerned about her, Kate. The gypsy's remark about the "dibs being in tune," taken together with Daniel's comment about someone named Lucky "calling them off" make me suspect that the real culprit is one of Daniel's gambling associates. I shall be very interested to discover why. Despite what the gypsy said, it cannot be gaming debts. Daniel may be nearly as chuckleheaded as Georgy, but he has always been punctilious about paying his debts of honor.

James was quieter than usual through the afternoon. When we retired for the evening and were quite private at last, I discovered why. First, he asked me to read your letter aloud (for of course it still looks to his eyes like a list of cough medicine receipts). When I finished, there was a long, thoughtful pause. Then he said, in the most expressionless voice possible, "Do you wish to return home to see for yourself that the children are safe?"

I fear I am a most unnatural mother, for until that moment, the possibility had not occurred to me. I considered the matter carefully for some while, for James only uses that tone of voice when he earnestly desires not to influence my response. Finally, I said, "No, I do not think it is necessary. I don't believe the children are in any danger. The gypsy woman only threatened Georgy; carrying off Edward was probably quite accidental. And if Kate had wanted me, she would have asked." I paused, working things out in my mind. "And if we were to race home now, it might give whoever is threatening Georgy the notion of threatening the children instead."

I am afraid my voice wobbled at the end, for James rose hastily and came over to me. "Now, Cecy, it's quite all right. Kate said everyone was safe."

"Yes," I said into his shoulder. "And I am sure she will keep them so. But do *you* think I ought to go back?"

Silence. I looked up, to find James's expression a study in conflict. He sighed. "I don't know. I think you are right about the children, but I am not sure it is safe for you to be here. If someone is threatening Georgy in order to squeeze money out of Daniel, they might well try the same with you."

I stared at him for a moment before I found my voice. "You think I am no more capable of dealing with such persons than *Georgy?*"

"No, not at all," James said hastily. "I mean, that is not what I meant."

"If it is safe enough for you to be here, it is safe enough for me," I said. "And if it *isn't* safe, I am *certainly* not leaving until you do. Especially since there is magic involved. Thomas is a very good wizard even when he is distracted by magnetism and good burgundy, and under the circumstances, he won't let himself be distracted by anything. The children will be spell-warded within an inch of their lives. You, on the other hand, can't even light a candle without a paper spill. And it is quite evident that there is *something* very odd going on at Haliwar, magically speaking. You need a magician here more than Kate and Thomas need one at Skeynes."

James tried to argue, but it was plain that his heart was not in it, and he did not keep it up for long. So we remain at Haliwar. I shall attempt to discover more at this end, and

I will let you know at once if Daniel returns. (And, if he does, what he has to say for himself—for I shall not be balked a second time, Webbs or no Webbs.)

Your determined,
Cecy

P.S. And *of course* you can only do three spells reliably. You have never cared for magic, only for what it can do, and there are only three things that you truly want to do, which can only be done by magic: find Thomas or the children, call Thomas, and keep your hair from falling down. If you ever find a fourth thing that you *want,* I will give you a new bonnet if you have the slightest difficulty in learning a spell to do it.

P.P.S. It is now Tuesday morning, and I am about to leave this letter for the post. Daniel has still not come back, and the Webbs are becoming quietly frantic at having mislaid so important a guest. I will let you know the *moment* I have worthwhile news; I trust you to do the same. —C.

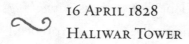

16 APRIL 1828
HALIWAR TOWER

(in cipher)

My dear Thomas,

Congratulations on retrieving your wayward offspring. Having heard Kate's account of the matter, I congratulate her even more heartily on not having had to retrieve any of mine, as well. I am, in fact, quite astonished that neither Arthur nor Eleanor attempted to join Edward's adventure, and I can only put it down to your wife's good influence, as I know better than to think you have had much to do with the nursery crowd.

You will be pleased to hear that the enchantments on your letters are working to your usual high standards, which is to say that your notes are quite impossible for anyone to read if they do not have the proper key. Indeed, your vile scrawl was barely readable even once the key was applied. It is a pity that magic cannot do anything about that.

I suspect its illegibility is the reason your missive was some hours later in appearing in the hall than the rest of the post; whoever has been intercepting our correspondence is still trying, despite our precautions. The only other letter to be so delayed, thus far, was one of Cecelia's missives from her father, due, I assume, to his execrable handwriting. I cannot think that our meddler would have much interest in his queries about the local antiquities—Viking campsites, Saxon ruins, and prehistoric standing stones—which Cecelia tells me made up the bulk of his letter.

I harp on the question of legibility for a particular reason. Though I have been over your letter several times, I am still unsure whether it was a Mr. Medway or a Mr. Medbury who made the arrangements for the house in Stroud where you found Edward. If it is indeed the former, I must tell you that a Mr. Harold Medway, of Stockton-on-Tees, is the man of business with whom Webb has been so involved of late.

Before you come charging up to the north counties, let me point out that Mr. Harold Medway cannot have been the multifaced person you so eloquently described. Tall, short, fat, thin, bald, red-haired—no matter the disguise or enchantment, this Mr. Medway has been here in Stockton since well before the beginning of this infernal house party and therefore cannot have been recently in Stroud. Yes, I have made inquiries, under pretext of looking for someone to work with regarding the supposed property I am pretending to wish to purchase. And since our arrival at Haliwar, Mr. Harold Medway has been out to consult with Webb every day. Not even magic could get him to Stroud and back, with time to arrange for a house rental, in between his visits here.

Nonetheless, if your vanishing renter is indeed a Mr. Medway, I find the coincidence of names disturbing. It may, of course, be simple coincidence, but I distrust coincidences of that sort. I think it more likely that someone borrowed the name, since it would be foolish indeed for anyone bent on threats and kidnapping to make rental arrangements in his own person. Or it may be a black sheep somewhere in the Medway flock. I will see what else I can discover in that regard; in the meantime, the northern connection may give you an additional angle for your own investigations. If, of course, it is Medway and not Medbury.

There is still no sign of our missing German. Peculiarities, there are in plenty. It has taken me nearly three weeks to collect even as little information as I have done. In part, this seems due to the understandable desire of the instigators of the Stockton and Darlington Railway to keep their difficulties quiet, so as to avoid panicking their investors.

One thing we have established with certainty: There is an extremely strong ley line running directly across the rail line, one end of which passes under Haliwar Tower. I believe, on the strength of Cecelia's observations, that the steam engine is interfering with the ley line (or vice versa, depending on how you look at it). Cecelia said the engine actually pulled the ley line sideways for a moment, like the string of a bow being drawn back. The extra load might well explain the unexpectedly high number of breakdowns. Unfortunately, the Webbs have made it impossible to investigate the railway line itself. So, for the present, we are at a stand.

Waltham has, as you may already know, seen fit to depart from Haliwar for parts unknown. The only surprising thing about this is that he did not do so weeks ago. His valet speaks of giving up waiting for his master's return and departing for Waltham Castle, on the theory that when His Grace reappears, he will either do so at his main seat or else send a message there. The Webbs are far more disturbed by this than Cecelia or I, but then, they cannot know His Grace so well. Despite his worries, Ramsey Webb continues his attempts to persuade me to give over looking at property and invest in his railway project instead.

I assume that by this time you have returned your superfluous child to her annoyed or worried parents—that is, assuming that she, like Edward, was lured away accidentally. If she belongs to your mysterious Medway or Medbury, you may have her on your hands some time.

Yours,
James

17 APRIL 1828
SKEYNES

(This letter faithfully enchanted by T.S., all his own work)

Dear Cecy,

I am so sorry to have alarmed you unduly. I wrote in haste. Now that I have leisure to write in more detail of these matters, I will try not to make such a mull of things again. You have much too much to worry about without my adding to the sum.

The children are all quite well. I shall enclose their latest missives along with mine when I render this up to Thomas.

If it is any comfort to you, it is a great comfort to me that you intend to stay with James. Difficult as the decision must have been, I believe it is the right one.

In addition, I have a purely selfish reason to rejoice. If you came here, there is the distinct possibility that Thomas would find some urgent reason James would need Thomas's help. In certain moods, Thomas can be distinctly mercurial, and he has done quite enough gadding about for now.

News of Daniel's disappearance does not alarm me as it might have done a week ago. Given recent events, very little alarms me as it might have done a week ago. I feel as if my supply of alarm has been exhausted, at least temporarily.

Your discoveries at Haliwar Tower astound us, however. In the seclusion of his study, I read your account aloud to Thomas. The look on his face at your description of the behavior of the ley line was such a compound of curiosity and frustration (for he longs to fling caution to the winds and go and interfere) that I cannot do justice to it. You may indeed trust us to let you know any worthwhile news. Be very sure that if any insight into the matter occurs to Thomas, he will communicate it with all speed.

The morning after our return from Stroud, Thomas invited me to accompany him on a horseback ride. It was a perfect spring morning. The breeze was pleasantly fresh, not raw. The meadows were invitingly green, not muddy. Even the stone walls seemed to glow golden in the sunlight.

There was such significance in his expression as he proposed the outing that I was not surprised when he drew rein the moment we were out of sight of the house.

"Will you help me cast the protective spell?" Thomas looked grave. "I'm going to ride the bounds of the park and the home wood. The barriers will be set deep and wide. No one will cross without my permission."

"I'll help all I can," I said.

Thomas looked pleased. "Excellent. Just stay close."

As we rode, Thomas cast his spell. It must take a master to work any kind of a spell from the saddle. I find it difficult enough to do it when I am sitting comfortably on the floor. The rhythm of the ride seemed to play a role in the rhythm of the spell. I had a sense that Thomas's spell used the life around us, the horses, the trees, the grass, the weeds—everything—to balance and to steady his intention.

I was very conscious of the way my ring felt on my finger. Had Thomas asked me to help in any active way, I might have found the sensation distracting. I could feel my heart beating, I could feel the ring, and I could stay on my horse. More than that, I could not have done.

We rode only the immediate perimeter of Skeynes: the grounds and gardens of the park to the east and west, the home wood to the north, and to the south, the home farm as far as the edge of the common. Truly, Arthur and Eleanor should pride themselves on the accuracy of their Map. I was pleased to note how faithfully they drew the boundaries.

By the time we returned to the house, Thomas was pale with fatigue, and I fear I have seldom been more disheveled. I had been at close quarters with every hedgerow and thicket en route, and my riding habit sustained considerable wear and tear.

Despite all this exertion, my hair did not come down, and I think you must have a point about the spells I have learned. The skill to keep my hair up reliably I count a true blessing. Calling and finding spells are important, but heaven forefend I need to use either of them again soon. My ears still ring from time to time.

The nursery is not the sanctuary I had hoped it would be, although it has helped me calm my fears for the children, spending so much time getting my hands sticky along with them. My advent has been accepted with visible tolerance by both Nurse Carstairs and Nurse Langley. Their patience is perceptible. I'm sure that they view my time in their stronghold as an indulgence to me. Indeed, it is.

Thank heavens for the charms of novelty. The children are not yet weary of my frequent presence among them, but soon the nurses will be. As a result, I am on my best behavior at all times, and when my presence is absolutely required elsewhere, the mutual relief is palpable.

Of course, we still have questions to answer. Thomas's enthusiasm for the inquiries in Stroud, I suspect, stemmed from his utter reluctance to question Georgy. Eventually, of course, the moment had to arrive.

Thomas and Georgy met (with me in the role of arbiter and referee) in the morning room, a spot as close to neutral territory as Skeynes can provide. Georgy had a bit of needlepoint with her and was seated in her favorite chair, her back to the window.

Thomas was having none of that. "Change places with Kate." As we obeyed, he added, "I need to see your face."

Georgy looked annoyed. "You enjoy ordering people about."

Thomas thought that over. "Doesn't everyone?"

"I don't," I said. "Oh, Georgy. I'm so worried. Please. Tell us what is going on."

Now, in all likelihood, I have said those words to Georgy a hundred times since her arrival. This time she answered me, but it was because of Thomas. I have never seen him show a more forbidding countenance. "I don't read Daniel's correspondence." The tone in which Georgy announced this suggested to me that she has done exactly that, more than once. "But he has been so . . . so different of late. Cold. More than that, he has been impatient, even surly at times. I know he is in financial trouble. He always grumbles about his investments, but this is different. I have begged him to confide in me, but he gets his mulish look and says nothing."

"Daniel was rich as Croesus when you married him," I protested. "What happened?"

"He has many investments," Georgy said. "Yet somehow Daniel's investments are not like other people's investments. Other people invest money, and it earns more money. Daniel's investments seem to demand more money, always more money, even for him to keep the holdings he has. He has shares in several railways. The only one that ever showed any promise is the Stockton to Darlington line. Five months ago, they demanded he double his stake."

When Georgy said "Stockton to Darlington," I could not help a glance at Thomas. His attention was all on Georgy, his expression grim.

Georgy continued, "That last afternoon, I was in the drawing room with Daniel as he read a letter he had received. It angered him. He crumpled it up and threw it into the fireplace. His aim was not of the best, however. When Daniel left the room, which he did very soon after, I was able to scrape it out again, smooth the page, and read it."

"So, whatever it was," I said, "Daniel could not have considered it of great importance. If he had, surely he would have kept it . . . or made certain to burn it. He would not have treated it so carelessly if it mattered to him."

Georgy paid no attention to me. Her gaze was fixed upon the needlework in her lap, but she seemed not to see it. "The letter was unsigned. It said, 'If you want a dead duchess, you've done all the right things.' I threw it from me as if it were a poisonous snake. This time the fire caught it at once, and it burned to ash before my eyes. I ought to have kept it as evidence, I know. A moment's reflection told me I was a fool."

"Unfortunate," Thomas agreed. "Did the letter come with a cover? Any sort of return address? A clue of any kind to the identity of whoever wrote it?"

Georgy shook her head. "It was a single sheet of paper, folded and sealed with wax. The direction was to His Grace, the Duke of Waltham. There was no frank. It might have been delivered by a footman. It must have been, for it was a Sunday. I didn't think of that then. I didn't think of anything. All I could do was leave at once."

"Thank goodness you came here," I said. "At the very

least, it referred to a threat against you. But I fail to see how it incriminates your husband. Harming you would only add to his troubles, not solve them."

"You forget the settlements," Georgy said. "When the marriage was arranged, Daniel settled a sum of money on me. It was a trifle to him then, but his circumstances are different now. The only way he can touch those funds is if I . . . die."

"Oh, nonsense," I exclaimed. "If Daniel needs funds so desperately, why can't he just sell a few thousand acres of land?"

"Most of the property is entailed," said Georgy. "No one could sell it."

"Well, suppose Daniel did mean to murder you for the money," I said. "Do you believe that is the sort of letter a hireling would write in reply to such a proposal? It hardly seems businesslike."

"Probably a mistake to assume Daniel means you any harm on the basis of that evidence," Thomas agreed, "but I think it was a sound decision to leave, given the circumstances."

Georgy twisted the needlepoint canvas in her lap. "That was the most odious journey I have ever undertaken. I thought at times I must surely be in a nightmare." She looked up at me, and I saw her eyes were full of tears. "It has no end. No matter how dull and safe and soothing you are, I'm still in that nightmare."

"You might have told us this when you arrived," I said, with what I considered commendable mildness under the circumstances.

Thomas was more nettled than I. "I suppose you thought it would all go away if you squeezed your eyes shut and wished with all your might."

Woebegone, Georgy protested. "I wanted to tell you."

"Then why didn't you?" Thomas demanded. "Has it never occurred to you that we needed to know about this in order to protect you—and the children?"

"You must believe me." Georgy began to cry. "I never dreamed the children were at hazard. Oh, dear. Oh, dear."

Thomas rose and set to pacing. His agitation was plain. The fact that he resisted the obvious desire to shout at Georgy did very little to diminish the thunderous atmosphere in the room. Given that I was torn between the urge to pat her hand and the passionate desire to box her ears, I did the best I could to soothe Georgy.

When she had collected herself, Georgy added, "I will do whatever you wish. Must I go?"

"Don't be an idiot." Thomas kept pacing. "If we let you out of our sight, there's no telling what nonsense you may engage in. You're to stay here where we can keep an eye on you."

"Where you will be quite safe," I amended. "Isn't that right, Thomas?"

"Completely safe," said Thomas. "No one can come

through the barriers I've put up without my knowledge and permission. At least, not unless we have a visitor with a great deal more ability in magic than I've ever encountered."

I will spare you the remainder of the interlude. You can imagine it all too easily. When your letter arrived, the information about Lucky (what an unsatisfactory nickname!—it could hardly give us less to go on) gave Thomas a reason to cross-question Georgy, but to no avail. Thomas and I agree with you. The Duke of Waltham isn't the threat to Georgy. His friends, if anyone has the bad taste to befriend him, are the place to look for a culprit.

Georgy assures us that she has told us everything she knows of Daniel's business associates. She has no better reason to suspect him of designs upon her than those given above. Thomas and I are convinced that the letter is nothing more sinister than an attempt to influence Daniel through a threat to Georgy. Still, that is sinister enough, all by itself.

My chief concern is the nursery. I will have the full story out of Edward yet.

Love,
Kate

P.S. Should the dastardly duke recollect his duty as a guest and reappear, try to leave some scraps of him. Enough for Thomas to conduct a few experiments upon, at least. —*K.*

P.P.S. Of course Daniel has always been punctilious about

paying his debts of honor. It's the other kind of debt that's ruining the man, the debts run up by a life of indulgence. I think Georgy is well rid of him. Perhaps she could live on the Continent, in something resembling respectable obscurity, once all this dreadful business is tidied up. —*K.*

P.P.P.S. Or perhaps Georgy can move somewhere within walking distance of Aunt Charlotte. Aunt Charlotte would welcome such a distraction, I am sure. I hope that last flight of fancy has made you smile, at least. —*K.*

 18 April 1828
Skeynes

(Enchanted by my own hand, T.S.)

Dear James,

From the mere words, you might think you know what *laid couching* is. You'd be wrong. (Unless I do you an injustice, and you do know what it is. In that extremely unlikely event, you have my wholehearted respect and a full apology. Not to mention my undivided attention, should you decide to explain to me why you know so much about stitchery.) Laid couching is the reason Kate and her escadrille of nurses are convinced that Drina, as everyone calls our superfluous child, is of good family, indeed, a rich man's child. No one in her right mind would work a child's petticoat with laid couching for the pure joy of it, I gather.

Oh, ask Cecy about it. This, like the mysterious business of when and where a woman must begin to wear her cap, seems to be one of those things all women know, yet even the best of them can't explain. I have every confidence that Kate's letters to Cecy will go into the matter of plackets and gussets and intricate embroidery in excruciating detail. Better her than me, that's all I say.

Kate says Drina has good manners and clean habits. If anything, the child has proven to be a beneficial influence on our children.

Arthur and Eleanor are fascinated by Drina's silence, for although we know from Edward's account that she can speak, she refuses to do so. (Kate suspects Drina is standing mute on principle, perhaps to protect someone.) As a result, they are quieter than usual themselves.

For Edward's part, Drina is the goddess of his idolatry. Enforced detention in the nursery could have vexed him, for it curtails his customary explorations. On the contrary, Edward hasn't even seemed to notice his confinement. He is far too busy adoring Drina.

Drina plays with Diana as if she were a highly satisfactory doll, which, thank God, the amiable Diana takes in good part. She is interested in both the babies, but the nurses keep her (as, in truth, they do all the rest of us) at a safe distance.

Edward has said very little of his adventure to me, which Kate informs me is my own fault, for roaring at him. Edward says a great deal to Kate. The problem is sorting it. Some of it seems to have come from a story by Mrs. Hannah More, of whom Kate has the lowest opinion imaginable, and some of it derives from the old story of Tom Tit Tot. I leave the matter in Kate's capable hands.

I have also left the matter of investigations at the house in Stroud in the hands of Piers and his redoubtable wife. My duty is here, protecting Skeynes and its denizens.

The rude wagon left behind on the premises in Stroud bears so little resemblance to the delightful vehicle Kate described, and the evidence of shape-shifting (a skill that requires a considerable degree of strength, as well as good solid training) is so marked, that I fear we are dealing with an accomplished magician at least, if not a full wizard.

I make my preparations accordingly.

Do take care of yourselves.

If Daniel should reappear at Haliwar Tower, strain every sinew to keep him with you. Reflection has done nothing to sweeten his wife's temper. One could almost pity the man.

Yours,
Thomas

P.S. Roaring. I like that. I make a few restrained observations and Kate calls it roaring. I wish she could, if only once, have heard my father when he was in top form. That was roaring, if you please.

21 April 1828
The Eagle's Nest, Stockton

Dearest Kate,

As you observe from the inscription, we are no longer stuck fast at Haliwar Tower. As you also observe, I am continuing to enchant my letters to be unreadable save to your eyes, or Thomas's. It is a nuisance, to be sure, but after recent events, both at Skeynes and here, I feel that it is better to be safe.

Our departure from Haliwar Tower comes, naturally, at the most annoying possible moment—just when it seemed we were about to discover something of interest. For Daniel's departure caused a good deal of talk among the servants, most especially when his valet left for Waltham Castle on Friday morning. Until then, the Webbs could speak with some plausibility, if not conviction, of their expectation that Daniel would return momentarily.

Walker was, of course, privy to the gossip, which she reported to us on Saturday morning. Most of it, she said, was of mysterious local disappearances of the past, largely sailors who vanished from the decks of their ships, entire ships that vanished, miners who vanished from the coal mines, and so on. Apparently, some of the staff felt that Daniel's evaporation should be added to the list, though at least one of the maids did not think it sufficiently sinister to warrant inclusion as yet.

"Just a lot of local legends," James said when Walker

finished. "The sort of thing people like to inflict on visitors at the least excuse."

"But of course, Monsieur," Walker replied. "I think, me, that they tried to frighten the little French maid. I pulled down my chin, so, and made my eyes very big so that they would continue talking. I thought that perhaps when they finished the stories, they would speak more of milord duke."

"Did they?" I asked.

"Not much," Walker admitted. "Only that Monsieur Webb was most put out, because he had finally 'wangled an invite' to Waltham Castle when no other guests would be there. That is interesting, no? For Monsieur Webb is of the sort who would very much like to visit a duke, yes, but for people to see and admire, and perhaps to meet other dukes." She sniffed. Walker disapproves strongly of *encroaching* behavior; I think it is because her late husband's parents thought it was what *she* was doing when she married their son.

"I am sure Waltham will honor his invitation when he reappears," James said.

"James!" I said. "Don't you think it odd at all?"

James frowned. "Now that you mention it, it does seem odd that anyone would want to spend a private week with either one of them. Though I can't say that I blame Waltham for disappearing, in that case. I'd want to vanish, too, if I'd been, er, wangled into inviting Webb for a visit."

"You are being deliberately provoking," I said. "Just because these disappearances have nothing to do with your missing surveyor . . ."

"But, Madame, I think they may," Walker said, a trifle diffidently. "One of them, at least."

James sat up suddenly. "What? What's that you say?"

"Most of the stories were old, old, and the footmen were telling them, but once the *fille de chambre* began to speak of an odd, foreign man who disappeared last October. Monsieur Webb's valet told her sharply that the fellow had merely moved on, but she said that her aunt in Goosepool said the foreigner and his things had disappeared in the night from the farmhouse where he was staying. One of the footmen said that was just like a foreigner, to leave without paying his bills." She sniffed again. "Then the valet told her to be quiet, in *such* a way, and she did, and me, I pretended to notice nothing."

"Walker, you are a gem," James told her, which is what he always says when she makes this sort of discovery. "Did she say where this farmhouse was?"

"Near a place called Goosepool," Walker replied. "I do not know exactly where, because of the interruptions, but I think I can find out more from the *fille de chambre* when Monsieur Webb's man is not nearby."

James and I looked at each other. "This valet was particularly concerned to keep her from speaking?" I said.

"Of a certainty, Madame," Walker replied. She sighed. "It is of all things the most unfortunate. He is a dried little stick of a man, not at all *sympathique*. I do not think I will learn more from him."

"Well, don't flirt with him on our account," James advised. "We don't want *you* disappearing." He spoke in an offhand tone, but he was frowning heavily enough that it was clear he meant what he said.

"No, indeed, Monsieur," Walker said.

Unfortunately, Walker did not have occasion to speak with the housemaid (nor with Mr. Webb's valet), for that very afternoon, Mr. Webb received a fat sheaf of papers from Stockton. He immediately summoned his valet, and the two were closeted for an hour in Mr. Webb's rooms.

Over dinner, we discovered what it was all about, at least in part. Mr. Webb announced that he had been called away most urgently and would leave in the morning for a day or two. We were all, however, most welcome to stay on, as he expected his business to be concluded quickly.

Adella Webb immediately endorsed her brother's position, saying that she did not know how she would go on without our company. I think that they must have settled it between themselves before dinner, for she was a little too prompt with her remarks. You can easily guess the conversation that followed. James and I demurred, Miss Webb pressed us to stay, the other guests allowed themselves to be persuaded, and we would once again have been all but forced to accept their continued hospitality had I not had the presence of mind to say that we would consider their very kind invitation and speak more of it in the morning.

James was somewhat put out, for he much prefers to make such decisions as they come to hand, if it is at all possible and wise to do so. I could see all evening how he felt, though I doubt the Webbs noticed anything amiss, and so I was quite prepared for a thundering scold when we retired to our rooms at last.

"Cecy," he said as soon as we were private, "what maggot have you got in mind now?"

I blinked, for this was not the opening I had expected. "None that I know of, James. To what are you referring?"

"To your behavior at dinner. We could be packing our bags now, if you had had enough resolution to inform the Webbs that we would be leaving in the morning."

"Why, James!" I said. "I believe that is the first time you have ever taxed me with a want of resolution."

"Yes, it seemed odd to—" He broke off, frowning at me. "Surely you can't wish to remain at Haliwar!"

"I thought the notion merited a private discussion," I said calmly. "Which, you must own, we could not have managed at dinner."

"No, but—Cecy, *why?* And don't tell me it's because you're concerned about Daniel and Georgy, for I won't believe it."

"But I *am* concerned about them," I said. "Especially since it seems very likely that whatever Daniel is mixed up in has also something to do with your missing engineer."

"Whom, you may recall, we were sent here to find. And how I am to do that with Webb forever at my heels—"

"That is exactly why I think we ought to consider staying," I said. "Not the way Mr. Webb follows you about, I mean, but to take advantage of the opportunity to discover more about what he knows and what is really going on."

"Cecelia—"

"You cannot deny, James, that the most promising information we have yet found is that story Walker brought us this morning about the foreigner who disappeared near Goosepool," I said.

James made the snorting noise that means he would very much like to deny whatever I have just said, but cannot in all honesty do so.

"Which we would very likely not have discovered had we not been staying here," I went on. "For I do not believe that it would ever have occurred to either of us to make inquiries about a village with such a name as Goosepool."

"Not, at any rate, until one of us heard the story of this disappearance," James said.

"Well, I cannot imagine how we *would* have heard the story if Walker had not discovered it," I pointed out. "No one has displayed the least inclination to talk to either of us, except for the Webbs, and they will certainly not tell us anything to the purpose if they can help it. And it was Mr. Webb's man who tried to turn the conversation. He can have had no reason to do so unless Mr. Webb told him to. Which must mean that Mr. Webb has some interest in the matter."

Before James could answer, there was a low rumbling noise from below us. "What on earth is—," James began, and then—

I do not properly know how to describe what happened next. I imagine that being hit by lightning must feel a bit the same way, if lightning came up from the ground beneath one's feet instead of down from the sky. Or perhaps it was more like being caught in the eruption of a geyser, such as they have in Iceland, except that this was not an eruption of hot water but of uncontrolled magical power. The room shook, knocking over a chair, the washbasin, and both of the night candles.

The shaking and the magical eruption continued for what seemed hours, though it could not have been more than a few seconds. When it stopped, the curtains were burning merrily, thanks to one of the overturned candles. James immediately grabbed a section of the curtains that was not in flames and pulled them down. "Out!" he snapped over his shoulder as he began stamping out the fire.

I did not immediately obey, as I was feeling quite dizzy. Having a great quantity of magical power pour through one unexpectedly is *not* an experience that results in a clear head and a calm ability to behave well in an emergency. James finished with the curtains and grabbed my arm. *"Out,"* he repeated. "If any other candles tipped—"

I managed to nod and stumble forward. Seeing the state I was in, James did not release my arm but merely shouted for Walker and his man. The four of us made our way down the stairs and out the main door, where we were soon joined by the other residents of the tower. Several of the maids were in strong hysterics, and so was Adella Webb. The fresh

air cleared my head, and I was therefore able to assist in removing the stunned and overset persons to a safe distance,
while James took charge of making certain everyone had
come out of the house and then got up an expedition to see
when it might be safe to return.

The shaking had started several small fires, and none of
us got any sleep that night. The gentlemen had some trouble
in extinguishing the various blazes, though there was never
any danger that the building would go up. The real damage
was done by the shaking itself. James reported that one of
the upper stairs had come loose from its supports; quite a lot
of the windows were broken; and in the dawn light, we
could see that much of the brick facing on the old portion
of the tower had peeled away, fallen, and shattered, reveal-
ing the underlying stonework.

Mr. Webb seemed quite stunned by the turn of events. I
think he must not be much accustomed to dealing with unusual occurrences, for once the fires were out, he actually
began to urge us once more to extend our stay—as if having houseguests after such an upset would be quite unexceptionable! James informed him in no uncertain terms that
we would be removing to Stockton at once, then advised
him to have a builder look at the "settling" before he
brought anyone else to stay in his ancestral pile.

So we are now in Stockton, occupying three rooms and
a private parlor at a pleasant little inn near the center of
town. I am still not at all sure *what* caused the upheaval at
Haliwar, but I am (for once) altogether in agreement with

James as to not remaining there a moment longer, information or no information. I do, however, hope to ride over in a day or two, to see what, if any, effect the eruption had on the ley line. (I shall, of course, pretend it is to reassure myself as to how the Webbs are going on after the unfortunate incident.) I can at least be sure that it was nothing to do with the railway, for the trains do not run after dark, and besides, the railway has been using horses to pull the coal wagons for the last three days, due to some mishap with the steam engine.

James is occupied in inquiring discreetly about Goosepool and the farm where the foreign gentleman disappeared. I fully expect to have more to tell you on that score in the near future. As soon as we have settled the matter of the surveyor, I shall try to persuade James to investigate Daniel's cronies. For after reading your letter (which arrived at Haliwar on Saturday, just before all of the excitement), I am more than ever convinced that it was one of them, and not Daniel himself, who was threatening Georgy. Indeed, only Georgy could have been so goose-witted as to leap from reading that note to the conclusion that her husband wished to have her murdered in order to retrieve the settlements he had made on her! I am quite cross with her for not having told us about it from the beginning. If she had, I would not have gone storming off to confront him, and he would very likely not have vanished, or at least, not until after I was able to pry loose whatever information he has. And even if that were only an account of how he came to be threatened and what they wish him to do, it would have provided us with some notion of what we ought to do next.

Yours,
Cecy

(in cipher)

My dear Thomas,

Cecelia and I retrieved your letter of the eighteenth from Haliwar this morning. I expect that you've had the dramatic rendition of our escape from that interminable house party in Cecelia's version—there was a bit of shaking and some small fires, which we used as an excuse to depart. I should have been perfectly happy never to see the place again, but Cecelia was sure that the shaking was magical in origin, and wanted to examine the house in daylight and with a bit of magical preparation.

So we rode out this morning, pausing half a mile short of the house for Cecelia to work her spells. Then we went on, paid our respects to Miss Webb (her brother having taken himself off on some "urgent business" or other), collected the post, admired the progress that had been made on cleaning up the place, and left.

Two circumstances alone cause me to provide so much detail regarding this boring little excursion. The first is that

Cecelia reports several changes in the flow of magic around the house. Previously, the ley line ran strongly north toward the river but disappeared when it reached the gates of Haliwar Tower; the house and grounds had little or no magic associated with them—"stagnant" was the term Cecelia used to describe the feeling. Now, she says, the ley line has dimmed noticeably, and the house and grounds have a decided, though disorganized, sense of magic about them.

The second matter of note was the curious nature of the damage to the house itself. Haliwar Tower is an odd building to begin with; the tower is a great squat, round, thick-walled thing in the Norman style, though it was built by one of Cromwell's followers in the 1600s. Two modern wings run off on either side, of somewhat later construction, and the tower had been faced in brick, presumably to make the contrast in style less obvious. In a reversal of the usual system, the family and guests are housed in the central tower, while the new wings are devoted to servants' quarters, kitchens, and so on.

Judging from the commotion on the night of the fires, and from the widespread locations we found smoldering at the time, the disturbance affected the entire building. But in the sober light of day, it was plain that only the central tower had suffered any real damage, apart from that caused by the fires. All of the tower windows were broken; along the wings, the glass was intact. More significantly, the brick facing had crumbled away from the tower, showing some deuced peculiar stonework behind it.

The tower is only three stories high. The upper floors are built of mortared stone, uncut and irregular but nothing at all out of the way. The ground floor, however, showed three enormous, irregular lumps of granite—single stones at least four feet wide and between eight and twelve feet high—set at even intervals, with the spaces between filled in with stones of a more usual size. I rode around the house, under pretext of inspecting the damage for Miss Webb, and found the rear of the tower to be in much the same condition—broken windows, and enough of the brick peeled off to show four more of these granite rocks embedded in the stonework there.

I was not able to get a look at the interior of the tower, but I would be surprised indeed if there are not several more of those large stones in the section of the walls hidden by the new wings. Their significance eludes me, but I have sent off an express note to Michael Wrexton in hopes of enlightenment. While I cannot say that either architecture or Cromwellian history is within his usual area of expertise, I have no doubt that the library at the Royal College of Wizards can supply any of his deficiencies.

Meanwhile, I ride out tomorrow to a village bearing the unfortunate name of Goosepool, following the latest scent of my missing surveyor. There is some rumor of a foreigner disappearing from a farmhouse there, and while it seems unlikely that a railway surveyor would find it preferable to lodge at a farmhouse instead of at an inn in Darlington or Stockton, the timing seems right.

Are you still afflicted with your superfluous child, or has the lapse of an additional week been enough to discover her appropriate residence? I am desolated to inform you that my familiarity with the term *laid couching* derives primarily from my father's occasional tirades on the rapacity of my mother's dressmakers, which he was used to punctuate by reading off details from the bills. From that alone, I conclude that one would be well-inlaid indeed to spring for a petticoat adorned with such stitch work.

Waltham remains among the missing, so far as I am aware. Should he resurface, I shall send him your way at once. In deference to your preference for a calm, well-ordered life, I shall try to warn you of his coming in sufficient time to make your escape before he arrives, but a taste of his wife's temper is the least he merits, after foisting that house party on us.

Yours,
James

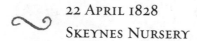

22 APRIL 1828
SKEYNES NURSERY

(This letter warranted to be enchanted against the unknown reader by the ever patient and always dutiful T.S.)

Dear Cecy,

This will make the third time I have begun this letter. The first time, Edward spilt ink on my opening lines. The second time, I spilt the ink myself. This time, I have taken steps to prevent a recurrence. I write to you from a table by the east window of the nursery, a table free of arrowroot biscuit crumbs and lead soldiers. I write to you whilst the children are having their naps. I write to you with the help of a sadly depleted inkwell. Even if I knocked this one over again, it wouldn't have much left to spill.

It rained yesterday, and it is raining today, the kind of soaking, cold rain that I am assured is good for the crops but that seems as if it will go on falling day after day after day, forever and ever, amen. I persuade myself this is an excellent thing, for if the weather were fair, it would be even more difficult to keep the children safely indoors. Still, I wish it would stop.

In truth, I see signs of restiveness amongst the infantry. Edward has squabbled disgracefully with Arthur over sharing his toy soldiers. This morning I heard Eleanor ask Drina if she is under an enchantment that forbids her to speak. Drina held her peace. Of course.

Yet I had the distinct impression that if Drina is not under an enchantment already, Eleanor would like to see that situation remedied, this time with an enchantment to compel her to speak. I must remember to warn Thomas. This is no time for him to indulge his niece's taste for spell casting. It would be just like Thomas—

I take up my pen again after a short interruption (a disagreement between Laurence and his last meal, alas). This time I do not write in solitary peace. No, the children are at the table with me, as we all write to you. A fresh ink pot is at hand, so anything can happen. As usual.

∽ 23 APRIL 1828

Cecy, at last I think we have established a reliable means of communication with young Drina. As we shared the new ink pot peaceably among us, Eleanor asked Drina if she would write to her mother, too. Drina's face lit up, and she seized pen and paper with such joy that I have been castigating myself ever since for not thinking to suggest it sooner.

Drina did not write to her mother. On the sheet of paper, she carefully formed the words, "If I speak, my mother will be harmed," and turned the paper so Eleanor could read it aloud.

"Goodness, who says so?" I demanded.

It required another dip into the ink pot, but Drina put her pen to paper and wrote, "Mister Scarlet."

It took time, persistent questioning, and quite a lot of paper, but I now have what I believe to be as much information about Drina as she is willing to give us.

I also believe I have a full account of Edward's experience and at least a partial one of Drina's. I take great pride in this feat, not least because I managed it despite Thomas's attempts to help.

You will forgive me, I hope, for forming a halting series of questions and answers into a narrative. I begin with

Edward's experience, on the grounds that while it may be less important in the grand scheme of things, it matters more to me.

What happened to Edward:

As has been speculated, Edward climbed into the tinker's cart whilst under the misapprehension that it was the most attractive and fascinating mode of conveyance in the world. His mistake was borne in upon him speedily, when the true nature of the wagon reasserted itself a few miles down the road. Edward found himself in a rattletrap of a cart, crowded in among a bale of rags, a roll of mildewed carpeting, and a few stoneware jugs.

The driver of the vehicle, such a convincing gypsy woman to our eyes, appeared to Edward as a man with ginger hair and a face flushed red as beetroot (he had to have been our Mr. Scarlet) when he discovered his stowaway.

"I don't believe it," Scarlet said. "*Another* brat."

For a moment, Edward was sure that Scarlet would hurl him out of the wagon, but the man relented. With a few muttered words, Scarlet put what I surmise to have been a sleeping spell upon Edward, for he grew drowsy and remembers nothing more of the journey. Edward denies this vigorously and claims that he saw a gnome spinning straw into golden jackstraws, but I believe this must have been a dream.

Once in Stroud, for that is the next thing Edward remembers at all clearly, Edward was rolled into the carpet and transported from the wagon to the house. Sputtering and indignant, he emerged to find himself locked in an upstairs room, Mr. Scarlet's prisoner.

At first, Drina was distinctly hostile. Edward had to explain to her that he had been kidnapped whilst protecting his Aunt Georgy before Drina grasped he was a fellow prisoner. Once she did so, however, she was prompt about ordering him to escape and fetch help immediately. The first stage of this plan pleased Edward enormously, as a leg up into the soot of the chimney was exactly what suited him.

Unfortunately, escape was not so simple. Although he was able to climb up high enough to elude any groping arm Mr. Scarlet cared to extend, Edward could not go very far without the risk of wedging himself into a flue that would neither let him advance nor retreat. Drina exhorted him mightily, but there was no help for it. He could hide, but he could not flee.

Edward would not be Edward, however, if some exploration had not taken place. Whilst discovering that he did not indeed have the entire run of every flue, Edward succeeded in climbing far enough to overhear a discussion from one of the rooms downstairs.

"Pretty work, Captain Crimson," a deep voice said, loudly enough to capture Edward's complete attention. I believe he thought the presence of a captain implied the possibility of pirates. "You were supposed to steal the lady, not tell her fortune."

In hope of hearing more clearly, Edward wriggled into a

perilously narrow spot. From there, he was certain he recognized the voice of Mr. Scarlet. "You were supposed to deliver your message and be on your way. I don't need advice from you."

"I can't leave empty-handed, Scarlet. You haven't given me your reply."

Scarlet sounded cross to Edward. "If I'm not nippy enough to suit him, tell his nibs to send more money. All this racing from one end of the world to the other takes time, and the faster I travel, the poorer it leaves me."

The deep voice laughed an unpleasant laugh. "I don't think you'd really care to send him that message."

"I don't think I really care what you tell him. If he doesn't like the way I work, he can find someone else."

"Brave talk. Now, in all seriousness, how shall I explain your delay to the old boy?"

Scarlet sounded angry. "What delay? The moment you gave me his orders, I carried them out."

The deep voice was patient. "You didn't. You only frightened her. Leaving that aside, you kept me waiting here for two days before I could give you the message. He's going to ask me where you were."

"I was making arrangements. Places like this don't just spring up like mushrooms, you know."

The sarcastic voice sounded surprised when Edward heard him speak again. "What the devil was *that?*"

Mr. Scarlet sounded brisk. "That's a finding spell, you gudgeon. Someone with the goods is headed this way. Either he's right on top of us, or he's powerful enough to turn us to stone from a mile away. Best not be around when he gets here."

"I was supposed to bring the chit back with me," the deep voice protested.

"You just look to yourself—you have your work cut out for you." This time Mr. Scarlet sounded sarcastic. "Who do you think the finding spell is for, anyway? You? I'm the one who stuck his neck out."

"You'll get it stretched one day."

"That's why I'm off out of here. Come along or it will be you for the jump."

From the sound of things, Edward judged Mr. Scarlet and the man with the deep voice left together. Edward extricated himself from that particular bit of flue but heard nothing more.

I gather that Edward's exploration of the system of chimneys fully occupied the rest of his time, for if anything, he seemed to feel our arrival cut his adventure short. Edward believes that but for our interruption, he might yet have found a way out. For me, our arrival came not a moment too soon. Given that my eldest son ran the additional risk of getting stuck up a chimney to be smoked like a kipper, I'm even happier we arrived when we did.

Now for Drina's story, much of which I have discounted on the grounds that it is all too easy for a youngster to exaggerate matters to earn attention. She views her family as the most important and influential in the world, with the possible exception (a grudging concession made to Arthur's persistence) of Lord Wellington. And King George, of course.

What happened to Drina:

Drina refuses to explain how she fell into the hands of the man she calls Mr. Scarlet. She seems embarrassed, as if she considers it to be her fault. I assure her that whatever happened, it is the fault of Mr. Scarlet and no one else, but this does not sway her. She writes that she found herself in the room where she met Edward, with no recollection of an arrival, let alone a journey. There must be more to tell than that, but that is where Drina begins.

Drina woke to find herself a prisoner in a strange room, in a strange house, in a strange town. I dread to contemplate what I would feel finding myself in such circumstances even now. At her age, I am convinced I would have wept myself into a spasm.

Drina, I judge, is made of stern stuff. She viewed her situation with aplomb. Her opinion of Mr. Scarlet is low. It was formed during their first encounter.

Mr. Scarlet performed a spell. He didn't tell Drina what it was supposed to do. Drina felt no different after than she did before. Mr. Scarlet performed a second spell, still to no effect, and then a third. Drina still felt no different, but Mr. Scarlet informed Drina that she was under an enchantment. If she dared speak to anyone of her family, they—specifically her mother and older sister—would be harmed. Silence was her duty.

If Drina dared to attempt escape, her mother would be murdered, her older sister sold into the stews. If Drina were recaptured, Mr. Scarlet promised her that by then she would be nothing more than a helpless orphan; thus he would deal with her as he saw fit, perhaps even unto selling Drina into the stews herself.

Monstrous as the stews are, shameful as the very idea of their existence must be to any decent man or woman, I find men like Mr. Scarlet more monstrous still. That he made threats of that nature to anyone—most of all to a child—brands him an unspeakable coward as well as a villain of deepest dye. How can the likes of Mr. Scarlet run free in the streets?

Reardon comes from Stroud. Even if her last relation there is gone, there remains a web of mutual acquaintance. I rely on Reardon to be our eyes and ears in the hunt for Mr. Scarlet. A creature like that deserves the fullest punishment.

Upon consideration, however, I will grant that Mr. Scarlet seems to have confined his villainy to bullying threats. Judging from Drina's account, and judging from the condition of her clothing, as well as of her person, Drina was in his hands no more than one or two days. She seems to have come to no physical harm whatsoever at his hands.

Indeed, Mr. Scarlet—or possibly an accomplice—went to sufficient trouble to prepare her regular meals. Mr. Scarlet delivered those meals on a tray, using each visit as a chance to confirm that Drina was secure in her cell and that she had sufficient drinking water as well as a change of chamber pot.

Mr. Scarlet was vigilant. The only meal Drina missed was luncheon on the day of Edward's arrival. There was no tray that afternoon. (I presume the cur was too busy threatening Georgy and abducting Edward.)

Fortunately, Thomas and I scared Scarlet off before he could harm either Edward or Drina.

Drina appears to consider herself to have been an involuntary houseguest, rather than a prisoner. I think she is now enjoying herself very much. The chance to be a figure of mystery plays a part in her enjoyment, but I suspect there is something more basic at work. From her deportment, I judge her to be almost painfully well brought up. Here at Skeynes, she has the opportunity to be a child among children. She enjoys being with the twins, who are of an age with her, so greatly that I am sure it is a novelty to her. She mothers our babies at every opportunity, showing little skill but great enthusiasm for the art. Where she comes from we are sure to learn in time. When we do, I am convinced we will find she is the baby of the family, lectured sternly as often as she is indulged.

I shall persist in my efforts to win Drina's confidence. Be sure that I will share every detail I discover.

Love,
Kate

P.S. Your letter of the 21st has just arrived. Thomas is beside himself with questions. I am relieved and delighted that you and James are safely out of Haliwar Tower. Take great care. —*K.*

148

P.P.S. Georgy is composing a letter of apology to you and James. She (belatedly but sincerely) regrets exposing your children to risk. From the amount of time she devotes to this missive, I fear it will be extremely long. It may even be in verse. I thought you should be warned. —*K.*

23 APRIL 1828
SKEYNES

(Enchanted by my own hand, T.S.)

Dear James and Cecelia,

I'll be brief, for I do not wish to delay Kate's letter. I add a line merely to ask a question. I address this letter to you both in the hope that if you cannot read my handwriting, James, Cecy (inured as she is to her father's penmanship) can decipher it.

Given your late experiences at Haliwar Tower, you may have made observations not included in your correspondence. How does a compass behave in the vicinity? Any marked differences between the way it behaves inside the tower itself? Did you smell anything (other than smoke) during the incident? What was the weather like? Did you note any change in wind direction? Any alteration in the appearance of the river itself? A change in flow or the color and turbidity of the water?

That seems to be more than a single question. I apologize and speed this missive on its way.

Thomas

26 April 1828
THE EAGLE'S NEST, STOCKTON

Dearest Kate,

The only thing more tiresome than Georgy's usual self-centeredness is Georgy in a penitent mood. You were quite right to warn me; her letter of apology ran to five pages, two of which were so tearstained as to be unreadable. Most unfortunately, the sections in verse were not among the illegible bits. (I wish I knew where she got the notion that sentiments expressed in poetry are somehow more sincere than sentiments said plainly or briefly.)

Forgive me if I sound unfeeling. I would be kinder, were I less certain that Georgy is greatly enjoying her orgy of remorse, and delighting in such an excellent excuse to wallow in overblown prose. What else can one make of comparing herself to a "faded blossom, trampled by the feet of guilt, awaiting the restoring rain of forgiveness"? It is just the sort of playacting she has always enjoyed. I have not dared to show the letter to James. I do not think he would be at all patient with it. (Please thank Thomas for franking it for her; it would have been the outside of enough to have had to pay the shillings for the extra sheets, especially the illegible ones.) I shall convey appropriately sympathetic reassurances to her under separate cover as soon as I have leisure to do so.

For a great deal has been happening here. We have—no, I must tell it in order, or I will surely leave out something important.

Two days after our removal from Haliwar, James and I rode over (ostensibly to see how they were going on). Mr. Webb had departed on his business trip, as scheduled, so only his sister was in residence, and she has been forced to move to a bedchamber in one of the wings. The central tower is presently an uncomfortable place to inhabit, though I think it will not take above a week to return the interior to order, provided they have no difficulty in replacing so many windows all at once.

Before we came within sight of the tower, James and I paused behind a little rise so that I could do the spells that allow one to sense ley lines. I wanted to see if that magical eruption had any lingering effects on that ley line I mentioned earlier. And *something* had affected it, Kate, for when we passed it on the way into Haliwar, the ley line did not feel as strong as it had the first time I detected it.

As we passed through the gates onto the grounds immediately around Haliwar, I got another surprise. The entire area was awash in magic—not strongly, only a little tingle, like the feel of a storm coming on or the hint of scent that lingers after Georgy leaves a room. It was very disturbing. Unfortunately, I could not tell anything more without making some actual tests, which I was unable to do because the place was full of workmen.

We did not stay long; there really was no point. Adella was quite useless as a source of information. All she could do was wring her hands and wish that her brother were there. She did make a halfhearted attempt to persuade us to

return, but I think she must have done so only because her
brother extracted some promise from her before he left, for
it was plain that she was hoping we would decline. Her relief when we did was palpable.

We had a pleasant ride back to Stockton, and the following morning, James left early to ride to Goosepool, in search
of the farmhouse that was missing a foreign visitor. He returned late in the day, jubilant. After three false starts, he
had found the very place, and while the farmer's wife had
been disinclined to talk much of the incident, he thought
she might be more forthcoming with another female. So he
had told her that we might wish to rent the room on behalf
of some mythical person but that I would have to look it
over first, then made arrangements for us to ride out again
at some convenient time in the next day or two.

The weather prohibited so long a ride on Thursday, but
Friday—yesterday—we went. Even on a hired hack, the
ride was enjoyable. The woman was waiting, and showed us
to a small room at the back of the house. James took himself
off almost immediately, leaving me to attempt to draw my
hostess into conversation.

It was considerably more difficult than you might think.
At first, she limited herself strictly to remarks about the
room, while I looked over the meager furnishings—a plain
bed with a chest at the foot. I said things like, "You must
have had many lodgers," and, "Will there be any difficulty
getting to Darlington from here?" and she replied, "Happen
I have," or, "Happen there may."

I was about to give up and rejoin James, when there came a rumbling and a noise resembling all of the horses at the Derby thundering past at once. At first, I thought it was another magical eruption, but it was plain that my hostess heard it, too. "Good heavens," I said when the noise at last began to fade, "what was that?"

My hostess gestured at the window and said something about "tha great noisy smelly gowk" that I did not at first comprehend. When I looked out of the window, however, I saw a string of coal wagons barely a quarter mile distant, disappearing in the direction of Stockton. "Oh, the *railway*," I said. "I had no notion you were so close to the line."

That was enough to set her off. The railway was, evidently, a sore point with her, as it cut up the grazing land and frightened the sheep. She was especially cross because the builders had revised the planned route of the railway just before it was actually built. The new route moved the rails some way north of the original plan, and had the surveyors changed just a few more miles of railway, the "great noisy smelly" trains would have passed well north of the house. The revisions, however, end just before Goosepool; from Goosepool east to Stockton, the railway follows the trail mapped out by the original surveyors.

"Dear me," I said when she ran down at last. "That is most unfortunate. Did the noise much disturb your last tenant?"

"Oh, aye; every time the wagons passed, he ran out to

scowl at them," the woman said. "That's when he wasn't off mucking with the circle."

"Circle?"

"Aye. The Dancing Weans, they're called. Nine great rocks in a circle, as old as old. Haunted, they are. He should no have been mucking about there."

"Very likely," I said. "Where is this stone circle?"

She looked at me suspiciously.

"My father is an antiquarian," I said with perfect truth. "He is interested in such things. If it is not too far, I thought my husband and I might ride past it so I could send Papa a description."

She sniffed, but obliged with the directions—half a mile east, atop a small hill overlooking the railway line. We then chatted amicably about the idiosyncrasies of male persons, which led with very little prompting to my obtaining the whole story of her missing tenant, such as it was.

Herr Magus Schellen—for it was indeed he who had rented the room—stayed only for three days before his disappearance. On the first day, he walked the railway line toward Darlington. On the second, he walked toward Stockton, and returned in a state of high excitement (or so I infer) to ask a great many questions about the Dancing Weans. On the third day, he took a large bag to the stone circle with him and stayed most of the day. On the fourth morning, he left for the circle, carrying his bag as before, and was not seen again. The bag vanished also, and that night, all of his belongings disappeared from the room.

"T' neighbor says 'twas a haunt took him," my informant said with another sniff. "And there's no sayin' it wasn't, the way he was on about the Dancing Weans, and all. But I say, whoever heard of a haunt coming back for a man's pipe and smallclothes?"

"It does seem unlikely," I agreed. James returned at that point, and the woman immediately returned to her initial reticence. As it was plain we would learn no more, we took our leave.

As we mounted our horses, I told James of the stone circle and my intention of investigating on the return ride. He was reluctant at first but soon saw the wisdom of making a casual-seeming stop on our way back to Stockton, rather than making a special trip out to look at it later.

So we turned our horses toward the railway line, so as to get within sight of it and then ride parallel to it until we saw the stone circle. (It is surprisingly easy to miss seeing a railway line that is running through a series of flatish country fields, if there is no train passing at the moment. Where there are cuts through the hills, or where the land has been raised to level the line, it is much easier.) As we rode, I told James what I had learned.

"Interesting," James said when I finished. "I wonder why the railway route was changed . . . and who selected the new path."

"Perhaps you should ask Lord Wellington," I said.

"I don't think Wellington knows anything about it," James replied. "The original plans had to be approved by

Parliament, but once that was done, the corporation wouldn't have had to inform them of anything but really major changes."

"*Somebody* must have known," I said. "Besides all the local people, I mean."

"Yes." James looked very thoughtful. "Perhaps I should visit Darlington tomorrow and see what I can learn at the corporation offices."

"I think—" I broke off. We were almost to the railway line, and I felt an unmistakable tingling. "James! The railway feels like that ley line—the one near Haliwar Tower."

"What?" James reined in his horse, and I was forced to follow his example. "How can you tell? You haven't done the sensing spells. Have you?"

"No, of course not," I said. "But I can feel it nonetheless. It isn't as clear as the line by Haliwar, but if I can sense it even without the ley spell, this ley line must be *far* stronger."

"You didn't sense it before, when we rode the train," James said skeptically.

"No, but I hadn't done *any* ley-line-sensing spells then," I pointed out. "I've done them twice since then. Possibly there's still a lingering bit of magical residue, or that burst of magic at Haliwar may have made me more sensible of the presence of ley lines."

"Or perhaps being aboard the train interfered with your ability to sense them at all," James suggested.

"Yes!" I said. "Remember the way the locomotive made the ley line bend? The train pushed it out of the way, or tried to—and then it snapped back. We were in the wagons well behind the engine, so we wouldn't have felt anything, except perhaps when the ley line jumped back into place, and that would only have been for an instant when it passed by."

"I wouldn't have felt anything, regardless," James said without rancor. "But don't get carried off by your theories. We don't actually *know* which of them is correct."

We rode toward Stockton in silence for a few minutes. "The ley line along the railway is fading," I said after a time.

"Ley lines don't change intensity as fast as that," James said.

"This one seems to be," I said. "Unless it's my sensitivity that's fading, but I don't think it is."

"Look! There are the Dancing Weans," James said.

We cantered forward to a low stone wall at the foot of the hill, then rode along it until we came to a gate. A man, a boy, and two sheepdogs were collecting a large flock of sheep from the slopes on the other side; the boy broke off work long enough to open the gate for us, and James rewarded him with a shilling. The horses picked their way along the sheep trails until we were almost at the top of the hill, where we dismounted. I handed my reins to James, then started for the stone circle a few yards away.

I got barely three steps. James shouted; there was a brown-and-white flash and one of the sheepdogs stood in front of me, blocking my way. I tried to go around him, but he blocked me again. And again. He didn't growl or bark,

just made sure that there was no way I could get any closer
to the circle.

The shepherd came puffing up at last. "Sorry, mum," he
said. "He's a good dog, for all he's new. Never acted like this
afore. Down, you!"

The last was said to the dog, who looked at him but did
not obey. The shepherd made a grab for him, but the dog
dodged. I took the opportunity to step forward, and instantly the dog was there again, this time gently but insis-
tently shoving me away from the circle.

I felt a shiver of magic. Frowning, I stripped off one of
my riding gloves and held out my hand for the dog to sniff.
He licked my hand and whined, and as he did I sensed the
magic much more clearly.

It was an enchantment, quite a strong one—wizard-
grade, in fact (I have felt enough of Thomas's spells to
know the difference in quality, compared to the sort of
thing a mere magician can cast). The dog whined again,
and something made me say, in a low voice, "Herr Magus
Schellen?"

The dog burst into a fury of barking. The shepherd
burst into a flurry of apologies, while attempting again to
catch the dog. The dog avoided him easily, keeping a wary
eye on me.

"Excuse me, Mr. . . . ?" I said to the shepherd.

"Williams," the shepherd said.

"Mr. Williams, how long have you had this dog?"

"He's never done anything like this, mum, I swear. I don't know what has got into him."

"Yes, you said that before," I told him. "But how long have you had him?"

"He turned up late last autumn," Mr. Williams replied. "I disremember the date."

"I thought as much," I said. I gave James a meaningful look. "I believe this dog belongs to a friend of ours, Herr Magus Schellen. His dog disappeared last October, didn't he, James?"

"Just so," James said smoothly. "I'm sure you will wish us to restore him to his proper owner." Mr. Williams began to make some protest, but James cut him off. "I am sure our friend would wish you to be compensated for your trouble in caring for his, er, valuable animal." He pulled a banknote from his pocket and held it out.

The shepherd took the note and was instantly reduced to speechlessness, from which I inferred that James had chosen to be most generous. Since the matter seemed settled, I looked at the dog. "Come, er, Franz," I said.

The sheepdog came instantly, but the moment I started toward the stone circle again, he blocked my way. Not wishing to make any more of an issue of the matter before Mr. Williams, I said, "Another time, then," and went back to the horses. James threw me up, and we rode off, with our new acquisition at our heels.

As soon as we were out of earshot, James demanded to know what queer start I was about now.

"Well," I said, "I am not perfectly certain. But I think—I am very much afraid that—I believe this sheepdog is actually Herr Magus Schellen."

The sheepdog barked once, as if to confirm what I had said. James looked from him to me. "Good Lord."

"It is quite a strong enchantment," I said. "And before you ask, I do not think it will be easy to remove."

"Once we get him back to London, that won't be a problem," James said. "I'm sure the Royal College of Wizards can handle it."

"First we have to get him to Stockton," I said. I turned to the dog. "Do you think you can walk so far, sir?"

The sheepdog barked once and trotted a few yards in the direction of the town. We took that as indicating agreement, and so rode slowly back.

That was yesterday; as I write this, James is making arrangements for us to return to London with Herr Schellen as quickly as may be. I hope that by the time you receive this, we will be on our way, so you may write next to the London town house. Do not, under any circumstances, mention the Herr Magus's situation in front of the children. It would not do for Arthur to take it into his head that we have acquired a sheepdog. He has quite enough dogs at home already.

I have every hope that this whole affair will be ended once we deliver Herr Magus Schellen to the Royal College and they disenchant him (though I shall be most put out if no one thinks to tell us all the details, once Herr Schellen is in a fit state to supply them). Another two weeks, at most, should therefore see the end of our children's visit (for which I am *deeply* grateful, Arthur's and Eleanor's new abilities at scrying notwithstanding).

I am, by the way, most impressed by your reconstruction of Edward's adventure. I can see why it took you something over a week to produce it—I can only imagine (and admire) the painstaking work it must have taken to compare his various accounts and eliminate the plainly fanciful. It is a pity that it sheds so little light on who Drina is, for it seems likely that she, too, was carried off by the odious Mr. Scarlet. Her family must be quite beside themselves with worry. But perhaps I will hear something when we arrive in London; the Season is at its height now, and while it is not what it was when we were young, it is still the best time and place for gossip of any sort. If Drina's family is so well-off, surely *someone* will have heard of them, and know that they are missing a child.

Your,
Cecy

P.S. —Why Thomas should think that either James or myself would commonly carry a compass about, I cannot imagine. As we do not, I cannot answer his questions about the behavior of such an item either inside, outside, or anywhere near Haliwar Tower. If we ever return there (a thing which seems most unlikely), I shall make a point of procuring a compass so as to provide the information he so urgently requested.

As regards his other questions—to the best of my recollection, the weather seemed coming on to rain earlier in the evening, but luckily when we all ran outside after the magical shaking, it had cleared. It would have been the outside of enough to have had to stand in the rain while the gentlemen worked at putting out the fires. It was quite calm, also; I remember thinking how fortunate that there was no risk of a spark being blown onto the roof of the stables. And if there was any alteration in the appearance of the river, or in the color of its water, it had passed off long before James and I saw it the following morning—it is, you may recall, some distance from the house.

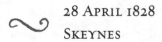 28 April 1828
Skeynes

(This letter enchanted by T.S.—entirely upon trust)

Dear Cecy,

I applaud you (and James, of course) for locating Herr Magus Schellen. One piece of the puzzle is solved, although many more remain. Thomas and I have (I hope) exercised the utmost discretion in the matter, so the children know you have carried out Lord Wellington's mission, yet they entertain no canine expectations whatsoever. Even if they did, it would take something rather startling in the way of pets to distract them from the salient point: In less than a fortnight, you will be reunited.

We have another salient point to consider. At last Drina has begun to speak freely, even in the presence of adults. This morning the children were engaged in one of their customary nursery debates, endless as it was pointless, when Eleanor referred to me as Aunt Kate. I can hardly do justice to the impatience in Drina's voice when she countered, "She isn't your aunt Kate. She's your first cousin once removed."

It surprised me to hear Drina speak at all. It startled me that a stranger should have divined the precise degree of our relationship with such accuracy. What astonished me was when Drina added, "Your other cousin once removed is only an ordinary duchess."

"Do you mean Aunt Georgy?" Eleanor's tranquility was entirely unruffled by Drina's criticisms. "She's not a bit ordinary. She's the most beautiful duchess there is, so there."

"No, she isn't." Drina noticed me staring at her and fell silent. She has spoken naturally enough ever since, no matter who is present. Yet she does not permit herself to answer further questions about her family. The threat to her mother still rules her.

I relate this incident in detail since I am certain you will find it full of interest. Georgy is the most beautiful duchess I have ever seen, without question, but how does it chance that Drina has such a decided opinion on the subject?

Reardon's inquiries have borne fruit at last. As you recall, the house in Stroud was hired three months ago by Mr. Adolphus Medway. It is perfectly possible that Mr. Scarlet and Mr. Medway are one and the same. According to the neighbors, Mr. Scarlet did entertain many visitors, but Thomas is inclined to dismiss all such descriptions as manifestations of Mr. Scarlet's chameleon-like talent for disguise. Why Mr. Scarlet should wish to bother to pay calls upon himself, Thomas is at a loss to explain.

Mr. Scarlet presented himself as a dealer in wool, interested in both bales of fleece and the finished cloth. Although Mr. Scarlet displayed no aptitude in the role—he arrived at quite the wrong time of year, for one thing—he went about his alleged business in a way methodical enough to excite neither comment nor interest from his neighbors. Then, a month or so ago, he disappeared for a week without a word to anyone. His reappearance occurred just after the full moon at the end of March. Mr. Scarlet made no reference to his absence beyond the flimsy lie that he had been abed with an illness the entire time. So ill that he took in no provender whatever? So sick he had no coal for his fire? You may picture for yourself Reardon's scornful dismissal of this tale. A farrago of lies, she calls it.

As the weather improved, Mr. Scarlet was seen to leave the house early, driving a smart curricle and pair, and to return well after darkness fell. If he had any attendant to see to the horses, no one knows of it.

The rest of the information is negative. No one saw Mr. Scarlet depart. No one has seen Mr. Scarlet since. So far as we can establish, no one ever saw the woman with the tinker's cart but us.

There is one detail Reardon and Piers turned up I find of considerable interest. Three days after Thomas and I took Edward and Drina from the abandoned house, a stranger arrived. He made inquiries very similar to our own. (Who lived in the house? Where had he gone? When?) Upon learning of Thomas's interest in the matter, the stranger withdrew. He said he intended to put up at a reputable inn. Wherever he went, it was nowhere in the vicinity. He has not been seen since. For what a physical description is worth under the circumstances, he possessed a handsome face, gentlemanly behavior, and a fashionable appearance. He expressed concern, no more, at the exciting circumstances surrounding the house, and he did not hint in any way that he had a connection either to the house or to its recent tenant. Yet he vanished from the scene at the first opportunity, despite his expressions of interest. What more could a discreet accomplice do?

Piers is of the opinion that the mention of Thomas's name put the wind up the fellow and caused him to retreat. Thanks to the excellent description of the man's curricle and pair provided by a boy who lives in Mr. Scarlet's street, Piers found an inn on the Cirencester road where the equipage put up for the night. At the inn, the man called himself Mr. Jones. He behaved as well as a fashionable young man with an interest in sport could be expected to behave, paid his shot promptly, and left at first light, last seen driving in the direction of Cirencester. All we have against him is his appearance at Mr. Scarlet's house and his abrupt loss of interest when he learned that the house was uninhabited and that Thomas was greatly interested in the whereabouts of the previous tenant.

Piers and Reardon did all they could, but they were unable to learn anything more about Mr. Jones. Thomas has written to Mr. Wrexton (who I fear will some day tire of being treated as Thomas's social vade mecum—I look forward to the day when we are together here again and I can show you his reply to Thomas's letter about Drina—it is a true masterpiece of sarcasm) to ask him to inquire about the possible antecedents of Mr. Jones.

Although he refuses to admit it to me, Thomas would much prefer to go to London and snoop into the matter himself. (How can I blame him? I would rather be in Mayfair myself.) But for all his impatience, Thomas remains here. He chides me when I seem surprised by his steadfastness. Although it has been quiet here, I know he views this interlude as the calm before a storm. I believe he would welcome a storm. Thomas may be at his best in a crisis, but he certainly does get thoroughly bored in the meantime.

If I keep on in this vein, I will be forced to ask Thomas to enchant this letter without reading it, and that would only pique his curiosity. So I will simply add that Arthur and Eleanor are thick as thieves with Drina. Diana and Edward are still their willing acolytes, and Alexander is exactly as sweet as Laurence. All are in bounding good health. All of us send you our very best wishes. We look forward to your return.

Love,

Kate

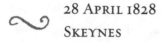

28 APRIL 1828
SKEYNES

(Enchanted by T.S.)

Dear James,

Finding a needle in a haystack is as nothing compared to finding a surveyor in a sheepdog. Congratulations.

I direct this missive to you at the London address Cecy provided Kate. May it find you both there safely.

Perhaps I should change "both" to "all," given the recent addition to your ménage. I trust that by the time you read this, the Royal College will have succeeded in restoring Herr Magus Schellen to his rightful shape. You know I am eager to hear all he can tell you. Do resist the urge to suggest I am dogging you for the story or panting after the details. After all, it would never do to jest at Herr Magus Schellen's misfortune.

Once you have Schellen sorted, and once you have turned someone at the College loose on the whole question of ley lines (Sulgrave would be my first choice—he's young enough to take direction, yet old enough to hold his own

against the true crustaceans at the College), I would consider it a personal favor if you would turn Cecy loose on her
aunt Elizabeth. Wrexton has been next to no help in the
matter of our superfluous young lady. Going by the clues we
have (her expensive clothing, her flawless deportment, and
a familiarity with duchesses Kate finds highly significant), it
beggars belief that a child like this could disappear without
raising an alarm somewhere. It's not as if the greatest gossips
of our time aren't already assembled in London for the Season. Surely between the pair of them, Cecy and Elizabeth
can learn something useful to us. You yourself, I seem to remember, have a way of soaking up scandal broth even as
you seem to have a mind for higher and nobler things. Stir
yourself.

Believe me, if I could, I would be shoulder to shoulder
with you, braving the boredom of the salons and assembly
rooms. Unfortunately, my responsibilities keep me here. If I
weren't here to chivvy her out of doors regularly, I fear Kate
would long since have gone mad from prolonged exposure
to the infantry.

In addition, there is the provoking fact that someone has
been making discreet inquiries about me. I have made it
clear in Stroud that anyone with any information whatsoever concerning Mr. Scarlet will be rewarded if they come to
me with it. My sources tell me that questions have been
asked about my intentions and antecedents. It would be
useful to know who has been doing the inquiring. Alas, no
word on that as yet. No matter what answers the questions

elicited, no one has come to me with anything, useful or otherwise.

All this may be moot in a fortnight. Kate thinks that all we need do is restore your children to you, persuade Georgy to take a repairing lease somewhere discreetly foreign, locate a Department of Lost Articles specializing in children of good breeding, and our problems will be solved. I fear the nursery is softening her brain.

Write with news. I will do as much, if I ever get any.

Yours,
Thomas

29 APRIL 1828
THE KING'S HEAD, LEEDS

Dearest Kate,

As you may see from the inscription, we are *not* in London, nor, it seems, is there any immediate chance of our returning there. We are in Leeds, with no prospect of moving further. In point of fact, it is quite likely that we shall soon be compelled to return to Stockton, or perhaps Darlington. I am quite cross and altogether out of patience with a great many persons, most of them decades dead. My temper is not improved by the certainty that any news you may have sent will have gone to the London address and will therefore take several extra days to reach us.

We left Stockton yesterday morning. Both James and I were anticipating a quick and easy journey to London, as the weather was fine and the roads good. We chose to travel by conventional methods, rather than take the railway, as we did not wish to draw any more attention to our sheepdog (and traveling by railway is a novelty that attracts attention all on its own; attempting to bring a sheepdog along would undoubtedly be a nine days' wonder in the village).

All went well for the first half of the journey, until the road turned away from the river, out of County Durham and into Yorkshire. Shortly thereafter, the sheepdog became restless. (I should mention that, as we chose not to travel on the Sabbath, I had spent much of Sunday attempting to devise a workable means of communication with Herr Magus Schellen. My efforts were of no avail; the transformation spell that affects him is quite thorough. Which is to say that, most unfortunately, Herr Magus Schellen is not a man in the shape of a sheepdog, who would perhaps be able to convey some useful information; no, he is simply a more-intelligent-than-usual sheepdog. So we had no way of discovering what the difficulty might be.)

As we continued on, the sheepdog went from restless to whimpering, and then subsided into a lethargy. By the time we reached the inn at Leeds, he was lying motionless on the floor of the carriage and I was growing quite worried. James was at first inclined to put the dog's behavior down to carriage-sickness (or the canine equivalent), but he, too, was concerned when Herr Schellen had to be lifted down and then lay panting on the ground.

Our situation attracted the attention of a number of

stableboys and various idlers, who made a great many un-helpful comments and suggestions about what to do with our dog. James responded more and more stiffly (a sure sign of irritation), while I was torn between trying to attend to the Herr Magus, wishing to avoid attracting more attention, and a strong desire to lay into the onlookers with my parasol.

And then I heard a voice that cut through the crowd eas-ily without being raised to any vulgar pitch: "Does all this uproar have some point of which I am not aware?"

The onlookers melted away like snow in sunlight. Only an erect figure in a modish burgundy walking dress and matching bonnet remained. "Aunt Elizabeth!" I said in mingled surprise, gratitude, and trepidation. "Whatever are you doing in Leeds?"

"We came to find you and James," Aunt Elizabeth replied, from which I inferred that Mr. Wrexton had accom-panied her. "I had not expected—" She glanced at the sheepdog, and her eyes narrowed. "I had not expected to find you in such an *interesting* position," she said, which I do not think was what she had meant to say to begin with. "You had better bring . . . everyone inside, where we can discuss matters without creating any more scenes."

As it was useless to protest that creating a scene had been the last thing we had intended, we followed her in. Or rather, I followed her in; James stayed with the sheepdog, at-tempting to persuade him to walk. When that failed, he was forced to bribe the lone stableboy who had remained within earshot to assist him in carrying the Herr Magus inside.

I will spare you an account of the discussion with the innkeeper; suffice it to say, he was initially much put out by the presence of so plebeian an animal as a sheepdog, and James had to turn all top-lofty on him—and even then, I am not sure we would have prevailed had not Aunt Elizabeth taken a hand.

Eventually, the five of us—Aunt Elizabeth, Mr. Wrexton, James, the sheepdog, and I—were served tea in a private parlor, while Walker and James's valet saw to the trunks. I was more than usually happy with the bustle of servants setting up tea things, for I was uncertain what tack to take when the discussion began. It is so awkward when one is involved in a secret matter and has no notion how much other people know, or whether they ought to be told more or not. Despite my worries, I was glad indeed to see Mr. Wrexton's cheerful face.

Fortunately, I did not need to mind my tongue for long. As soon as the door closed behind the last of the servants, James turned to Mr. Wrexton and asked, "What brings you to Leeds?" (just as if he had not heard Aunt Elizabeth say, only a few minutes before, that they had come in search of us).

"This business of Wellington's," Mr. Wrexton replied. He frowned at the sheepdog. "Though I suspect my news will wait. What *have* you stumbled onto?"

James looked at me. I began an account of finding the sheepdog, but Aunt Elizabeth stopped me before I had gone three sentences. "From the beginning, Cecelia, please," she said firmly. "Official reports are useful, but too often they sacrifice relevant details for brevity."

She was very careful not to look at James as she said this, but since his are the only official reports there have been of this matter, it was quite clear what she meant. She added, "I need not fear that *your* narrative will suffer from a lack of description."

(Dearly as I love Aunt Elizabeth, and much as I appreciate her sterling qualities, I confess that I *cannot* like the way she has of making me feel as if I am once more a scrubby ten-year-old with torn stockings and muddy petticoats.)

So I did as she asked. I began at the beginning—with Lord Wellington's summons to James—and recounted the entire business in order. Aunt Elizabeth and Mr. Wrexton listened with great attention, and when I finished, they looked at each other.

"I believe this is more your area, my dear," Mr. Wrexton said, gesturing at the sheepdog.

Aunt Elizabeth rose and went over to the dog. She felt very gently behind its ears and at the back of its neck, then frowned. Then she made a chopping motion with her left hand and said, *"Aperio."*

The sheepdog howled. Aunt Elizabeth closed her hand into a fist and the sound stopped abruptly as the sheepdog collapsed once more.

"Aunt Elizabeth, what—"

"Hush, Cecelia. In a moment." She rose, dusted her

skirts, and hastily reseated herself. Giving me a warning look, she began to speak in a voice rather louder than normal, and much more in Aunt Charlotte's style than her own. "Now, about the shameful way in which you and Georgina have been neglecting the London Season—"

The door of the parlor burst open. The innkeeper stood there, sputtering apologies; behind him, the scowl on his wife's face made clear who was responsible for their abrupt appearance. I blessed Aunt Elizabeth's quick wits; for of course if she had not started in on the Season in that nonsensical way, the innkeeper and his wife might well have heard something they ought not.

Aunt Elizabeth fixed our hosts with an imperious glare. "Gracious me," she said in a forbidding tone. "What *is* the reason for this intrusion?"

"Begging your pardon, ma'am, but you'll have to be keeping that dog quiet," the innkeeper said. His wife punctuated his remarks with emphatic nods.

"Has there been some disturbance?" Mr. Wrexton asked with great politeness.

The innkeeper looked quite taken aback, but his wife was made of sterner stuff. "That dog was howling, but a minute gone," she said. "And we can't be having it. Begging your pardon," she added grudgingly after a pointed glance from her husband.

Aunt Elizabeth put down her teacup and sniffed. I am sure you remember that sniff, Kate; we surely heard it often enough after our childhood adventures. "Nonsense!" she said. "Does that dog look capable of such an effort as howling?"

Everyone looked at the sheepdog. The dog blinked but did not raise his head from the carpet. He gave every appearance of being incapable of lifting so much as an ear. Throwing back his head to howl was plainly beyond him.

The innkeeper seemed willing to accept this evidence, and repeated his apologies. His wife was more reluctant to retreat, but it was clear even to her that she was no match for Aunt Elizabeth. When they had gone at last (and when we were quite certain that the wife was not listening at the door), I looked at Aunt Elizabeth and said, "Aunt Elizabeth, I never thought to hear such a string of bouncers from you, of all people."

"It has long since become clear to me that I failed, in your upbringing, to impress upon you properly how unattractive it is for a lady of quality to use slang terms adopted from her brother," Aunt Elizabeth observed. "And I must point out to you that no word of falsehood passed either Michael's lips or my own."

"A masterly job of misdirection," James said. "But what, if anything, did you learn about our involuntary guest?" He nodded at the sheepdog.

"Cecelia is quite right; this is a case of transformation," Aunt Elizabeth replied. "I cannot, of course, determine who he is, or was, prior to becoming a sheepdog, but I think it likely that she is also correct in assuming him to be your missing engineer. Unfortunately, I fear he will not be easy to disenchant. The spell is linked to a power source somewhere northeast of here."

"Ah. That will explain the animal's lethargy," Mr. Wrexton said. "The spell is drawing on the dog's energy to maintain the link over too long a distance."

"Good heavens!" I said, appalled. "You mean that he's like this just because we brought him this far south? However are we to get him to the Royal College?"

"I don't believe you will, dear," Aunt Elizabeth said. "Not without disenchanting him first."

"We can alleviate the problem, but only very temporarily," Mr. Wrexton said. "Not long enough to get him to London, I'm afraid."

The sheepdog whined. James and I looked at each other. "I don't think Wellington is going to be pleased about this," James said after a moment.

"That's another thing," Mr. Wrexton said, and his tone drew James's and my attention at once. He cleared his throat and went on, "There's a bit of a bother at the prime minister's office."

"Michael, dear," Aunt Elizabeth said in a tone of mild reproof.

"Yes, all right," Mr. Wrexton said. "I've been dancing around the facts for so long that it's become a habit," he said apologetically to James and me. "To give you the matter without any bark on it, information has been leaking out of the prime minister's office, and we don't know yet who is responsible or why."

"Wellington's staff?" James said in tones of horror.

"Doubtful," Mr. Wrexton told him. "The problem seems to date back to some months before Wellington took office. That's not much help, though; there are dozens, if not hundreds, of clerks and functionaries who could be behind it. And the fellow's been careful, to get away with it this long. We won't be able to narrow the field until we find out what he's after."

"What he's after?" I said. "Can't you guess from the sort of information that has been leaking?"

"That's the problem," Mr. Wrexton said. "The things we've traced have been very . . . miscellaneous. Everything from the progress of trade discussions to the prime minister's opinions of quite minor bills in Parliament. Some of the gossip about that last argument between His Majesty and the Duke of Cumberland was traced to the office. Nothing important, but Wellington was furious. And now this latest incident—"

Apparently, James sent off an express packet to Mr. Wrexton last week, after the incident at Haliwar, asking him to check at the Royal College for information about the tower, ley lines, and all the rest of the things that have been puzzling us. As the request was part of our investigation, he sent it through Lord Wellington's office. Lord Wellington sent it on at once, of course, but the next morning there were signs that someone had tried to enter his office. (Lord Wellington naturally takes magical precautions to prevent this; James says it is a habit he acquired long ago, during his India campaigns.) Since his secretary's desk, which did *not* have any protective enchantments, was also rifled, and since the message packets appeared to have received considerable attention from the rifler, Lord Wellington and his aides concluded that someone wanted rather badly to find out what had been in James's urgent letter.

And so Mr. Wrexton and Aunt Elizabeth made some hasty preparations and set out on the North Road, to act as a combination of reinforcements and messengers. I believe that Lord Wellington also had some hope that, because Aunt Elizabeth and I are related to Georgy and because there have been some garbled rumors flying about London regarding Georgy and Daniel (everything from murder to runaway matches with the groom and governess, Aunt Elizabeth says), it would seem natural for Aunt Elizabeth to come north to assist me in confronting Daniel, or some such. (I do not think that this is at all likely to fool whoever is rifling desks in the government offices, but it may do for an explanation to Society.)

Which brings me to the last of Mr. Wrexton's news. James had, as I mentioned, asked for information about ley lines and Haliwar Tower. As Mr. Wrexton is no antiquary, nor any sort of expert on ancient magic or history, he went straight to the archives at the Royal College of Wizards. And what he found there is quite dreadful.

"You have to understand," he said, "that the archivists at the Royal College are fanatics in regard to completeness. They write *everything* down. There's even a thorough description of those experiments of Sir Hilary Bedrick's, because even though they were illegal, unethical, and got him kicked out of the College to boot, he performed some of them while he was a member."

James made a disapproving noise. I did not say anything, but I shared his sentiments. Sir Hilary's "experiments" in stealing other wizards' magic and driving people mad do not seem to me to be the sort of thing that the Royal College ought to preserve, and I do not believe that I feel this way *only* because I was one of the people he intended to drain and drive mad.

Mr. Wrexton nodded as if we had both spoken. "Just so," he said. "But this time, it's very much to our advantage. You see, there was quite a lot of experimentation on ley lines right after they were discovered in 1641. It wasn't limited to the Royal College, either; I found a variety of accounts sent in by an assortment of magicians. One of them, Lord Charlton White, was proposed for membership in the College on the strength of his spell for measuring the intensity of different ley lines."

Aunt Elizabeth sniffed again. James looked from her to Mr. Wrexton. "What was wrong with White's spell?"

"Nothing," Mr. Wrexton said. "It's still used. The problem is with what came after. He and another fellow, a magician named Steven Morris, came up with the theory that some ley lines had been artificially constructed."

"*Artificial?* You mean, some of them were made by wizards?" I was stunned. Just tapping a ley line is dangerous enough; controlling one long enough to move it or create a new one . . . well, if ley lines are like rivers of magic, then creating a new one would be like digging a canal, except that the canal would be for a strong acid that threatened to eat you and your tools at any moment.

"Exactly," Mr. Wrexton said. "If they *were* artificial, they'd have to be prehistoric, of course, or we'd have records of how the lines were constructed. Morris and White spent five years roaming around mapping assorted ley lines in an attempt to prove their theories. After about four years, their project was interrupted by the Civil Wars."

"It *would* be a bit difficult to wander about casting detecting spells with Cromwell's army marching back and forth," James said dryly.

"That's what everyone's thought for years," Mr. Wrexton said. "Especially since Lord White was killed during one of the early clashes. After the Restoration, of course, King Charles II sent Lynne and a corps of wizards to do the mapping job properly. So no one paid much attention to those early maps."

"Except you," I said. "What did you discover?"

Mr. Wrexton sighed. "The Royal College was as divided by the Civil Wars as the rest of England," he said. "There were Royalists and Parliamentarians among wizards, the same as everywhere else. And Morris and White—"

"Were on opposite sides?" I guessed.

Mr. Wrexton nodded. "Lord White was a Royalist; that's why he lost his head when Cromwell caught him. Morris was, it seems, secretly one of Cromwell's advisors from the very beginning."

"And their political persuasions have something to do with ley lines and Haliwar Tower?" James said.

"Possibly," Mr. Wrexton replied. "I found a summary of their work and theories by accident, apparently misfiled among a series of maps showing the incidence of sheep-cursing along the Tyne in 1653. The archivist was most upset."

"Good Lord!" James said. "What were you looking for in there?"

"But what did they *say*?" I demanded at the same time.

"Lord White was quite sincere in his desire simply to prove the existence of a prehistoric network of man-made ley lines. Morris, however, seems to have wanted not merely to find them, but to control them."

"He was going to use all that magic to help Oliver Cromwell!" I said.

"In a way," Mr. Wrexton replied. "It's clear from Morris's notes that he believed the artificial leys weren't simply set out at random or for the convenience of a particular wizard or group of wizards. He thought they formed a pattern, a spell, that bound the whole country. And still does."

James's eyes narrowed. "Bound it to what?"

"Bound it together," Mr. Wrexton replied. "Think about it. Over the centuries, England has been invaded by Romans, by Danes, by Saxons, by French—and all of them have either left again or settled down and become English."

"That's the spell's doing?" I said.

"Morris and White believed it was," Mr. Wrexton said. "And when the fighting started, Morris thought that the spell would keep Oliver Cromwell from winning unless something was done about it."

"Hmph," Aunt Elizabeth said. She had been listening with evident interest; plainly, Mr. Wrexton had not previously informed her of his discoveries. "You needn't mince words, Michael. They were a pair of lunatics. They left out anything that didn't fit their notions, and added in lines that weren't there. Unless you think that several new ley lines simply *appeared* out of nowhere after they made their maps."

"I regret having to contradict you, my dear," Mr. Wrexton said. "But they were not lunatics. Or at least, if they were lunatics, they were partially *correct* lunatics. Lord White left extremely clear notes along with the maps. I didn't have time to verify all of it, but I managed enough. Artificial or not, there is a spell powered by a network of ley lines that does exactly what Morris thought. And I cannot see how such a thing could have arisen by some natural accident."

There was a stunned silence. At last James said, "Does the duke know about this?"

"Lord Wellington? Of course. I went to him right

away," Mr. Wrexton said. "He verified my results himself, and some of his comments were extremely insightful. The College lost a great wizard there, when he chose to devote himself to public service, though of course he's still a member."

There was another pause. After a moment, Mr. Wrexton went on. "Morris was quite as capable as Lord White of demonstrating the spell and its effectiveness. It's how he persuaded Cromwell to meddle with the ley lines."

Aunt Elizabeth *hmph*ed again. "I'll wager they hoped to make their version of Parliament proof against change," she said.

Mr. Wrexton nodded. "Morris had been doing some experiments on his own. He thought he'd learned enough to manipulate the artificial ley lines himself, so as to change the pattern and make it do what he and Cromwell wanted. They planned to begin by controlling one or two of the larger ley lines that Morris thought were keys to the spell and then redirect others to solidify the changes they wanted. Lord White found out and sent his notes, maps, and information to the Royal College just before he was caught and killed."

"And by the time anyone looked at it, Cromwell was in charge and the Royal College was keeping out of politics," James said. "I'll hazard a guess that someone misfiled those documents deliberately."

Mr. Wrexton nodded. "The archivist at the time thought a record should be kept, and disapproved heartily of the crew of magicians Cromwell had collected to help him. He knew Cromwell would order the documents confiscated if word of them got out, so he made sure that it didn't."

"A little too sure, perhaps," Aunt Elizabeth said.

"Fortunately, the process of controlling and redirecting ley lines proved to be longer and more difficult than Morris expected. He and his magicians were only about a quarter of the way through when Oliver Cromwell died."

"The ley line under Haliwar Tower!" I said. "The Webbs said that the tower was built in Cromwell's day. That ley line is one of the keys, isn't it?"

"So Morris's map indicates," Mr. Wrexton said. "It was one of the first to be altered."

"And now the railway is affecting it every time a steam train passes across it," I said.

"But affecting it how?" James asked.

"The train is the least of the matter," Mr. Wrexton said. "I don't think it's an exaggeration to say that tampering with the ley spell could result in chaos. I don't mean simply bringing down the current government; I mean having it fall apart altogether. And Wellington thinks that someone's been deliberately tampering."

"Recently?" Aunt Elizabeth said. "This can't be some relic of Cromwell's nonsense?"

"Within the last five years," Mr. Wrexton said. "The resonance traces were quite clear, once we realized we should look for them."

"Who?" said James. "And why?"

Mr. Wrexton spread his hands. "If we knew, things would be much easier to sort out."

"And how are they doing it?" I added. "From everything I've read, it is *exceedingly* difficult to tap the power of ley lines safely, and this sounds like considerably more than mere tapping." A thought occurred to me, and I straightened in my chair and nearly spilt my tea. "Earthquakes! Tapping ley lines can cause earthquakes, I remember, and one of them runs directly under Haliwar Tower! James, you don't suppose . . ."

"I try not to reason in advance of my data," James said in a dry tone. "But I admit, the coincidence bears looking into."

I considered everything we had just heard for a moment. Then I looked at Mr. Wrexton. "And do you mean to say that all this important information has been hidden in the archives at the Royal College of Wizards for a hundred and fifty years, or more, and *no one noticed*?" I said. "That is appalling!"

But appalling or not, that is the case exactly, Kate. And Lord Wellington, via Mr. Wrexton, wishes James and me (and Mr. Wrexton and Aunt Elizabeth, thank goodness) to "see what we can do about it."

This entire situation could have been avoided if anyone in the past hundred years had bothered to clean out the archives at the Royal College. Or if the college had paid proper attention to what its wizards were up to. And it is *most* annoying to be caught out like this, just when we were on our way back to London. For of course, we cannot say no, under the circumstances.

So today James is making arrangements for the lot of us to return to the vicinity of Haliwar Tower, and Mr. Wrexton and Aunt Elizabeth are trying to make poor Herr Magus Schellen more comfortable. *I* shall go shopping. Leeds may not have the variety available in London, but its weavers are second to none. If I am to miss the Season altogether on Lord Wellington's business, I intend to have a few good lengths of merino and linen to show for it, at least.

I will confess, in your ear alone, Kate, that I am not so thoroughly displeased by this development as I might have been. For while it is most aggravating to have all our plans overturned like this, I cannot be sorry that we shall have a chance to unravel all these mysteries *completely,* instead of simply turning Herr Magus Schellen over to the Royal College and hoping they remembered to let us know what happened. Aunt Elizabeth is quite right; official reports *never* contain the details one is particularly interested in knowing.

I need not caution you to share this information with Thomas alone. (If he asks, you may tell him that Mr. Wrexton approved my providing it to you both, and also highly commends our caution in making our letters unreadable.) You can imagine the possible difficulties if any of this were to become known.

Pray convey my apologies to the children. I hope they will not make your life a misery with their disappointment. I am much afraid that my only hope of redemption in their eyes will be to bring them back a sheepdog after all (though of course *not* the Herr Magus!). That would put the cap on this whole misadventure, to be sure.

Your most annoyed,
Cecy

May

(in cipher)

My dear Thomas,

You will by this time have been apprised of our latest change in plans. I delayed writing so as to provide you with our new direction, in the certainty that my dear Cecelia would pour out the entire business to Kate early on, who would doubtless inform you of the salient details.

Our entire ménage—myself, Cecelia, the Wrextons, and our much-tried surveyor-turned-sheepdog, together with assorted servants—are currently ensconced in a rented property in Darlington, it having proved impossible to arrange satisfactory quarters for so many, with such peculiar requirements, at any of the local inns. Assuage whatever disgruntlement you feel over this turn of luck by dwelling on the difficulties of finding a suitable place and settling the arrangements in less than a day—the job fell to me, as Wrexton was naturally busy with the spell on the sheepdog. I shall spare you the details. I'm sure your imagination is up to the challenge.

We chose Darlington for two main reasons: First, it is as near to Goosepool (and the stone circle called the Dancing Weans, where we discovered the sheepdog) as is Stockton, which will make Wrexton's work on de-transforming Herr Schellen simpler, and second, Darlington is the home of the Stockton and Darlington Railway offices, which I mean to investigate next.

Once disenchanted, our sheepdog-surveyor will no doubt clear up a good many puzzles, but Wrexton's news about the possible effect of the ley lines on the stability of the government has cast the whole situation in a far more serious light. Since nothing in the Herr Magus's background indicates that he is an expert on ley lines, and since neither Wrexton nor his wife is more than normally acquainted with ley theory, I am considering calling in a specialist.

Unfortunately, Wrexton says that the greatest living expert on ley lines is an Irishman, one Sean Skelly by name, who has persistently refused to have anything to do with the Royal College, or, indeed, anything or anyone English. I believe, however, that I have a possible solution to the problem.

You remember that insufferable puppy we rescued in Rome ten years back? Theodore Daventer, who had the infernal cheek to make sheep's eyes at Cecelia? The Royal College of Wizards spent a long time working to remove the spells of persuasion and leadership that that Italian woman cast on him, but they were only partially successful. It is, I suppose, to his credit that he never wanted to be emperor of Europe, or we might have had much more trouble than we did. Instead, it seems, he has used his abilities to establish an international fraternity of sorts, an academy to facilitate the free exchange of all kinds of knowledge: scientific, historical, and, to the point, magical. He's recognized now as one of the rising intellectual lights of Europe. If anyone can persuade Mr. Skelly to assist us, it is Daventer.

In the meantime, I plan to return to my study of the railway, since that is what brought Herr Magus Schellen up here. There are a number of prospective investors for the proposed Manchester-Liverpool line in town, studying the performance of the Stockton and Darlington line. I shall present myself as one of them, and if that will not serve to pry loose some useful information, I warn you that I will sacrifice you as well. The opportunity to hook a peer of the realm, with the added benefit of obtaining his vote in the House of Lords, will no doubt open a good many doors. I shall not, of course, mention your utter refusal to take your seat in Parliament, save on those rare occasions when something strikes your fancy. What has it been, twice in the last fifteen years?

So if you should receive any inquiries about your interest in investing in railways, kindly do me the favor of responding with circumspection. That is to say, I'd appreciate it if you'd tell them you'd like more information, instead of telling them to go to the devil.

Yours,
James

4 MAY 1828
SKEYNES

Dear Cecy,

Such an unfortunate turn of events. But how fortunate that Aunt Elizabeth and Mr. Wrexton arrived when they did. And only think of the effect it would have upon your children to learn that the dog you had secured for them (don't ask how they contrived to divine this—your prediction has proved uncannily accurate—they know about the sheepdog and view it as their rightful property) had died en route. The demise of Herr Magus Schellen would have been a tragedy, of course. The demise of Arthur's dog ("My faithful hound," I overheard Arthur say) would have been unmitigated domestic disaster.

Thank goodness today's post brought us your new direction from James, for if I could not relate my news to you and send it off at once, I think I might shatter into small pieces. Small and silly pieces, so put aside any expectation that I have news of importance. I have nothing but nonsense for you. Be warned. I intend to burden you with it in painful detail, for otherwise it will buzz around inside my head for days. I know you are much too sensible to permit anything so foolish to buzz around inside your head for even five minutes, so I look forward to hearing your opinion of the matter.

I gather we may count ourselves fortunate indeed that we are neglecting the London Season, as Aunt Elizabeth puts it, for I have learned that the London Season has not, alas, been neglecting us. You must keep this news in strictest confidence.

Alice Siddington (you remember Alice Grenville that was, I hope?) is a tolerably regular correspondent of mine. She does not generally devote much of her attention to the gossip in town, but when she does, her information is to be relied upon.

The most recent newspapers have confirmed, with their usual mixture of speculation and inaccuracy, a rumor I had heard from Alice in her last letter. A most mysterious volume of poetry has taken the fancy of the Ton. (Not for its quality, I assure you, but because the identity of the poetess is shrouded in secrecy.) Some speculate that the verses were written by a peeress, some that the author is a foreign noblewoman, still others that the poetess is someone belonging to the throng of King George's cousins, half rackety, half royal, or both.

Demiroyal or demirep, the anonymous poetess has taken the Ton by storm. Copies are selling in the dozens, and hardly a fashionable gathering goes by without some reference to the mystery.

Dear that she is, Alice sent me a copy of the slim volume so that I could speculate, too. A handsome article it is, bound in limp red leather. If the verses matched the quality of the paper they are printed on, it would be an impressive object. They don't. The moment the curiosity of the Ton has been satisfied, all interest in the poetess and her work will go where dew goes in midmorning. For now, however, it is a nine days' wonder, perhaps even ten.

I'm sure you are well ahead of me, Cecy. It would have taken you a few lines only to detect the identity of the mysterious authoress. I had to read an entire page before I came to these lines, written ostensibly upon the topic of an ornamental fountain, although the author's determination never to fall in love again has been hammered at relentlessly throughout the verse:

> *Falling I rise again*
> *And rise to fall no more*

Even I could hardly fail to guess the author, could I? Georgy once embroidered those words on a sampler. If her handkerchiefs had been large enough, she would have embroidered it on each of them, she was so proud of her poetical efforts.

When I recovered my breath, I locked the slim volume safely away with Alice's letter. If I have learned anything from Thomas, it is the importance of keeping vital evidence safe while one considers the ways and means with which one might put it to the best possible use. No wonder Georgy enjoyed wagering. If there was ever anyone with such luck—

to find herself all the rage for her poetry, of all things—I have never heard the like.

I found Georgy in her bedchamber, trying which bonnet suited her best. When I closed the door and leaned against it, she turned to me from the looking glass with visible reluctance. I showed her the passage in the most recent *Gazette*. "No more penitent poems to James and Cecy, I fear, or all will be discovered."

Georgy blushed. "I don't know what you mean."

"Don't try to dissemble. Is that why you ran away? To create some sort of cause célèbre to sell more copies of your book? You might have warned us of your impending notoriety." I was not nearly so stern as the words make me sound. Indeed, I could hardly keep from laughing at her indignation.

"I would never do such a thing!" Georgy snatched the *Gazette* from me and hurled it across the room. That is, she tried. As I have often observed from Thomas's attempts to do the same, newspapers do not hurl well. They flutter and come down on the carpet in pieces, so that one has to bend repeatedly to pick it all up before one is discovered midtantrum.

Georgy did not stir herself to pick up even a single page of the scattered *Gazette*. She held her head as if it pained her. "People are so dreadful!"

"Which people? Those who buy your book?" I tidied up the scattered sheets. "Or those who shelter you from the curiosity of the Ton?"

"The trifler who betrayed the confidence of a lady," Georgy snarled. "You can't think I intended my most intimate letters to be published?"

"Do you mean you did it by accident?" I asked, before reason caught me back again. "Wait—did you say your letters?"

"Yes, my letters," Georgy said defiantly. "I wrote to—a friend, confiding my distress to him only under conditions of strictest secrecy. That my thoughts took the form of verse only proves how intimate, how private they were. He betrayed me. He had the bare decency to suppress my identity, but when I could not—would not!—meet his terms, he carried out his threat! I only meant to make Daniel jealous. I thought he would send the letters to Daniel, never that he truly intended to have them published."

The dramatic vigor of Georgy's lament was not lessened by the fine disdain with which she took the *Gazette* away from me again. The interest with which she reread the passage I had pointed out to her spoiled the effect a little, but under the circumstances I could not blame her for her curiosity.

"It seems he has fulfilled his threats to the last degree," Georgy exclaimed when she had read the passage twice. "What am I to do?" She said a good deal more, but I will spare you what I can.

"What a mercy you are here, safely away from the scandal," I told her. "We may scrape through with our reputations intact. It's not as if anyone ever saw you read poetry, let alone write any."

"You are heartless!" Georgy informed me. "What can you know of the finer feelings?"

I ought to have shown Georgy more sympathy, I own. Very likely I would have done so if she had not been watering our carpets for months on end now. My patience deserted me, as usual, just when I needed it most. "I don't see what your feelings have to do with it," I confessed. "It's your infernal verses that are causing the trouble."

"You have taken on a harder stamp since your marriage," Georgy said. "I blame your husband."

"Oh, do you?" I retorted. "Then be sure to blame him for the roof over your head and the food on your plate, too, for I don't see anyone else lining up for the privilege of entertaining you, Your Grace, particularly not your husband."

I was a fool to lose my temper. But there it is. I am a fool. I flew out of Georgy's bedchamber as if a swarm of wasps were after me, and only pouring out the whole silly tale to you has made me feel any more composed about the matter. I am sorry to burden you with these starts when you have the whole weight of English history, ley lines and all, upon your shoulders.

I will write again, and in a more temperate vein, as soon as I have something of genuine value to say. In the meantime, thank you for existing. At least I have one relation (other than Aunt Elizabeth) with some sense. I find it a great comfort.

Yours,
Kate

Dear James,

Thank you for settling down in one place long enough for me to learn your direction and write to you properly. You've earned so much commiseration from me over your trials that I won't bore you with any. Instead I send something far more to the point—news.

In my unceasing efforts to protect your offspring (I sometimes forget why I bother, particularly when we have had to purchase a fresh supply of India ink for the third time in a fortnight), Kate and I cast and recast the warding spells daily. This requires us to ride the bounds every morning, which I grant you proves no hardship, given the season of the year. As we rode past this morning, our gamekeeper, Josiah Penny, gave me one of his sidelong glares.

Remember Colonel Ettrick of the Seventh? Come to think of it, perhaps his name wasn't Ettrick. Remember the chap who looked like a broomstick topped by a hatchet? You'd remember him if you ever saw Penny, for not only does Penny have the same hatchet profile, he usually possesses a similar air of half-scandalized disapproval whenever he sees me. Not, however, of late. Indeed, if Penny were capable of beaming at me, he would certainly have done it by now. Our riding the bounds has made his duties far easier, as the local poachers can't cross the boundary spell. The pheasants are safe for months to come.

I have just come from an exchange of intelligence with Penny. My contribution to the dialogue took the form of a small quantity of ale and a few questions.

Penny has sources of information you and I can only dream of. Someone he will not name to me (several some-ones, I suspect) reports that a foreigner has been seen at the very edge of the estate these past two nights. (Don't take the term to heart. To Penny, anyone not from his village quali-fies.) It is possible, I suppose, that some gudgeon is out birds-nesting. I think it more likely someone has come to test my attention to spell-casting detail.

Penny proposes we go out this evening and watch, just to see if the would-be intruder returns. If the third time is the charm, we will question the visitor. If he seems likely to possess useful information concerning the goings-on here of late, either I will try the good old *dicemi* on him, or Penny and I will roast him over a small fire until he shares all he knows with us.

If he turns out to be an innocent passerby, I will send Penny about his business and tip the fellow half a crown for alleviating my boredom.

In either event, I will write again if the results yield any-thing of interest.

Yours,
Thomas

∽ 6 MAY 1828

Dear James,

Damn. I regret that I posted my last letter so promptly. If I had it to hand, I would destroy it and write you a far less falsely confident one. As it is, I will compound my error by writing you yet another hasty missive. When I'm done, I intend to sand it, seal it without troubling to reread it, and go straight to bed, where I should have been hours ago.

Here is what happened with no bark on it.

As I planned, I joined Josiah Penny after dinner. It was raining, but I was dressed for it. With some grumbling, he led me to the stone wall that marks part of the southern boundary of Skeynes. Within the wall lies my ancestral property, specifically a bramble thicket of exceptional ferocity. Beyond the wall, centuries of sheep have trimmed the grass on the common to a rough carpet.

You would find the place unworthy of interest. Lumps of raised ground, which optimistic antiquarians believe to be traces of an ancient earthwork, make a ring. At the center of the ring is a biggish slab of stone, tall as a tall man and about twice as wide. This is called the Tingle Stone.

No, don't ask me. I don't know why they call it that. It's always been called that, just as it's always been there, a monument to masculine pride, I suppose. As it provides the only proper cover for several hundred yards, I kept most of my attention on it, and the earthworks that circle it, as the time passed and pints of rainwater ran down my collar.

Penny and I didn't have much to say after the first two hours. By the time another hour passed, despite the miserable conditions, I was beginning to grow sleepy. I'll swear Penny scented the man on the wind before I detected the first glimmer of magic. Once we knew he was there, I could feel him—almost hear him breathe—as he crouched at the foot of the Tingle Stone. I sent out my holdfast cantrip as slowly as I could, hoping to entangle him in it before he noticed it rising from the grass beneath to grip him around his ankles.

I needn't have wasted a moment on caution. From the first touch of my spell, the visitor was as aware of me as I was of him. He sprang up like a salmon. I let the holdfast run thin, enough to trail along behind him as he sprinted away from us. My intention was to bring him down with it and let the rough grass hold him for me while I built its strength.

It should have worked. Very possibly, if only Kate had been with me, it would have worked. As it happened, it did not work. Despite all my efforts, our visitor found the strength to run—well, to shuffle—away.

Penny and I were somewhat hindered by the wet and the brambles, but that is no excuse. The visitor's strength was beyond what I would consider possible.

Penny gave chase. As soon as he'd fired his ancient fowling piece, he scrambled over the wall and tried his best to bring the visitor down. I was playing the holdfast with all my skill, trying to slow the fellow's flight, but I spared the time to put up a fool's light, a burst of cold fire to give us a look at the man.

The rain made it hard to make out detail in the greenish glow, but I judge the man was young, of medium height and slender build. He had a workman's cap pulled down as far as one can pull a cap and still see beneath it. His stockings were falling down around his ankles with the force of my holdfast, but he didn't let that slow him enough for Penny to catch up.

By the time my fool's light faded, he was long gone into the outer darkness. Penny tracked him a few hundred yards, but even Penny's skill has its limits. A search of the place brought us nothing more than some trampled mud and tufts of wet grass to show for our efforts.

You will understand that the last touch that crowns all my disgust with myself is the one I will hear first once I explain this to Kate. If I had mentioned a word of this to her, she would have insisted on sitting in the rain with us. (My chief discomfort rises from the fact that it was my reluctance to subject myself to Penny's sighs and grumbles about the presence of a lady that prevented me from including her.) Given the strength she lends my ability to focus, my holdfast would have held fast. I would still be wet and cold and covered in bramble scratches, but I would have a prisoner to question. Interrogation would have been no inconvenience, even given this most unreasonable hour.

Enough. I'll hear all about my misjudgments tomorrow—no, I mean later this morning.

You now know all I know—at least for the moment. This letter will be on its way to you by the time I wake up. I hope it provides you some slight amusement. Where friends are concerned, I spare no expense.

Oh, hell. I'm going to bed.

Yours,
Thomas

7 May 1828
Wardhill Cottage, Darlington

Dearest Kate,

It is a good thing for Georgy that I am currently in the northern wilds, for if I were anywhere nearby I would most certainly box her ears. Anonymous poetry, indeed! It will all come out eventually, Kate, you know it will, for Georgy has never had the least discretion, and it would suit her down to the ground to be toasted by the Ton as a poetess. No other possibility would ever occur to her. It would not surprise me in the least to learn that her "friend" behaved exactly as she wished in publishing her poems, for it would be just like Georgy to think that she would escape censure so long as she had someone else to blame for bringing her poems out in public.

And even if Georgy's mysterious correspondent really did publish her poetic attempts out of revenge, as Georgy claims (and one must ask, revenge for what? It is too much to hope that it was in revenge for sending him such drivel in the first place), his revenge will hardly be complete until the Ton knows the identity of the poetess.

Aunt Elizabeth is of the same mind as I—you may well imagine her reaction when I told her that Georgy's anonymous poetry was the talk of the Ton. Of course I had to tell her; she saw that sampler of Georgy's as often as we did, so even if Georgy's identity has not been discovered by the time she returns to town, she would recognize the work at once, and I could not leave her unwarned.

I believe she intends to write Georgy a stern letter, to be followed, undoubtedly, by a lecture when they at last meet face-to-face. And do not be surprised if Aunt Charlotte arrives unannounced. I shall do my best to talk Aunt Elizabeth out of writing to her (for your sake, Kate, not for Georgy's!), but with all of Aunt Charlotte's correspondents in London, it is inevitable that she, too, will discover Georgy's transgression. And when she does, she will not give a fig that Georgy is a married woman and a duchess, and has been no charge of hers these nine years. Aunt Charlotte will descend in righteous wrath. It is a mercy she is not there already, which I devoutly trust is due to the unfashionable nature of the watering hole where she currently resides.

James finds the matter quietly amusing, though he is inclined to take more seriously the misdeeds of Georgy's correspondent. He said something about horsewhipping the fellow when he finds him. I told him that would only encourage Georgy, but I do not think he took my meaning. Fortunately, we shall probably be stuck here for a considerable time yet. A bout of fisticuffs would only add to whatever scandal is going to result from all this.

James has found us the prettiest little cottage just outside Darlington, with whitewashed walls and a thatched roof. With four people, the servants, and a sheepdog, the accommodations are a trifle cramped. There is, however, a large room at the back that is perfect for magical experimentation—convenient to run off and fetch any ingredients one may have forgotten, but private and thick-walled enough to keep any mishaps from discomfiting anyone in the rest of the house.

The place is called Wardhill Cottage. This naturally made me wonder whether it had once been owned by a magician or wizard, but Mr. Wrexton found no magical residue when he set our wards. James says the name is very old, having been taken from the name of the previous house, which was replaced in the 1500s, so any magical associations cannot be recent.

This is probably just as well, as I do not need any more distractions. Studying Herr Schellen's transformation spell is proving quite enough of a challenge. (And I can think of only two ways for Arthur to have learned of him: Either he is reading my letters to you, which is not possible unless Thomas has been tutoring him in the more advanced magic he would need to decode them, or else he is using that *very fine* scrying spell Thomas taught him to watch James and me. I must remember to thank Thomas for providing Arthur with such a *useful* way of practicing his spell casting.)

Mr. Wrexton was only half right in his suspicions about Herr Schellen's transformation: The spell is linked to, and

powered by, not merely one ley line, but several. Mr. Wrexton says that the leys must themselves be linked in some sort
of spell network, and in a day or two we plan to ride out toward Goosepool to see whether we can identify which spe-
cific lines are involved.

Herr Magus Schellen seems much more comfortable
now that we are further north. Mr. Wrexton and Aunt Elizabeth are very pleased by this evidence of the correctness of
their theories. They are less pleased by the prospect of having to work directly with ley line power to disenchant Herr
Schellen. So we decided that our first task would be a cir-
cuit of the town to map the lines nearby, for though Mr.
Wrexton brought several charts with him (including a copy
of the maps Mr. Morris made in 1653), he felt that under the
circumstances it would be wisest to confirm their accuracy
before proceeding.

So Mr. Wrexton, Aunt Elizabeth, the sheepdog, and I
have spent the past several days riding about Darlington. Or
rather, Mr. Wrexton rode; Aunt Elizabeth and I were in a
hired carriage, as it is far easier to mark maps in a carriage
than on horseback. The sheepdog ran along beside. All
three of us performed the sensitizing spells. Aunt Elizabeth
had a fresh map on which to mark whatever we found, and
I had copies of the official survey to use for verification.

We began with the area around the railway station.
There were some faint traces that ought not to have been
present, but Mr. Wrexton said that they were just "shad-
ows," and that this is a well-known phenomenon occurring

chiefly in the spring and autumn, when—and so on. One can never stop being a teacher, I suppose.

From there, we worked our way through the town. I must say, Kate, that if this is the sort of thing Herr Magus Schellen does for a living, I do not envy him in the least. Granted, he is not an expert in ley lines, but mapping ley lines cannot be so very different from mapping railroads, and I assure you that mapping ley lines is the most tedious task imaginable. It was not until yesterday that we finally discovered something interesting, and even then it was only because of a mix-up between James's investigations and our own.

While we were searching out ley lines, James spent his days haunting the offices of various business concerns in town, mostly connected with the railway. He does not intend any implied criticism of Mr. Wrexton's magical abilities by this, he was careful to explain, but since he can be of no assistance magically, he thought he ought to busy himself with something he *is* good at.

Yesterday evening, Mr. Wrexton, Aunt Elizabeth, and I had planned to look over our maps. There are rather more of them than you might expect, as Mr. Wrexton had brought several varieties. An ordinary map of all the ley lines in a particular vicinity usually bears a strong resemblance to a diagram of the straw in a haymow. Often, only the strongest ley lines are drawn in, to avoid confusion (though the official surveys are quite complete—and as a result, nearly impossible to read). The top of the table was covered three deep in maps, and Aunt Elizabeth kept scolding Mr. Wrexton for shifting them and smearing the marks we had made.

Mr. Wrexton was reviewing the maps of the area east of Darlington. I believe he has been growing as impatient as I with the pace of our mapping (at the rate we have been progressing, it will be *weeks* before we reach Goosepool). Suddenly, he frowned. "What's this?" he said, gesturing at one of the maps.

Aunt Elizabeth glanced over. "It must be one of Mr. Morris's hopeful sketches," she said. "The lines don't look like any of the official maps."

"I told Simmons to label all of the Morris copies," Mr. Wrexton said crossly. "I do hope I won't need to have words with him when we return to London."

"There will be a good many words when we reach London," Aunt Elizabeth muttered, which I took as a reference to Georgy's indiscretion (for she did not seem to be speaking of the maps, and she has been muttering about it from time to time all day). "Is the label on the back?"

Mr. Wrexton turned the map over. "No, there is nothing. Simmons is usually much more reliable."

Just then, James came in. "Cecy, have you seen—oh, you have it."

"This is yours?" Mr. Wrexton asked, lifting the map slightly.

James joined him at the table. "Yes. I picked it up at the railway office yesterday. It's a chart of the two routes proposed for the railway—the original and the one Stephenson finally built. And it wasn't easy to pry loose, let me tell you. How did it get in here?"

"The maid must have gathered it up and put it with the rest of the maps," I said. "I'll speak to her in the morning."

"Don't speak too strongly, dear," said Aunt Elizabeth, of all people. "This is very interesting. Look, Michael." Her finger traced one of the lines. "That route is the same as the ley lines on Mr. Morris's map. And this one"—her finger ran along the other line—"I believe only crosses them in one or two places."

"What?" said James and I together. We both bent forward over the map, and our heads bumped together sharply.

Once we sorted ourselves out, we sat down to study the maps with more care. Aunt Elizabeth was, of course, entirely correct. A large section of the original route planned for the Stockton and Darlington Railway ran right on top of two of the major ley lines marked on Mr. Morris's chart. The actual railway route was different; parts of it had been built some way south of the original plan. As a result, the tracks merely crossed the two lines in places, instead of following them.

"Who changed the route?" Mr. Wrexton demanded. "And why?"

"Stephenson changed it," James replied absently. He was still studying the various maps with a frown. "Wrexton, how could the official surveyors miss ley lines as strong as those?" He indicated the thick slashes on the Morris maps.

"I don't believe they did," Mr. Wrexton said. "There are leys in the right places on the official maps; they just aren't as strong as Morris indicated."

"Wishful thinking on his part," Aunt Elizabeth sniffed.

"Perhaps," I said. "Or perhaps the strength of the lines has changed since Mr. Morris made his maps."

Mr. Wrexton shook his head. "Ley lines have been known to change in strength, it is true," he said. "But not so significantly, nor so fast. I think Elizabeth is correct; Mr. Morris was puffing up his theories, trying to make the leys in his network seem more important than they were."

"If so, he was remarkably consistent," James commented. He picked up one of the other maps Mr. Wrexton had brought with him. "All of the lines he's marked heavily are of minor strength, according to the official surveys."

"All of them?" Mr. Wrexton said with interest.

James nodded.

"Perhaps he didn't intend to mark how strong they were," I said. "If he thought something else was more important . . ."

"Just what were his theories?" James asked. Everyone looked at him. "I don't mean in general—ancient artificial ley line networks and spells holding England together. You explained that very clearly, Wrexton. But how did he think they worked? Even if you don't have his notes, you must have some notion."

Mr. Wrexton frowned. "Speculating on Morris's ideas would not be—"

"Then don't speculate on *his* theories, dear," Aunt Elizabeth said. "Tell us about yours."

"Yes, well, I admit, I *have* spent a good deal of time, since we discovered Lord White's notes, thinking about the question," Mr. Wrexton admitted. Aunt Elizabeth nodded, and James and I did our best to look expectant, and so Mr. Wrexton really had no choice but to tell us what he thought.

He began with the basic magical theory of spell diagrams (as if none of us had ever heard it before!). All spells need a diagram to contain the magical power and shape it properly, at least the first time they are cast. Everyday spells, like the one you use to keep your hair up and the scrying spell the children have been playing with, only need the diagram the first time, when the wizard is learning the spell. More complex or more powerful spells must have a diagram drawn every time they are cast.

Mr. Wrexton thinks the ley lines *are* the diagram for the old spell that binds the country together. That is part of what makes the spell so powerful and dangerous—unlike a normal spell, where magical power flows through the diagram when the wizard casts the spell, and is used up, the ley lines have enormous magical power flowing through them *all the time*. It's as if the spell were being cast over and over— not just from time to time, the way we reinforce warding spells, but continuously, without ever stopping.

"There is only one problem with this theory," Mr. Wrexton finished. "In order for the ley lines to act as a spell diagram, they have to have been linked together in certain places. And I can see no way to do that without the linkage becoming unstable very quickly."

"If those ancient wizards could actually create artificial ley lines—" I began, but Mr. Wrexton was already shaking his head.

"It's not the same sort of problem," he said. "Magical power behaves in certain ways, just as water does. We can dig canals—artificial rivers—but we can't make water flow uphill. I can believe, just barely, that those ancient wizards knew how to create new, artificial ley lines. To work as a spell diagram, though, they'd have to be linked, and without something to contain the linkage, it would become unstable very quickly."

"This is interesting speculation, to be sure," Aunt Elizabeth put in. "But it doesn't get us any further ahead with our current problems."

"Maybe it gives us a place to start," I said. I put my finger gently on the map I had been looking at, right where three of Mr. Morris's heavily marked ley lines came together.

Aunt Elizabeth looked across the table. "I don't see the significance, dear."

"Well, I am not perfectly certain," I said. "But I believe this is the location of the Dancing Weans."

"What?" Mr. Wrexton said.

"The stone circle where James and I found the—found Herr Schellen. It's just past Goosepool, a little way from the railway line, on top of a hill. And it does seem a bit of a co-

incidence that so many of Mr. Morris's leys come together
there, doesn't it?"

"And look here," James said, pointing to the next junction, southeast of Goosepool on the opposite side of the
river. "That's—"

"Haliwar Tower!" I said.

"And there is another stone circle built right into the
tower walls," James said. "I noticed it after the facing fell
away in the earthquake." He looked at Mr. Wrexton. "Would
a stone circle be enough to contain your linkages? There are
certainly enough of them scattered all over England."

"I suppose it's possible," Mr. Wrexton said cautiously.

You may imagine the flurry of comparing maps that followed. There are several other junctions in the vicinity, so
Mr. Wrexton, Aunt Elizabeth, and I are going to visit one of
them tomorrow, to see what, if anything, is there. We decided not to begin with either of the places James and I had
already been, as that might arouse suspicion. In a few days,
if all goes well, we shall return to Goosepool, and eventually
to Haliwar Tower.

Meanwhile, James continues his investigations into the fi-
nances of the Stockton and Darlington Railway (which, I
must confess, I find nearly as tedious as all of the ley line mapping that the Wrextons and I have been doing this past week.
I will be vastly relieved to be doing something different, even
if it is only a sedate carriage ride through country scenery).

Your bored but busy,
Cecy

9 MAY 1828
WARDHILL COTTAGE

(in cipher)

My dear Thomas,

I had forgot that there was yet another of those ancient stones near Skeynes. I say "yet another" because in course of their magical inquiries, Cecelia and the Wrextons have unearthed a third stone circle of interest near Darlington. (The first two, your lamentable memory may remind you, were the one built into Haliwar Tower and the one near which we discovered the sheepdog.) The three of them rode out yesterday to investigate the spot where, according to Wrexton's old maps, several ley lines of some importance came together. They returned with the news that a stone circle sits squarely atop the meeting place, but that they had been unable to examine it closely as the owner of the land has fenced off the entire area due to a strong dislike of fox hunts.

Wrexton is now convinced that there is some connection between the old standing stones and the ley lines that Wellington is so concerned about. I believe he means to write you in extensive technical detail, as a preface to requesting your assistance. He seems to think that any tampering with the leys is restricted to the north country, but since he has no basis for comparison, he cannot be certain. When I mentioned your adventures with that prowler at the Tingle Stone this morning, he conceived the notion of persuading you to provide the basis—that is, he means to ask if you will ride out to the nearest circle in your vicinity and make some observations. Let me add my pleas to his. Anything that can speed the end of this tedious business would be welcome.

For tedious it is, in the extreme. I have spent the last week poring over the financial records of the Stockton and Darlington line. I now know more about the shipping of coal from the northern fields than you would believe possible, and I am positively looking forward to my next meeting with that inquisitive bore Lord Cheffington. For once, I shall not need to hold back when he starts his interminable questioning.

Two promising lines of inquiry have emerged from this flood of involuntary education. First, I have finally got hold of a list of the stockholders in the Stockton and Darlington Railway. In addition to "Stephenson and his lot," there are a number of persons associated with the Religious Society of Friends, or Quakers. Several of the locals have made recent trips to London; I have arranged a meeting with one of them this coming Monday, in hopes of discovering why they have developed such an urge for travel.

Second, there are plans afoot to provide the Stockton and Darlington with some direct competition. A man named Tennant has proposed building a second railway line from the coal fields to Stockton, along a route some fifteen to twenty miles north of the current system. He has been at work on this proposal for several years; indeed, the incorporation act comes before Parliament soon. The recent spate of accidents on the Stockton and Darlington may or may not work to his advantage. On the one hand, he can argue that he will do a better job than the current railway line, but on the other, the accidents give reactionaries like Sheridan and Fitzhenry the chance to point out that steam railways are unsafe.

Tennant's proposal is also in competition with the corporation the Webbs have proposed. The more I find out about their scheme, the more absurd it seems. They intend to build a southern line, but both the docks at Stockton and the western coal fields are on the north bank of the Tees, so such a route would require building two expensive and unnecessary bridges. Nevertheless, they have scraped together funds and completed all the preliminaries in near-record time. Their bill of incorporation, too, is to be presented to Parliament this session.

I am in hopes that my meeting with Mr. Pease on Monday will provide some insight, if not some answers, in regard to both Tennant and the southern line. Mr. Pease has a reputation as a knowing one, and is deeply involved in the affairs of the Stockton and Darlington. He'll have as much information about his competition as anyone, and perhaps more.

In the meantime, I must acknowledge that the years have improved young Daventer's manners. I am in receipt of a note from him promising to persuade Mr. Skelly (the obstreperous Irish ley line expert) to take an interest in our problem, and no impertinent questions, either. He goes so far as to promise Mr. Skelly's arrival within the month. This of course means that we shall be stuck fast in the north until then, but I have long since given over hoping for a speedy resolution to this affair, and am currently trying simply for a satisfactory one.

Yours,
James

5 MAY 1828
SKEYNES

(Enchanted by T. Schofield, his mark)

Dear Cecy,

How tiresome it is sometimes, losing one's temper. I am still out of sorts with Georgy for the remark about my harder stamp, but I am more out of sorts with my own foolishness. I have come to try my hand at nursery life again, to see if the squabbles of the younger set can teach me anything about my own tantrum.

6 MAY

Please excuse the blotted page. Yesterday I put the pen down with too much haste when I went to answer the latest alarum.

Edward has inherited his father's youthful fondness for heights. On this occasion, Edward attained the cornice over the dining room door. I think he must have climbed up the curtain of the nearest window and edged his way along the molding. When the servants were laying the table for dinner, he struck a heroic pose on his perch and declaimed one of the improving verses I set him to learn. This poetic outburst was unexpected, to say the least. Only one wine glass was broken. It's a miracle the damage wasn't greater.

Thomas gave Edward a fine scolding, partly for startling the servants but mostly for reciting verse. Thomas didn't *say* he found it alarming that there may be a family turn for poetry, but given recent events, he doesn't need to.

I have promised Thomas upon my honor that Edward will be given no more improving verses to learn. If there is a bent toward poesy, the poor child does not have it from me.

Except for another squabble about toy soldiers (Eleanor has commandeered all Edward's favorites to stand guard over the twins' famous Map of Skeynes), it has been peaceful in the nursery of late. I like it here at the top of the house. It's comfortable to sit here by the fire, an impartial observer as the nurses direct bedtime preparations. I feel a bit like one of those domestic goddesses the Romans were so good at inventing, a very minor goddess. Perhaps they had a goddess of nightcaps, or hearth rugs, or candlesticks. I feel a little like that.

Oh, dear. Inspired by recent events, Diana has been moved to compose her first couplet. She proclaimed it proudly just now over her cup of warm milk: *Drina tells God / Arthur smells odd.* Diana appears to view this as an adequate substitute for a bedtime prayer. Fortunately, I can leave it to Nurse to disabuse her of this notion.

I should seal this letter and give it to Thomas to enchant for me. Nothing else worthy of putting in a letter, even a letter as inconsequential as this one, has happened. (Arthur gave Edward a bump on the forehead with a battledore when they were playing shuttlecock this morning, but there was nothing premeditated about it.) Nothing seems likely to happen, either. At last we are enduring a break in our run of fine weather, the sort of day that we ought to have had back in March. It is raining in a sullen way, not hard but not stopping, either, which matches my mood perfectly. What a good thing this ugly streak of weather held off until now. Had it arrived during the races at Cheltenham, it would have ruined the gaiety. The king himself was in evidence. His horse did not distinguish itself, but His Majesty does not seem to have permitted that to interfere with his usual amusements.

Yes, it's come to this. I have been reading the newspapers, and not just for titbits concerning the mysterious poetess. I have been reading them because there's nothing else to do here. Nothing that I can accomplish with the moments snatched from the demands of "Only look, Mama!" that is.

If nothing else, such titbits of gossip are useful when I am taking tea with the Cramptons. They were in Cheltenham, ostensibly for the races, but in fact to get a look at the king. Their reward was also their punishment, for in addition to His Majesty, they also saw his brother and heir, William, Duke of Clarence. The Duchess of Kent was expected to be there, as well, the better for her daughter Alexandrina to become better acquainted with her royal uncles. Unfortunately the duchess could not attend, for her daughter caught a streaming cold a few days before the event.

The Cramptons were voluble in their praise of the consequence and dignity of the king and his brother. I think that the presence of a young girl with sniffles would have lowered the tone of the occasion considerably, but the Cramptons seem disappointed to have missed a sight of her all the same.

꩜ 7 MAY

I take back every word. To think he was laying his plans even as I wrote that last page by the light of the nursery candles. I could scream.

This morning, for the first time in weeks, I was not awakened at dawn by Thomas and the necessity to ride the bounds before we indulge in so much as a cup of tea. Indeed, this morning I woke of my own volition to find the sun well up and the household abustle.

Puzzled and not a little alarmed by this change in routine, I woke Thomas. This took some doing, I can tell you, and when I finally succeeded in bringing him to a sense of where he was and who I am, he buried his face in the pillow with such a groan that I contemplated sending for a physician.

Thomas emerged before I could take serious fright. "Forgive me, Kate," he said, words I have never yet learned to hear with any degree of equanimity. Only think of the things Thomas wouldn't dream of asking my forgiveness for.

I am asked to forgive him for being a half-wit, it turns out. To spare himself the inconvenience of my company last night, Thomas went out alone to watch for an intruder the gamekeeper alerted him to. (To do him credit, it has not even crossed Thomas's mind to use the foul weather as an excuse for leaving me behind.) As he was alone, Thomas was quite unable to stop the intruder, who made a neat escape while Thomas was casting some sort of spell on the man's garters. I may have that detail wrong. I freely confess I had given up listening closely by the time Thomas's narrative had proceeded so far. Fury distracts me.

I held my tongue, over all but the absolute essentials, through the entire ride of the boundary. (Thomas assured me that his spell would lose little efficacy through his tardiness, though like most magic, it seems to work better the more discomfort the maker of magic endures.) By the time we were back in the stable yard, I was able to view the situation with a degree of detachment. Not a great deal. Enough to keep from giving Thomas a piece of my mind in front of the servants. But only just.

Were Thomas not possessed by a devil of self-indulgence, we might have captured the intruder and be possessed of fresh knowledge at this moment! I could tear my hair.

To ease my mind, I have taken up my customary post at the nursery worktable. This is viewed with tolerance by Edward, Diana, and Drina. Arthur, I fear, finds my presence a dampening effect on some scheme of his. (Need I say this only makes me the more determined to stay right where I am?)

Yours,
Kate

〜 9 MAY 1828
SKEYNES

(Enchanted by T. Schofield)

Dear Cecy,

I have your letter of 7 May in hand and will make up for the undisciplined nature of my last letter with the brevity of this one.

Thank you for explaining matters to Aunt Elizabeth. I value your opinion of Georgy's exploit. Even Thomas does not appreciate the true enormity of her behavior. He will when Aunt Charlotte stirs herself to come lecture Georgy in person.

Thomas is beside himself with curiosity. If it were not for his recent exploit, I'm certain he would be thinking of excellent reasons to visit London, the better to conduct some research into the historical Mr. Morris's doings himself.

I could almost envy your sedate carriage rides. If only they weren't to view the torrents of magic that run through ley lines. Do be careful. Aunt Elizabeth isn't always over-cautious, you know.

Yours,
Kate

(Message received in inkwell, 10 May 1828)

GO AND FETCH AUNT KATE RIGHT NOW.

K.: Keep T. away from the stone circles. They are a trap for wizards. Letter follows with details. *C.*

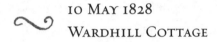

10 MAY 1828
WARDHILL COTTAGE

Dearest Kate,

I trust you received my message in a timely manner. I held the scrying spell long enough to watch Arthur write it out and run off in a tearing hurry, and he is usually quite reliable when it comes to really important things, but I shall not be quite easy in my mind until I hear from you. We are all well, thanks to James's quick action, though it was a near thing.

The stone circles are, as I said, a trap for wizards and magicians—that is how poor Herr Schellen came to be a sheepdog. And when James told me at breakfast that he and Mr. Wrexton had asked Thomas to investigate any circles near Skeynes, and that the ley spells (including the trap) might well extend to any similar junctions linked to this one,

I simply had to warn you as soon as I could. Of course we cannot be *certain* yet that the spell net extends so far as Gloucestershire, but I thought it best to be safe. Now, when you receive James's letter, you will know enough to keep Thomas away long enough for this explanation to arrive.

Forgive me; I am still a little overset by everything that has happened. I am sure it will make far more sense if I tell it in order.

Our investigation of Mr. Morris's ley map did not begin well. We had chosen a spot some miles north of Darlington and the railway line, as we did not wish to attract the attention of whoever seems to have been tampering with the leys. The Wrextons and I rode out on Thursday, but we were unable to examine the junction as closely as we had wished. The landowner had fenced the entire area most thoroughly, and we could not come any nearer than the roadway. However, that was near enough to see that, just as at Haliwar Tower and Goosepool, there was a tumble of ancient stones on the spot where, according to the map, the ley lines converged.

And I will confess, in your ear, Kate, that I am rapidly becoming heartily sick of maps. We spent the early part of yesterday shuffling various large and awkward sheets of paper from one side of the worktable to the other in pursuit of stone circles and possible ley line linkages. Aunt Elizabeth had to forcibly dissuade Mr. Wrexton from sending an express letter to London at once for more maps—maps of ley lines in other parts of the country, maps of ancient building sites and known magical locations, and even maps of ley lines in other countries!

He was persuaded at last when James mentioned that he, James, has sent for an expert on ley lines, a Mr. Skelly, who should arrive within a few weeks at most. (You remember that nice boy Theodore Daventer, whom we met on our wedding journey? He had a hand in arranging the matter.)

Aunt Elizabeth was initially inclined to take umbrage at James's action, which she saw as a slur on her husband's abilities, but when she saw that Mr. Wrexton was pleased by James's foresight and quite looking forward to having a knowledgeable person with whom to exchange speculations, she accepted the matter with tolerable equanimity.

This left us with the question of where to look while we await Mr. Skelly's arrival. We selected the Dancing Weans at Goosepool, that being closer and less likely to be under observation than Haliwar Tower. As the hour was still early and the day fine, we determined to set out at once—the four of us and the sheepdog. (James chose to accompany us, on the grounds of being unable to further his own investigations until some meeting he has arranged for on Monday.) I was not altogether certain about the advisability of bringing the sheepdog, as he had prevented me from entering the circle before; however, I did not think he would be able to stop all of us at once.

When we arrived at the farm outside Goosepool, we had to leave the carriage and climb a stile into the field, then walk to the little hill where the stone circle was located.

Fortunately, the farmer and his sheep had moved on, though they had left many traces behind, as sheep do.

We cast the ley line detection spells and set off. As we picked our way across the close-cropped grass, the sheep-dog became more and more agitated, running around us and plainly trying to herd us away from our course as if we were so many sheep.

Finally, Mr. Wrexton paused and looked sternly at it. "Herr Schellen," he said, "I can see that you are disturbed and I can understand your reluctance to revisit a place that must of necessity bring back unpleasant memories. However, if we are to remove the enchantment that affects you, we must examine these unusual ley configurations."

The sheepdog paused (standing between us and the stone circle) and whined.

Suddenly, I remembered something. "Mr. Wrexton! Didn't you and Aunt Elizabeth say that the transformation spell is tied to more than one ley line? And three of them come together at that stone circle. Is there some test we could do to see if these are the leys that are affecting Herr Schellen? Because if they are—"

"Then more may be ailing our friend here than bad memories," James finished. "What about it, Wrexton?"

Mr. Wrexton looked thoughtful for a moment. "Yes, I believe that would be possible. Elizabeth, did you bring any comfrey?"

Aunt Elizabeth dug in her reticule. "Yes, I have it. You're thinking of the Foxcroft inversion?"

Mr. Wrexton nodded. "It will be simpler if we test each ley line individually," he murmured half to himself. Aunt Elizabeth handed him the comfrey. He frowned at it and said, "Yes, if we make a circle outside the stones . . . Cecy, wipe this on your palms. Now, all we need is—" He looked around and found the sheepdog, watching us alertly. At least, its bearing was alert; it is rather difficult to tell more than that with sheepdogs. "Herr Schellen, if you please?"

The sheepdog cocked its head, then rose and walked over. Mr. Wrexton held out the comfrey. The dog sniffed it. Slowly, it nodded. Mr. Wrexton rubbed the comfrey over the dog's paws and on the back of its head, muttering in Latin the whole time.

We began tramping in a wide circle around the hill. We had gone no more than two yards when we sensed the first of the three ley lines. It was, as the official maps indicated, a small one. Mr. Wrexton had the three of us—Aunt Elizabeth, me, and himself—link hands, while the sheepdog sat inside our small ring. Mr. Wrexton and Aunt Elizabeth chanted. My studies have been worth this much; I was able to understand a good deal of what they were saying, and it was plain that the invocation they were using required the participation of three persons. Nonetheless, I felt very nearly useless.

I did not have long to mull over these sad thoughts, for Mr. Wrexton and Aunt Elizabeth finished abruptly. The sheepdog barked once, deep and short, and began to glow.

"I take that as a positive indication," James said.

"Yes," Mr. Wrexton said with satisfaction. "You were quite right. That's definitely one of the lines that's supporting the transformation spell." He waved a hand and the glow ceased. "Two to go."

The sheepdog had the same reaction to the second ley line. When we reached the third, however, Mr. Wrexton frowned. "This cannot be right," he muttered, and pulled out the official ley map. "It's in the right place," he said after a moment, "but it's much stronger than it should be."

Aunt Elizabeth looked over his shoulder. "The flow indicators are all wrong," she said.

The sheepdog barked once, as if it agreed, then growled.

"What does Mr. Morris's map show?" I asked.

Mr. Wrexton put the official map away and took out the older version. "Hmm. You may have hit on something, Cecelia. He's marked this one twice as heavily as the other two—though that's still not as strong as it should be."

"But if he was mapping ley lines according to their importance, the thickness of the line wouldn't have anything to do with how strong it really is," I pointed out.

"Very true. That doesn't explain why the official maps are off," Mr. Wrexton said.

"It is puzzling, to be sure, but the strength of the ley line shouldn't affect the Foxcroft inversion," Aunt Elizabeth said. "Let us finish one set of tests before we commence another."

As we formed our little circle around the growling sheepdog, I heard a distant whistle and a rumbling noise.

The rumbling grew steadily louder as Aunt Elizabeth and Mr. Wrexton chanted (to no one's particular surprise, the sheepdog glowed just as brightly as it had for the first two). "What *is* that noise?" Mr. Wrexton said.

"The steam train," James said. "It should be here in another minute or two."

"Perhaps we should move a little," I said. "The last time the train came by when I was sensing ley spells, it shifted the ley line, and I don't think I want to be standing right on top of one if it happens again."

"An excellent notion," Mr. Wrexton said, and we all moved away from the ley line. The steam engine pounded past, trailing a dozen coal wagons and a plume of damp smoke like Mrs. Gordon's prized ostrich feathers. And as it reached the ley line, we all felt the ley catch and begin to stretch.

"My word!" Mr. Wrexton said, and started forward. Just then, the engine surged forward and the ley line snapped back into place, vibrating like a bowstring that has just been released, or like one of the wires in Georgy's pianoforte when it has just been struck. Mr. Wrexton, Aunt Elizabeth, and I all jumped, and Mr. Wrexton lost his footing and sat down unexpectedly in the damp grass.

"My word," he said again. "Cecy, I had no idea." He scrambled to his feet and in three strides was back at the ley line, muttering softly. After a moment, he looked back, his expression one of keen interest. "I cannot be certain without the proper measuring tools," he said, "but I *believe* this ley is very slightly stronger now than it was a moment ago. We must come back later and measure it properly."

"The train makes ley lines stronger?" James said.

"I would not go so far as that," Mr. Wrexton said. "It has certainly affected *this* ley line, and the unusual interaction seems the likeliest explanation for the difference between what we sense and what the official maps show. We must find some other leys that cross the railway line and see whether they show the same sort of influence."

"Not today," Aunt Elizabeth said firmly. "We came to examine this junction"—she waved at the stone circle—"and we had better do so."

The sheepdog growled loudly. Mr. Wrexton looked from it to Aunt Elizabeth. "That is an excellent notion, my dear," he said after a moment. "However, given the reaction of our friend and the undeniable fact that all three of the ley lines involved are tied to the transformation spell that affects him, I think a few additional precautions are in order."

The precaution Mr. Wrexton had in mind, it turned out, was chiefly that he should enter the stone circle alone, while Aunt Elizabeth and I remained outside. James heartily endorsed this proposal, of course, but he was sensible enough to point out that it provided no particular safeguard for Mr. Wrexton.

So we spent the next half hour casting every ward and protective spell we could think of on Mr. Wrexton, even the ones that are seldom used because they last so short a time. "That will do," he said at last. "Any more, and I'll have so many enchantments interfering with my magic sense that I won't be able to feel anything more than James here."

Aunt Elizabeth frowned slightly but nodded. We all walked nearly to the edge of the circle. The sheepdog was still growling softly, so James took hold of it. Then Mr. Wrexton went on into the circle, and a great many things happened very rapidly.

There was, I thought, a flash of light as he crossed the ring of stones. Aunt Elizabeth agrees with me, but James says he did not see anything, so it may well have been some unexpected effect of the ley line detecting spells that let us see what James could not. At the same time, there was a surge of magical energy inside the stone circle. The sheepdog howled and leapt toward the circle, dragging James with it. And Mr. Wrexton gave an exclamation and began to twist horribly.

Aunt Elizabeth cried out and tried to reach her husband. I grabbed her arm and pulled her back. James let go of the sheepdog and dove forward, knocking Mr. Wrexton out of the circle and himself further in.

Mr. Wrexton fell backward and rolled away from the circle. I could sense the spell that he had triggered stretching after him, but the wards we had set left very little for it to cling to. It snapped back into the stone circle and subsided.

Mr. Wrexton shook himself, then tensed and looked up. "Tarleton! Get out of there immediately!"

"If you insist." James said from the middle of the stone

circle. He stood up and brushed himself off, then walked over to join us. "What was all that about?"

"That circle is a trap," Aunt Elizabeth said with considerable emphasis.

"If it weren't for all those protective spells, and your quick thinking, Tarleton, I'd have joined the canine club," Mr. Wrexton said, nodding at the sheepdog. "What I don't understand is why you haven't. You're not immune to magic, after all."

"No, but I've no ability of my own," James said. "Magic calls to magic; that was one of the first lessons in the theory classes. Something has to trigger that spell, and it can't be just crossing into the circle, or there surely would have been an unusual number of unexplained sheepdogs in the area by now, along with a selection of missing shepherds, sheep, and who knows what else."

"It's a trap for magicians!" I said.

"Very likely," Mr. Wrexton said. "We should be able to confirm that much with a few tests. From out here," he added when Aunt Elizabeth gave him a Look.

And we did. As a result, it was quite late when we arrived back at Wardhill Cottage, but we had learned considerably more than we had expected. Not only do three ley lines meet at the stone circle, they join there, just as Mr. Morris's map describes and Mr. Wrexton's theory says they should. That stone circle, at least, acts to contain and stabilize the junction, and it seems very likely that the same is true elsewhere.

Furthermore, someone has tapped into the power at the junction to create a trap that turns any trained wizard or magician—and *only* a trained wizard or magician—into a dog when they cross into the junction point (that is, the stone circle). Because three ley lines are concerned, Mr. Wrexton thinks it likely that Herr Schellen can only be disenchanted at the place where they meet—which is, of course, not possible, as any magician who crosses into the stone circle will instantly become a dog, just as Herr Schellen did.

And not just magicians and wizards who enter the Dancing Weans. According to Mr. Wrexton, the transformation spell does not have the proper confines and boundary limitations, and as a result he thinks it highly probable that it has leaked out into the entire ley line network. This means that any magician in England who enters a stone circle is very likely to turn into a dog.

As soon as we realized this, and remembered the request James made of Thomas, we realized we had to warn you. It took us some time to determine how, and by then it was far too late in the evening to try. We could, however, lay out the India ink and the little silver tray we needed for a scrying spell, and early this morning, Mr. Wrexton, Aunt Elizabeth, and I cast one. I had hoped that the children would decide to look in on us early, as well, but they did not, so we took turns watching the ink until Arthur and Eleanor finally cast their own spell to see what we were doing. With two wizards and a magician working together, it was not much trouble holding the spell so long, even over such a distance, especially since two of us (Aunt Elizabeth and I) are blood relatives of Arthur and Eleanor.

As soon as I was certain Arthur was watching, I pointed at the note, which we had written out in very large black letters. I waited long enough to see his eyes widen; he nodded vigorously and there was much rushing about the nursery for paper and quills. And so I trust you know Thomas's danger now, and all is well.

There remains the puzzle of Haliwar Tower. If the ley line under Haliwar is part of the network (which seems unquestionable, since it runs straight from the Dancing Weans to Haliwar), and if there is a stone circle actually built into the walls of the tower, then I, at least, ought to have turned into a dog the moment I set foot in the place. We are not yet certain why this did not happen; however, I have my suspicions. You may recall that I wrote you that Haliwar seemed to have a dampening effect on magic, most especially on ley lines (at least, while I was inside, I could not sense them, though I certainly ought to have been able to do so).

I think, therefore, that there is some protective spell on the tower itself. If it is specifically a protection against the transformation spell, then the Webbs are not only wizards after all, but responsible for Herr Schellen's transformation and goodness knows what else. Mr. Wrexton says it is too early to reach such a conclusion. I think he is only trying to prevent me from confronting the Webbs prematurely, which I *assure* you, Kate, I will not do. Anyone who can manipulate ley lines and cast spells that affect all of England must be approached with great caution. For one thing, I do not intend to go anywhere near the Webbs until I am sure that I will not turn into a dog, or, at least, that Mr. Wrexton and Aunt Elizabeth know how to reverse any such spell immediately.

Disenchanting Herr Schellen remains an interesting problem. I left Mr. Wrexton and Aunt Elizabeth discussing the possibility of creating a spell that could be performed by someone like James, who has *no* magical ability (such a pity—he is so good with theory. I have often thought that having no magic must be rather like being tone deaf; one can learn all the theory one likes, but when it comes to actually performing, one ends up sounding like Aunt Charlotte). A person without magical training would be perfectly safe within the stone circle, despite the ley lines and transformation spell, and so could perform the disenchantment. Despite Mr. Wrexton's optimism, I cannot think it likely that someone of no magical ability whatever would be very good at casting a de-transformation spell, but it has occurred to me that an *untrained* magician might—

Please forgive the blot. The most astonishing thing has happened. I was sitting here, at the writing table, composing my letter to you, with Herr Schellen—the sheepdog—lying by the hearth on the other side of the room. With no warning, the sheepdog sat up and howled. I turned sharply (that was when I blotted the page) just in time to see his shape blur and expand from that of a dog to that of a stocky, bearded, extremely scruffy-looking man.

"*Gott im Himmel!*" the man said.

"Good heavens!" I said. "Herr Schellen?" And then I shouted for James and Mr. Wrexton, and things became very busy.

As near as we can tell, Herr Schellen has been entirely disenchanted, though he is still more than a little dazed by his return to humanity. Mr. Wrexton can find no traces of the transformation spell; not the smallest link remains. He is a bit disgruntled by this, as it means there is also no trace of whatever caused this abrupt change, and he had been quite, quite certain that the spell could only be unraveled by some complicated counterenchantments cast within the stone circle where the original enchantment took place. (I believe he is also a touch disappointed that he will not be called upon to invent the countercharm.)

And so things seem to be looking up at last. I have every hope that within a day or two, when Herr Schellen has had time to rest and to recover his wits, we shall have a full explanation of many of the things that have been puzzling us. I fear, however, that I shall have to purchase a sheepdog for the children after all. It will not do to disappoint them when their scrying has come in so very useful after all, and really, what difference will one more dog make at Tangleford?

Your hopeful,
Cecy

🌀 10 May 1828

(Enchanted by T.S.)

James and Cecy,

Send Wrexton at once. I will write to him under separate cover, but add your urging to mine, I beg you.

Kate seems unhurt, so far as I can ascertain under the circumstances, but as she has been transformed into a healthy female foxhound, I cannot say she is unscathed.

When the children received Cecy's efficient and unusual message, Kate was with me, recasting the protection spell on the bounds. Arthur rode out to warn us, leaving the others to trail after his pony on foot. As their omniscience did not extend so far as our precise location on the route, they very sensibly went for the point at which the boundary passes closest to the Tingle Stone and its circle.

While they were waiting for us to arrive, Edward, as is his wont, climbed the nearest eminence. The first we saw of the children, as we rode toward them along the outside of the stone wall, was Edward waving cheerfully to us from atop the Tingle Stone.

The children shouted to warn us. Kate and I stopped at a safe distance. As Arthur and Eleanor and Drina delivered your message verbatim to me, Kate rode into the ring. I assume she meant to help Edward descend from the Tingle Stone by taking him up behind her in the saddle.

The trap did its work with terrible swiftness. Before I

could shout a warning, Kate's horse shied. Edward fell off the Tingle Stone and landed (unhurt, the jackanapes) beside a frightened foxhound bitch—Kate. I promise you, it was the worst moment of my life.

I could only watch from a distance while Edward coaxed Kate out of the ring. She growls at everyone else, including me, but has not bitten anyone. (Although back at the house, I confess I had a moment of wild surmise when she encountered Georgy, who screamed and burst into tears once she understood the true state of affairs.)

I have Kate safe in my workroom for now, and great damage she has already inflicted upon the place. She will be most unhappy when she sees what she did to the carpet there, not that she ever liked it above half.

Yours,
Thomas

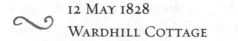 12 MAY 1828
WARDHILL COTTAGE

Dear Thomas,

Of course we will send Mr. Wrexton as soon as possible. Poor Kate! He and James are at a meeting with a Mr. Pease about the railway, but I will show them your letter as soon as they return.

In haste,
Cecy

13 MAY 1828
WARDHILL COTTAGE

(in cipher)

My dear Thomas,

Cecelia gave me your news when Wrexton and I returned from meeting with Mr. Pease of the Stockton and Darlington line. I am sorrier than I can say. I blame myself, in part, as does Wrexton. If we had not had the notion of asking you to investigate the stone circle, this very likely would never have happened.

I will spare you a description of the breast-beating that ensued. Suffice it to say that Wrexton and I spent the greater part of yesterday evening—and several bottles of port—in considering what would be best to do. We settled it that Wrexton would come down to Skeynes immediately, while Cecelia, Herr Schellen, and I remain here to await our tardy ley line expert, who might have some useful contribution to make.

Unfortunately, the ley line expert arrived a few moments ago, just as Wrexton was preparing to set out. I say "unfortunately" both because of his temperament, which is poor, and because even after being fully informed of the current situation, he insists that Wrexton, and no one else, take him out to the stone circle at Goosepool to examine this "supposed net of ley lines." As he may be our best hope of understanding (and reversing) the ley spell,

Wrexton and I thought it best to delay his departure for another day.

You see, Herr Schellen was unexpectedly disenchanted last Saturday morning, shortly after Cecelia sent her inkpot message to Skeynes. Wrexton has been unable to determine the reason for this sudden change of condition, though he is positive that no ley linkages remain. Herr Schellen is therefore in no danger of reverting to being a sheepdog as abruptly as he ceased being one. Wrexton suspects that it may have something to do with our recent visit to the stone circle and the various tests we ran, but he is very nearly as out of his depth as I where ley lines are concerned and so cannot be sure. I believe he hopes that Skelly can confirm his theory, or offer one that is more sound.

In the meantime, I have some rather suggestive information from Mr. Pease to look into. He says that several years ago, when the Stockton and Darlington was having difficulty winning Parliament's approval, Mr. Webb approached him and offered to see to it that the bill was approved, in return for a sizable share in the railway. As Webb had neither the acquaintance nor the means to influence Parliament, Pease and Stephenson wrote him off as one more of the many cranks who seemed drawn to the project, and rejected his proposal.

When the accidents and breakdowns on the railway began, Mr. Pease had Webb discreetly investigated. He could find no evidence that Webb was involved—but he and his investigators had, at that time, no reason to pay any special attention to ley lines. The first to do so was Herr Schellen. When Mr. Pease heard that he was to survey the proposed route between Manchester and Liverpool, he quietly hired him to look into the layout of the Stockton and Darlington as well, with particular emphasis on the changes to the original route. It seems unlikely to be mere coincidence that Herr Schellen was promptly turned into a sheepdog.

Mr. Pease had no further revelations regarding the Webbs, but he has referred me to a Mr. Thornton in Leeds. As for Herr Schellen, he has provided no certain insight into the question of who was responsible for his transformation. He seems well-suited to his profession, which is to say that he is far more aware of, and informative about, rock formations and land grades than people. Circumstances point more and more to the Webbs as the culprits.

The horses have been brought round, so I will close with the promise that, one way or another, I shall see the Wrextons on their way to you tomorrow. I trust that this expedition to Goosepool will provide them with the information they need to break this transformation spell once and for all.

Yours,
James

~ 13 MAY 1828
WARDHILL COTTAGE

Dearest Kate,

I am enchanting this letter so that either you or Thomas can read it, just in case. I thought you would want to know everything that has happened as soon as possible.

After Thomas's dreadful news arrived, we all spent an agitated night. Aunt Elizabeth and I occupied ourselves in assisting with packing up the Wrextons' things for their hurried departure, though I think Walker and Aunt Elizabeth's maid would have been better pleased had we retired to the parlor with a bottle of port, as the gentlemen did. But that would not have *done,* even so very far from London, and we both felt a strong need for some useful occupation. So the maids had to put up with us.

Alas, for our good intentions! The Wrextons were in the very act of stepping into the carriage to depart for Skeynes when a tall, lanky man with curly brown hair rode up and demanded—there is no other word for it—to know the way to Wardhill Cottage.

"This is Wardhill Cottage, sir," James replied.

"Which of you is this Tarleton fellow, then?" the man said.

"I'm James Tarleton," James told him. "I am sure you will enlighten us as to your own name and business in good time."

"My name is Skelly. I'm to understand you'll be having a puzzle for me," the brown-haired man said.

"Ah, Mr. Daventer's ley line expert," James said, far more politely than Mr. Skelly deserved. "No doubt you've merely forgotten to present the letter he will have given you."

Mr. Skelly glared, but he could hardly deny that he had such a thing, nor that he ought to have presented it straight-away. He fumbled through his pockets and handed the let-ter to James, who scanned it briefly and pronounced himself satisfied. James then made introductions all around. Mr. Skelly scowled throughout, though he ventured a curt nod in Mr. Wrexton's direction.

As soon as the introductions were finished, Mr. Skelly looked pointedly at the carriage and said, "And what is it you are at? Daventer gave me to understand the matter was urgent; I've come a long distance, and I'll not be put off."

"The Wrextons are just leaving for Gloucestershire," James said. "I'll join you as soon as we've made our farewells."

"Leaving?" Mr. Skelly contrived to sound as if he had been personally insulted. "The Royal College of Wizards is too high-and-mighty to be speaking with a mere Irish magi-cian, then?"

"I'm not here as a representative of the Royal College," Mr. Wrexton replied. "And I have urgent family matters to attend to. If you will excuse us—"

"Indeed not," Mr. Skelly replied. " 'Tis no more than I'd expect from a parcel of Englishmen. I've half a mind to post back to Ireland at once."

By this time, Aunt Elizabeth was bristling visibly. I had been having the greatest of difficulties in keeping my own temper, but Mr. Skelly's final words gave me the notion that he was *trying* to provoke us all, so as to have an excuse to leave. I could see from the way James's eyes narrowed that the same thing must have occurred to him, too, for before Aunt Elizabeth could say anything untoward, he took Mr. Skelly's arm.

"I'm sure you won't wish to leave at once," James said with sudden affability. "Not with the state the roads are in. Besides, it's a pretty little puzzle that will no doubt interest you. Ah, Herr Schellen!"

Herr Schellen had emerged from the house to find out why James and I were delaying. James proceeded to introduce the reluctant Mr. Skelly, finishing with the provocative remark, "Herr Schellen has only recently ceased being a sheepdog."

"A sheepdog?" Mr. Skelly said skeptically.

"Just so," Mr. Wrexton replied. "It was quite a thorough transformation spell, which I believe to have been propagated through a network of ley lines from a local junction point. We have reason to believe that the spell is still active, as there has just been a report of a similar case in the southern counties. Until we are certain of the circumstances, I strongly advise you to avoid entering any stone circles while you are in England."

The effect of this statement on Mr. Skelly was remarkable. "Ley network?" he said eagerly. "Then Daventer wasn't exaggerating? You've actually found a workable ley network?"

"Two of them," Herr Schellen put in unexpectedly. He has been very silent and gloomy since he was disenchanted. "Both artificial."

"Artificial?" Mr. Skelly said in patent disbelief.

"Not in the street," Aunt Elizabeth said firmly. "If you *must* discuss these matters now, let us do it inside, where we can talk in comfort and privacy." She turned and marched into the house. Herr Magus Schellen looked at Mr. Wrexton, who nodded. The Herr Magus followed Aunt Elizabeth, and Mr. Wrexton waved the incredulous Mr. Skelly forward.

James and I remained out of doors for a hasty consultation, after which he set the coachman to walk the horses while I departed to see a tea tray prepared. I had no desire to emulate Mr. Skelly's dreadful manners, and I was determined that he should be able to find no fault with our hospitality.

Having given the proper orders and overseen the beginning of the preparation, I went up to the parlor, where I found Mr. Skelly arguing with Mr. Wrexton and Herr Schellen over their theories regarding the ley lines. In the

face of so much testimony, he could not deny that Herr
Schellen had been turned into a sheepdog (though I think he
would have liked to do so). He scoffed openly, however, at
the notion that the spell was linked to and sustained by more
than one ley line. He attributed Mr. Wrexton's "mistake" in
this regard to interference from the railway, and he was incredulous when we informed him that a second magician—
you—had been turned into a dog in the same manner as
Herr Schellen (by stepping into a stone circle). And he was
flat-out disbelieving when we told him of the peculiar way
the ley lines moved as the railway engine ran across them.

Finally, Mr. Wrexton reached his limit. "Very well, sir,"
he said. "You have heard my observations in detail; there is
no more that I can tell you. Go to Goosepool and see for
yourself."

"That I shall," Mr. Skelly said. "And I'll be pleased to
show you where your error lies. Ley lines are tricky things;
'tis not surprising you were misled."

Aunt Elizabeth snorted. Mr. Wrexton frowned. "I am
leaving for the south," he reminded Mr. Skelly. "Lady
Schofield's condition requires urgent attention."

"Perhaps so," Mr. Skelly said, "but you'll be giving it the
wrong sort of attention if you go on as you intend. Ley
lines—"

"Are tricky things; you've said so several times," Aunt
Elizabeth said. "If you are such an expert—"

Fortunately, the tea tray arrived just at that moment. I
say "fortunately" because Aunt Elizabeth was plainly pre-

paring to give Mr. Skelly a dressing-down, and though I quite agreed that he deserved one, it seemed evident to me that it would not be of the least use.

The tea settled everyone wonderfully, though it did not settle the argument. At last Mr. Wrexton agreed to accompany Mr. Skelly to Goosepool to examine the Dancing Weans, provided they went that very day so that the Wrextons' departure need be delayed no longer than absolutely necessary.

So the baggage was unloaded and the carriage brought round once more. Aunt Elizabeth elected to remain behind, as did Herr Schellen, so we were only four—James, Mr. Wrexton, Mr. Skelly, and I.

Mr. Skelly did not improve on closer acquaintance, though he at least sank no further in my estimation than he had already. He spent the drive questioning us all, over and over, regarding the details of what we had seen, sensed, and suspected. He was quite put out when it became clear that he could neither persuade nor bully any of us into altering our tales, and at last retreated into silent sulking, which was a great relief to us all.

The train and its steam engine were not in evidence during our trip. I was not sure whether to be relieved or disappointed. On the one hand, I was quite pleased to be spared Mr. Skelly's inevitable observations; on the other, I should have liked to have seen him discover that we had all been telling the exact truth regarding the effect of the engine's passage on the ley lines.

We reached the lane near the stone circle at last, and climbed out of the carriage to cast the ley-line detecting spells. As Mr. Wrexton began his work, Mr. Skelly stopped him. "I see it's the usual ley-detecting spell you've been casting," he said. "I've a better notion than that, I think."

"What notion would that be?" Mr. Wrexton said, sounding a trifle annoyed.

"The spell I use is a bit out of the common way," Mr. Skelly said smugly. "It's my own design."

Mr. Wrexton hesitated, as if torn between his eternal thirst for magical knowledge and his desire to give the odious Mr. Skelly a thoroughgoing put-down. His thirst for knowledge won, but not, I think, without considerable struggle. "Do proceed," he said after a moment, and Mr. Skelly did.

Like Mr. Wrexton, I watched Mr. Skelly's spell casting very closely. It was not so very different from the usual ley-detecting spell; he used juniper springs instead of comfrey, and altered the order of "seeing" and "perceiving" in the incantation. Nor were the results so obviously superior to the usual spells as he had made it sound. I did think the edges of the ley lines were a little sharper and clearer than I had previously sensed, but it did not seem so great a difference as to justify the fuss.

As soon as the spell was active, Mr. Wrexton began a running commentary regarding the ley lines and the things he had noticed on our first visit, as much to keep Mr. Skelly from making any further inflammatory remarks as to inform him of our observations. The tactic served admirably, and we made our way across the intervening field without incident.

Mr. Skelly's manner changed sharply as we neared the stone circle and began to sense the ley lines. He frowned slightly when Mr. Wrexton turned and began to walk around the outside of the stone circle, but said nothing. When they reached the first of the three ley lines, he took a small notebook from his pocket, along with an odd device that looked much like a compass attached to a slim silver chain with a bone-white plumb bob at the far end.

Holding the compass part over the center of the ley line, he made several adjustments to the chain, then waited while the plumb bob swung in lazy circles. He made several notations, then went on to the second ley line and repeated the process.

When he finished with the third ley line, he shook his head. "There's naught unusual about these lines," he informed us smugly. "That one is stronger by a quarter"—he waved at the first line, the one that crossed the railway— "but that's not out of the common way. Now let's see about this circle."

"No!" Mr. Wrexton said as Mr. Skelly started forward. "You can't cross that circle. You're a wizard; that transformation spell is still active. Check for yourself if you don't believe me."

"Ah, yes, the transformation spell." Mr. Skelly muttered under his breath, and I sensed magic intensifying around him, though I did not recognize the spell he was casting.

"That should take care of the matter," he said after a moment, and before anyone could stop him, he stepped briskly into the stone circle.

You can certainly guess what happened next. Despite his precautions, the transformation spell struck with great force. An instant later, a bewildered terrier stumbled out from between the stones.

"Now, *that* is interesting," Mr. Wrexton murmured.

"What is?" James demanded.

"That spell. Come here, sir!" Mr. Wrexton said, snapping his fingers at the terrier.

Whether out of bewilderment or embarrassment, the terrier came. "James, would you do me the favor of retrieving Mr. Skelly's notebook and ley compass?" Mr. Wrexton asked without looking up. "He dropped them inside the circle, and I've no wish to make the same mistake he did."

"My pleasure," James replied.

With the compass safely in hand, Mr. Wrexton repeated Mr. Skelly's measurements, comparing each with the notation Mr. Skelly had made moments before. "I thought so," he said with satisfaction when he finished.

"Thought what?" I said.

Mr. Wrexton hesitated. "There is one thing more I'd like to do before I answer your question, and I can't do it here. Please oblige me by waiting until we reach Wardhill Cottage."

Naturally, we agreed, though I was positively afire with

curiosity during the whole drive back. When we reached the cottage, Mr. Wrexton disappeared into the workroom at the back, leaving us to explain Mr. Skelly's disappearance and the presence of the terrier to Aunt Elizabeth and Herr Schellen.

Aunt Elizabeth nodded as we finished, then looked down at the terrier. "Let that be a lesson to you, sir!" she said sternly. "In future, mend your manners."

"Hah!" came from inside the workroom, and a moment later Mr. Wrexton threw open the door. He was smiling broadly, and in one hand he held a large bowl of ink. "All's well; Lady Schofield is herself again."

"Michael!" Aunt Elizabeth said. "What do you mean?"

"See for yourself," he said, extending the bowl of ink with great care.

We all crowded around as he refreshed the scrying spell, then saw you, Kate, sitting in the library at Skeynes, surrounded by the children. As we watched, Thomas came in with a strip of sticking plaster across his knuckles, looking somewhat rumpled but insufferably pleased with himself.

"How is this possible?" Aunt Elizabeth said as the scene faded. "What did you do?"

"I didn't do anything," Mr. Wrexton said with some regret. "Except, that is, observe the behavior of the ley lines when our Irish visitor allowed himself to be transformed. There was a distinct surge in the southernmost of the three just as the spell hit him, and afterward it was measurably drained. And the spell affecting him had resonances that were identical, insofar as I could determine without more precise measuring tools, to the one that we studied on Herr Magus Schellen. That's not impossible, but you'll allow that it is vastly unlikely."

"You thought it was the *same* spell?" Aunt Elizabeth frowned. "But what—"

"And Herr Schellen was disenchanted at the same time that Kate was transformed!" I said. "So it's been the same spell on *all* of them, just jumping from wizard to wizard!"

"I thought it might be," Mr. Wrexton admitted. "But I didn't wish to raise hopes until I was certain."

We assured him of our understanding, then retired to the parlor for a suitable celebration of your disenchantment (which was more difficult for the gentlemen than you might expect, as James claimed that the occasion was worthy of French brandy, but there was none to be had so far north at short notice). It fell to Aunt Elizabeth and me to make more sensible plans while James and Mr. Wrexton considered which of the readily available vintages would make the most suitable substitute. We decided that it would be best for Mr. Wrexton and Aunt Elizabeth to travel south tomorrow, as planned, so that they can convey a personal warning to the Royal College of Wizards on their way to Skeynes. When they arrive, which should be on the heels of this letter (if indeed they are not already there), Mr. Wrexton will examine both you and the stone circle to make certain that there are no lingering spell tendrils that might make future trouble. He expects not, as there were none on Herr Magus Schellen, but he wishes to make absolutely sure.

The terrier and the Herr Magus remain with us in Darlington—the terrier, because (as has already been demonstrated with the sheepdog) it would be as much as his life is worth to take him too far from the vicinity of the circle where he was enchanted; the Herr Magus because his surveying equipment is still missing, and much as he has come to dislike the north of England (for good reason!), he will not depart until he has recovered it.

James and I remain because someone knowledgeable must have charge of the terrier (if he suddenly resumes being the obnoxious Mr. Skelly, we shall have to scour England for a missing wizard and a superfluous dog) and because we have not yet discovered who is behind all these enchantments, what is causing the breakdowns and accidents at the railway, how this is all related to Parliament, or why someone should be doing any of the mysterious things that have occurred.

Do write as soon as ever you are able. Despite Mr. Wrexton's scrying spell, and my confidence in his theories, I shall not feel truly reassured as to your well-being until I see it written in your own hand.

Your,
Cecy

13 MAY 1828
SKEYNES

(Enchanted by T.S.)

Dear James,

Excuse my handwriting. If I use my other hand, the result would be worse, I promise.

I have sent to London for help. I've written to everyone I can think of, from Old Hookey to the College. Our prowler is confined to the coal cellar, bound hand and foot and hung about with every spell and cantrip I can devise. Peace rules the infantry at last. Thus I will spare a moment of my well-earned rest to relate what happened today. Details can wait until we meet. Here are the bare bones.

I was in my study with Kate. I was trying to find a spell to turn Kate back to her right shape. Kate was destroying one of my old boots. I never cared above half for that pair, and it kept her quiet. She was gnawing away as I thumbed through spell books, when I was interrupted by a full chorus of "Uncle Thomas!" augmented by Edward's "Papa!"

I unlocked the door and emerged, Kate at my heels, to discover Arthur, Eleanor, Drina, and Edward in a state of wild excitement. I tried to make them state their business in a methodical way, but they fell upon me and urged me toward the nursery. Much ado about the map, the soldiers, someone coming—bedlam in miniature. Imagine Kate dancing about us barking, and you have the scene exactly.

I resisted them just long enough to lock the study door, but then I was borne away helpless by the pack of shouting children.

In the nursery, peace prevailed. The nurses were chatting, the babies were asleep and thereby rendered harmless, and all seemed orderly to the casual visitor. I was hauled to the big table by the window, the one Kate has employed as a writing desk of late, where the plan of the house and grounds the children have drawn in such detail was spread out with Edward's toy soldiers to hold the edges flat.

You must let Wrexton have the tutoring of your twins, James, however he protests the notion. The thought of that pair growing up with no more magical supervision than Cecy was given makes my blood run cold. With no formal training to speak of, and nothing more in the way of informal training than their mother's general advice, my casual scrying lessons, and a few visits from some scrub of a tutor, Arthur and Eleanor have contrived a simple but effective warning spell.

The toy soldiers were placed along the route of the wards Kate and I rode each day. The spell was designed to move the soldiers to point at any place where a ward was disturbed, the way a magnet moves iron filings. As we watched—all of us but Kate, who was more interested in smelling Edward's feet—the soldiers nearest the place where the Tingle Stone was marked on the map were moving to point their weapons at something crossing my boundary spell.

Impossible as it ought to have been to cross my boundary spell undetected, something—or someone—was doing just that.

I can't remember precisely what I told the children. I know I ordered them to remain in the nursery, come what may. I ordered Kate to stay with them, but she paid even less attention to my wishes than usual. No, she came bounding downstairs after me and stood in the doorway barking while I marshaled the resources in my study.

Once made aware of the intruder, I was able to locate the place he had breached my defenses. It was the magician Penny and I had watched for, no question, the man who fled my best holdfast spell. I could almost smell his style of magic. He was coming slowly but steadily across the grounds, his route a beeline for the house. All the power at his disposal was focused on countering my spells. If the children hadn't set the soldiers to guard their map, I would have had no warning until he was upon me.

I freely admit to a moment of indecision. Better to go out to meet him and engage him in the gardens? Or better to lie in wait and marshal the protective spells laid on the house itself? I always prefer the direct approach, but this time there were children to consider. I hesitated a moment too long, and he was at the door.

The Greater Cessation didn't stop him. I ran to the door of the entry hall and cast it with all my might, then watched as he opened the front door despite my spells on lock and hinges, threshold and lintel. For the size of his magic, our intruder was not a very big man. His face was red as beetroot, but not with exertion. He was not even breathing hard when he stepped into the hall.

Kate growled most hideously as he entered our house. I agreed with her sentiments. This was the man we knew as Mr. Scarlet. Whatever the source of his magic, it was my duty to stop him.

Mr. Scarlet drew on formidable power. In the process of taking one another's measure there in the entry hall, I learned his intent was not only to enter my home but to invade the very nursery itself. It took all my strength, training, skill, and cunning to counter him.

I have no use for false pride. It would be quite possible, given a sufficient quantity of magicians, to outmatch me, even on my home ground. I have no use for false modesty, either. On that day, in that place, Mr. Scarlet crossed the threshold, but he could go no farther. I met him and matched him. Locked in one another's spells, with Kate circling and snapping at Scarlet, we battled to a stalemate.

I held him there, held my spell steady, and groped for reinforcements. I heard Georgy screaming behind me, harsh as a teakettle on the boil. No help there. I held Scarlet's power locked in mine, my vision narrow with the need to concentrate, but from the corner of my eye I thought I saw grass snakes and bullfrogs coming to my aid. In addition to a plague of frogs, I gave Scarlet a plague of boils. That made him bellow, but his efforts held steady, and our deadlock continued.

Kate has, on occasion, accused me of an inability to take proper notice of the finer points of her wardrobe. She may well be right. I'm afraid that the precise moment of Kate's transformation from foxhound to her true form all but escaped my notice. All I know is, one moment she was a foxhound, crouched and snarling at Scarlet's feet. Fierce as a wolf, she sprang for his throat. Scarlet did his best to hold her off.

The next moment, she was my Kate again, in her proper shape but still at his throat, doing her best to throttle him with her bare hands. I had all I could do to keep him from striking her, but I held him fast.

Kate, bless her, did not permit her transformation to discompose her in the slightest. She kept her grip on Scarlet's throat even as she repeated the spell she uses to keep her hair up. If there was a growl in her voice, a snarl in her words when she spoke it, it only strengthened the spell she cast on Scarlet's cravat, the twist and lift she gave it.

Scarlet's chin came up as the cravat rose and tightened. The fabric twisted. Scarlet's face grew purple. His breathing grew ragged. His eyes bulged as his gaze locked with Kate's. What I read there, even as I used his distraction to overwhelm him, was terror.

All his fear was warranted. No foxhound could defend her young more valiantly than did Kate. Kate may not practice many spells, but the spells she can cast are not to be trifled with, and neither is she.

It was not until Scarlet was fully at Kate's mercy that I had leisure to notice that the children had joined us. Drina was closest, only a few yards from Scarlet. She said nothing. She didn't have to. Her cold stare expressed all possible contempt.

I roared at the children, "I told you to stay in the nursery. Go back at once!"

As they thundered back upstairs, I used great care in binding Scarlet magically, hand and foot. Kate was back in her right shape, but the front door was in flinders, the magical wards on Skeynes in tatters. All that had to wait until I secured our intruder.

Scarlet's breathing slowed to a rattling wheeze. I felt it necessary to remind Kate that if she strangled him, he couldn't answer any of our questions. I had to say it twice, the second time right in her ear, before she turned her attention from Scarlet to me. Scarlet fell at our feet, wheezing horribly.

Kate's eyes were wild, but as she regarded me, her expression softened. She came into my arms, Kate again, safe and sound.

I felt the moment Kate released the spell on Scarlet's cravat. As she slumped against me, Scarlet gasped and coughed, breathing freely again at last. He seemed to swoon. Between relief and exertion, I felt a little light-headed myself.

For now, Scarlet is locked away safely. He will stay that way. Still, my exertions have depleted my resources sufficiently that I think it is wise to wait until morning to question him. I will write again when I have his full confession.

Yours,
Thomas

~ 13 MAY 1828
SKEYNES

(Enchanted by T.S.)

Dear Cecy,

Aunt Charlotte always told us there can never be sufficient excuse for tardy correspondence, but even she could not deny that being transformed into a dog must prevent one from writing letters. If I could have written sooner, I would have, I promise you.

What little I remember of being a dog makes me wish I could have set some of my impressions down on paper. When I try to put them into words now, they fade away into incoherence. There was a sense of order, I do remember that much, something that made it important that Thomas keep me near him. My hearing was extremely acute. In addition, there was a sense of possibility—any detail could have been of vital interest, every object held fascination—a fascination that had everything to do with the way it smelled. I confess, to my own disgust and embarrassment, I miss the smells.

I think it is fortunate I was a dog for only a short period of time. Herr Schellen was a dog for months on end, in circumstances that must approach dog paradise. I do not wonder that he seemed disoriented at first, nor that he seems silent and gloomy now, poor man.

Do not mistake me. I am happy to be myself again. No scent on earth could compensate for such a transformation. Nothing could match my joy when I discovered I had my own shape back again, for when the moment arrived, I was at Mr. Scarlet's throat. It would have been vexing to be able to do no more than sink in my teeth and worry at it until I ripped his flesh.

No, I promise you, it was with delight that I remembered I had hands. As I clung to him, and as he struggled to throw me off, Mr. Scarlet pulled my hair cruelly. I fancy that was what reminded me of the spell to keep my hair up. My mind was not so clear that I was able to give the matter anything resembling rational thought.

Upon consideration it seems meet and proper that having just enough expertise to qualify as a magician for purposes of suffering canine transformation, I should have enough ability to employ one of the very few spells I know fluently.

Thank goodness Thomas was there to bring me to my senses. I let the spell go before Mr. Scarlet was damaged beyond repair. Thomas took him into custody with his usual enthusiasm. Indeed, the one serious struggle Mr. Scarlet put up after I released him provoked Thomas to such violence that I fear Arthur's interest in fisticuffs has been renewed.

Since then, I have been restored to my usual state. Despite Georgy's efforts to play at chatelaine, Belton kept the household running smoothly while I was indisposed, and the nurses had little trouble from the children, as they were feeling guilty about the role they inadvertently played at the Tingle Stone. When I was washed and properly dressed, I returned to the nursery and explained in terms that even you could not have bettered for clarity and firmness that none of this was their fault. Indeed, they have behaved admirably throughout. "The dog is gone?" Diana asked. Arthur and Eleanor confirmed this fact and hardly scoffed at her.

"You were a jolly good dog, Mama," Edward told me comfortingly.

I thanked him for his thoughtful reassurance.

"Mr. Scarlet is no wizard," Drina observed. "I have never seen him do magic."

"Perhaps he isn't a true wizard," I countered, "but he has done enough magic to be very dangerous."

Once Thomas feels his strength entirely restored, we will question Mr. Scarlet. This letter has waited so long to be written that I might as well delay it still further so a full account of the interrogation can be included.

Yet I find that even as I take comfort in the familiar pleasure of writing to you, I take comfort in bringing this to my customary close. I shall write another letter to accompany this one as soon as the inquisition is complete.

For now, I remain your,

Kate

15 MAY 1828
LEEDS

My dear Thomas,

As you perceive from the inscription, I am once again in Leeds. I left a few hours after the Wrextons departed for Skeynes; I trust they will have arrived by the time you receive this. I arrived last night, and spent the morning interviewing Mr. Thornton. You may recall, though I am skeptical of it, that he is the gentleman Mr. Pease of the Stockton and Darlington referred me to for more information regarding Mr. Webb and his improbable railway proposal.

You will be surprised to learn that the trip here has been exceedingly fruitful, though not entirely in the way I had intended. Mr. Thornton was a fount of information and ancient gossip. His family hails from Stockton, and has an interest in the shipping docks, which led inevitably to his involvement with the Stockton and Darlington Railway enterprise.

As a result, he was full of information about Mr. and Miss Webb. I shall not bore you with the endless particulars, but it is evident that they aspire to heights of wealth and society that they have been utterly unable to achieve out of their own birth or merit. They are, he claims, particularly bitter because an ancestor of theirs chose to renounce his title and throw in his lot with Oliver Cromwell instead of romantically siding with the king and getting his own head cut off, or at least sensibly holing up at home to study magic.

Yes, I thought your ears would perk up at that last. Quondam Baronet Webb was not only one of Cromwell's passionate Parliamentarians, he was one of Cromwell's wizards. Furthermore, it was he who built Haliwar Tower.

According to Mr. Thornton, the current Mr. Webb had nothing good to say about his ancestor until about ten years ago, when he inherited Haliwar Tower from a great-uncle. Shortly thereafter, he made that extremely puzzling proposal to Mr. Pease, offering to use some unexplained "influence with Parliament" to assist the passage of the Stockton and Darlington bill of incorporation. It seems possible, perhaps even likely, that Webb, having learned of the ley line network and its ability to affect the government, expected to influence Parliament magically. Naturally, he did not say so straight out.

When Pease refused, Webb's reaction was not temperate; indeed, if Mr. Thornton is to be believed, there was a good deal of shouting and name-calling involved. This is, of course, why Pease had him investigated. Mr. Thornton is of the opinion that the investigation did not go far enough, though he can offer no evidence for his opinion beyond the assertion that Webb has been acting "too damned smug" since the railway's troubles began.

All of this information is, you will agree, extremely suggestive, and well worth making yet another trip to Leeds to obtain. Nevertheless, the best is yet to come.

On my way back to the King's Head, I was accosted in the street by a fellow who began by demanding to know whether I was "the cove what took off the dog up by the Williams' farm." When I acknowledged that I was, he offered to buy the animal from me for the princely sum of five pounds.

"That will not be possible," said I. "I am afraid the dog has run off."

Much disgruntled, the fellow went on his way. I went on up the street, then nipped around behind a drayman's cart and doubled back. Fortunately, he had not gone far, and I followed him for another ten or fifteen minutes before he disappeared into a business establishment. No, I am quite sure he did not see me. Though you still may doubt it, I have learned a thing or two in these past ten years from my dear Cecelia regarding "sneaking about."

Once the fellow went inside, I was at a stand. To linger would be conspicuous, and I had no idea how soon he might reappear. I chose not to risk tipping my hand, and strolled on. I was, however, able to make a note of the establishment, and the innkeeper at the King's Head identified it for me later. It is a branch office of Maxwell and Medway— the same firm that handles Ramsey Webb's business.

There can be no reason for anyone at Maxwell and Medway to have need of a sheepdog. Indeed, it seems extremely unlikely that anyone at all would pay five pounds for an ordinary sheepdog. It borders on the incredible that someone would follow me from Darlington to Leeds simply to purchase a dog. It is clear, therefore, that it is not just a dog that they want, but Herr Magus Schellen in the shape of a dog. Presumably, the intention was to prevent me from discovering who and what the dog was, or, failing that, to discover what I have learned. Maxwell and Medway have no reason I know of to be interested in either sheepdogs or surveyors, so it seems most probably that Webb was behind the attempt to get hold of the dog.

If that is true, then another visit to Haliwar Tower is clearly in order. I expect to spend the night here in Leeds, then return to Wardhill Cottage tomorrow with my news and the few letters that had not been forwarded. Once I have consulted with Cecelia and Herr Schellen about the proper magical precautions, we shall decide on the best approach. If we can clearly establish that the Webbs are behind this extremely murky business, I shall consider my job complete and hand the whole sorry mess over to Wellington's wizards.

Yours,
James

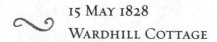

15 MAY 1828
WARDHILL COTTAGE

Dearest Kate,

What adventures you have had! I confess I do not envy you your transformation, despite your interesting description, but the capture of Mr. Scarlet sounds most dramatic. I am agog to hear what you have learned from him—for I am sure that however firm his resolve to remain silent, it is nothing compared to Thomas's resolve to force him to speak. And yours.

Things have been quite dull since the Wrextons left. There is little I can do to assist James in his investigation, as all of the magical matters seem to be tied to the ley lines in some fashion and James will not hear of my experimenting with them so long as that transformation spell is active. Herr Schellen agrees, though in his case I fear it is not concern for me that motivates him, but rather a wish to be spared the company of Mr. Skelly, who is far more personable as a terrier than he was before his transformation.

In consequence, I remain here while James is off to Leeds to talk to yet another railway gentleman. I expect him back tomorrow. In the meantime, I have been busying myself in reviewing for Herr Schellen what we think we have discovered.

Apart from Herr Schellen himself, it is a very *mixed* assortment of things, beginning with Herr Schellen's disappearance. At least we have located him (and while your mishap at the stone circle was certainly most dreadful, it *did* have the happy result of disenchanting him, so that we have been able to send notice to Herr Schellen's Prussian friends, who can now persuade their people to stop pestering Lord Wellington).

The question remains as to whether the transformation spell was meant especially for Herr Schellen, or whether he fell afoul, as you did, of a spell meant for some other wizard. On the one hand, the spell is plainly new, or wizards would have been popping in and out of canine form all over England for years and the Royal College would surely have heard of the matter before now. Also, it seems most suspicious to me that Herr Schellen's bags vanished from the farmhouse the night after he was transformed. That was not the work of the transformation spell. Someone was watching Herr Schellen and absconded with his luggage in order to give the impression that he had slipped away without paying his bill.

But if the spell was meant for Herr Schellen, it seems unutterably foolish to tie it to ley lines and stone circles all over England. Indeed, if it affects *any* wizard who enters *any* stone circle, the transformation spell cannot possibly have been intended for a particular person, for who could say that a wizard in Cornwall would not walk into a circle there, seconds after the intended victim had been enchanted (thus returning the first victim to his original form)? As a trap for one particular wizard, it is a singularly chuckleheaded arrangement. But what else could its purpose have been?

More important, who arranged the spell . . . and when? If, as Mr. Wrexton thinks, the ley lines and stone circles are part of a magical net created 170 years ago by Oliver Cromwell's wizards, was the transformation spell part of some defensive ward intended to keep the king's wizards from disrupting his plans? Could it, perhaps, have been set off by the regular interference between the railway engine and the ley lines, or was it Herr Schellen's probing that activated the ancient protections? (Herr Schellen denies it, but I do not see how he can be certain. So despite my murmurs of agreement, I intend to keep an open mind on the subject.)

Herr Schellen is a most provoking man. Now that he has had time to recover from the enchantment, I had hoped he would have some useful detail to impart regarding his activities, or at least that he might have remembered something more useful than measurements related to the construction of railways. But it is no such thing. Our conversation ran something like this:

"Herr Schellen, I trust you are fully recovered?"

"Recovered, Madam Tarleton?"

"From that dreadful enchantment."

"Oh. Yes, Madam."

"Then it would not be an imposition to ask you to speak of it? It could be so very useful."

"Useful, Madam?

"To the investigations James is making."

Herr Schellen nodded stiffly, the way people do when they have not understood, but do not wish to admit it.

"Did James not tell you that he is looking into these problems with the railway?" I asked.

"Yes, Madam Tarleton," Herr Schellen said cautiously.

"Well, if that enchantment is connected to the difficulties in any way, you must see how helpful it would be for us to know all the details."

"No, Madam."

I looked at him, and after a moment he was moved to expand on his statement.

"Turning into a hound has nothing to do with railways," he said.

"Not in the general course of things," I said. "But in this case, you were investigating the problems with the railway. If someone wanted to stop you, he might use the transformation to do so."

"Mr. Tarleton has also been investigationing of the railway, and he is not turned into a hound," Herr Schellen pointed out.

"No, but he is not a wizard," I said. I did not even attempt to explain that a sheepdog is not a hound of any kind; I was having enough trouble persuading Herr Schellen to stick to the point, without adding more complications. "If someone wishes to set a trap for James, it will need to be of some other kind."

"Ah!" Herr Schellen's face took on an annoying expression of tolerant benevolence. "You are the wife, and so you worry." Clearly, he thought this a charming female foible.

I decided that if he was willing to answer my questions, he might think what he pleased. "Yes, very much," I replied. "So if you would not mind describing your experience—"

"Naturally, Madam."

I waited, but he said nothing more until I prodded him, and then his answers were all just as unsatisfactory. What exactly had happened to him? He walked into the stone circle and turned into a hound. Had he seen anyone just before? No, Madam. Had he noticed anyone following him? No, Madam. Had anyone taken an interest in his work? The gentleman who hired him, Madam. Had anyone *other* than Mr. Pease seemed interested? No, Madam. Had anyone seemed disturbed or agitated, then? The farm wife at Goosepool was always agitated about something, Madam. Had anyone seemed disturbed or agitated about the work he was doing? No, Madam. What about the time when he was enchanted—did he remember anything interesting from that? Sheep, Madam. Sheep? Sheep are very interesting to a hound, Madam.

And so it went. To hear Herr Schellen tell it, he might just as well have stayed in Prussia. All he has discovered are boring reassurances regarding the changes that Stephenson made to the originally planned route of the Stockton and Darlington Railway line. (The new route is, he says, equal or superior to the original in terms of grade and distance and a number of technical things, which he described at great length, and which both Thomas and Arthur would no doubt have considerable interest in. I doubt, however, that you are any more interested than I, and so I shall spare you the details.)

This leaves us no further along regarding the variety of accidents and problems with the steam engines, which have plagued the railway from its opening. It seems likely that at least some of the problems are the result of the interaction between the railway's steam engines and the ley lines. Herr Schellen confirms that the engines are only capable of pulling a certain load (rather like horses, though of course the load is far larger); if the engine drags along every ley line it encounters, it is very likely working much too hard, even if the ley lines snap back into position once the train has passed.

It is also possible, however, that some of the problems are the result of deliberate interference, perhaps by a disgruntled landowner (old Lord Darlington rode all the way to London several times in order to vote against the railway's incorporation bill in the House of Lords, so one might well expect him to be very disgruntled indeed when the bill passed and the railway was built despite his efforts). I think that if this were indeed the case, James would have had some hint of it before now, but it cannot yet be ruled out entirely.

So the ley lines appear to be the most likely explanation for the railway's troubles. Indeed, everything keeps coming back to them—not only Herr Schellen's enchantment and the steam engine breakdowns, but the earthquake and fire at Haliwar Tower and that enchantment involving Parliament that Lord Wellington is so worried over.

I do wish Mr. Skelly had been more informative when he was still able to speak. He was apparently much surprised by our ley line network, but he did not give any reason for his opinion, and I should like to know what it was (though since he also did not believe that the transformation spell would have any effect on him, I confess to wondering whether his expertise would have been as helpful as we had hoped. However, Walker informs me that as a terrier he has become the bane of the rats in the stables, so at least he is of some use).

∽ 16 MAY

You may have noted that in all my maunderings of yesterday, I did not mention Georgy's poetry or the odd way in which Daniel vanished from Haliwar Tower. I confess that they had quite slipped my mind, but no longer.

When James returned from Leeds today, he brought with him several letters that had not been sent on from the inn there. Three of them were for me, all from Aunt Charlotte. The first had been sent from the watering hole where she has been staying, and you may easily guess its contents. Just as we feared, she has discovered Georgy's book of verses and guessed the authoress, and she was in even more of a taking than I had anticipated she would be. I am able to report this with equanimity only because in her agitation, she crossed and recrossed her lines, making her letter all but completely illegible.

Both of the other letters were written in Leeds, in a somewhat more temperate (and hence more readable) fashion. It is a wonder she did not meet James in the street while he was there; the final one was dated only yesterday. And the reason she is in Leeds is that she has, through her various connections, traced Daniel there. I was quite wrong to think that she would come directly to Skeynes to blame you for

Georgy's behavior. No, she is evidently well aware that she cannot hold a mere marchioness responsible for the behavior of Her Grace, the Duchess of Waltham, however much she would like to do so.

Since Georgy's behavior is quite beyond the bounds of what is acceptable in Polite Society, and since Aunt Charlotte must hold *someone* to blame, she has settled on Daniel, who, as Georgy's husband, ought to have controlled her better. (I think this is quite unjust of Aunt Charlotte. *She* never controlled Georgy's flights when she was the one responsible for rearing you both, and since it is plain enough that she would never own herself inferior to anyone less exalted than a royal duke, I cannot see why she thinks Daniel should have any better success than she did.)

I do not know how she discovered that Daniel had gone to Leeds, nor how she learned that we were there and had dined with him some weeks ago. Still, she did it. Much of her final letter was taken up with scolding me for not sending Daniel in pursuit of his errant wife, with a fine disregard for the fact that at the time, none of us knew or even suspected that Georgy had been erring.

But the worst of it is that she has very nearly tracked Daniel to Haliwar Tower—"He went off to a house party near Stockton with some jumped-up northern Cit" is the way she put it (not without some justice, though how she managed to obtain such an accurate character of Mr. Ramsey Webb, I cannot imagine)—and she proposes to follow him, find him, and confront him there! "Since none of the rest of you appears to have any Notion what is Due to the Family," if you please!

James is quite put out, as the information he gained at Leeds indicates that the Webbs may well be deeply involved in this railroad business, and he is most anxious that they not be warned or set on edge before he can get at them again. Since Aunt Charlotte is certain to set *anyone* on edge, we are going back to Stockton tomorrow to find and stop her. Poor James is growing quite tired of all this gadding about, but at least we shall not need to move our entire establishment this time. It will only be an overnight trip, so our trunks may stay here at Wardhill. (Walker, needless to say, comes with me.)

Your much-traveled,
Cecy

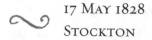

17 May 1828
Stockton

My dear Thomas,

You will be pleased to learn that you are to be spared a visit from yet another relative-at-law. For my sins, I shall not. Charlotte Rushton is somewhere in Stockton, having taken some hen-witted notion that the Duke of Waltham needs her instruction to deal with his erring spouse. In fairness, I must admit that Daniel frequently strikes me as needing instruction on a good many topics, but with the best will in the world I cannot see Miss Rushton as the proper person to do the instructing.

Having tracked His Grace this far, Miss Rushton is likely to discover the name and location of Haliwar Tower at any moment. How she has managed it, I do not know. I am half minded to recommend her to my lord Wellington for his special staff, provided I am never required to deal with her myself.

Cecelia and I have, perforce, come to Stockton in an attempt to locate her aunt before she descends in fury on the Webbs. It is a great pity I did not know of her presence or intentions when I was in Leeds on that railroad business. I might then have headed her off quite easily, but as she addressed her screed to Cecelia rather than to me, I did not discover the matter until I had returned to Wardhill and handed over the reserved letters.

I am more than a little tempted to refer Miss Rushton to Goosepool and the Dancing Weans, but it would not do. Even if her magical talents and training are enough to activate the transformation trap, it is unlikely that she would remain in canine form for long. Once she reverted to her natural shape, I would have both her and the difficult Mr. Skelly to deal with—for I place no dependence on any change in his behavior as a result of his time as a terrier. There is also the probable reaction of my dear Cecelia and your unexpectedly dangerous Kate to the transformation of their aunt. No, on the whole I think it better not to mention the matter.

I do not expect that it will take us more than a day or two to find Miss Rushton. It had better not. We came away with a minimum of baggage, and my valet will not be pleased if I run out of cravats. So your correspondence may continue to be directed to Wardhill Cottage as usual.

Yours,
James

14 MAY 1828
SKEYNES

(Enchanted by T.S. on general principles)

Dear Cecy,

I fear I write only to tell you I have nothing to write.

Mr. Scarlet remains mute, despite all Thomas's efforts. The man smirks. That is the only sign he even hears what Thomas is saying to him. The *dicemi* spell that has served Thomas so well in the past only makes Mr. Scarlet smile disdainfully.

Thomas will try again in the morning.

15 MAY 1828
SKEYNES

Dear Cecy,

Thomas has shown such patience I can scarcely credit it, yet Mr. Scarlet sits mumchance. The beastly fellow seems to find our coal cellar very much to his taste.

I cannot send you so meager a letter. I will wait another day in hope I may add genuine news to it.

∾ 16 MAY

Still nothing. Thomas is dogged. Mr. Scarlet may be stubborn, but I will back Thomas against him any day. It is only a matter of time. I will write when there is something that merits the ink and paper for me to tell you.

∾ 17 MAY 1828
SKEYNES

Dear Cecy,

I promised I would write when I had something to tell you. Now I scarcely know where to begin.

We have solved the problem of our superfluous child. Drina is safely reunited with her mother. That Thomas and I are safely here at Skeynes with the children, we owe largely to Mr. Wrexton and Aunt Elizabeth, and perhaps a trifle to Reggie Winters, as well.

I think you may recall Colonel Winters? He was mere Captain Winters when we met him in Paris back on our Grand Tour, a good-tempered young man with a mustache. He was dogged (if perhaps a trifle dense, at least in Thomas's estimation) in the pursuit of the miscreants who broke into the Sainte Chapelle to conduct their clandestine magical ritual. If you do remember Reggie Winters, I am impressed, for

I haven't given him a thought in years. Fortune has favored him, and he is now liaison for Wellington, the army, and those members of the Royal College who advise the military.

This morning (hard to believe—it seems a lifetime has passed since then) the children greeted Thomas and me on our return from riding the boundary. They were agog with excitement over the behavior of the toy soldiers that guard the Map. Thomas came with me to the nursery, where the soldiers were all in motion. It was exceedingly slow motion, such that we had to hold our breath and watch in silence for minutes on end, but it was just as Arthur and the others said. All the soldiers were moving, at a rate of mere inches per month, around Skeynes as the children have it marked on the Map.

Thomas retired to his study to scrutinize the bounds we've set around Skeynes. Nothing he did could detect any threat to correspond with the phenomenon. After one last thorough inspection of the Map in situ, he concluded that the spell was failing.

Thomas detailed Arthur and Eleanor to make careful observations of the toy soldiers' motion, both in distance and in time, on the grounds that further study was required before a hypothesis could be formed. I think you would be pleased and surprised by the patience and respect Thomas displays toward the twins where magic is concerned. Certainly it pleases and surprises me.

"That should keep them busy," Thomas confided to me. "The remarkable thing is that they were able to create the

Map in the first place. After all, Arthur and Eleanor have had no formal magical training. If their creation malfunctions before it stops working entirely, I suppose it's not surprising."

We had only just finished in the nursery when we were informed that a carriage had drawn up at the door. Thomas joined the children at the window. "It's the Wrextons at last," he told me over his shoulder as he turned for the stairs. "From the look of things, they've brought half the army with them. Not before time, either. I've been writing to London daily for help from the Royal College. Perhaps someone has finally troubled himself to open the post."

When I followed Thomas out to meet the Wrextons, I was taken aback to discover that he had only been exaggerating a trifle. To the great annoyance of our servants, there were troops of red-coated soldiers everywhere. The Wrextons, both looking as neat as wax despite their travels, were in a far grander carriage than is their wont, an elegant barouche with a coachman and footman in the front. Riding in the barouche with the Wrextons was a lady wearing a veil that concealed her features utterly. The officer only too obviously in charge dismounted and greeted Thomas with starched formality.

"Reggie Winters," Thomas exclaimed. "Haven't you sold out yet?"

The name, once uttered, jogged my memory sufficiently that I was able to make a more formal greeting. "Colonel Winters, how nice to meet you again."

Colonel Winters ignored us both as he drew forth a letter and read it aloud to us. I freely admit any memory I might have had of the formal opening phrases was displaced by my astonishment when I heard these words read out:

"Thomas Schofield, quondam Marquis of Schofield, I do arrest you on the charge of high treason."

I was gaping at Colonel Winters, so I felt Thomas's surprise more than I saw it. He stiffened beside me, caught utterly off-guard by the accusation, and exclaimed, "Winters, is this your idea of a joke?"

Mr. Wrexton sprang down from the barouche. "Thomas, I do beseech you to moderate your language. Clearly there has been a mistake. But irreverence will only compound the difficulty."

Aunt Elizabeth descended from the carriage and came to my side. "Dear Kate, I'm so glad to see you in your best looks. Michael, do apologize to Thomas for your error."

"This is partially my fault," Mr. Wrexton conceded, "and I do beg your pardon for it most sincerely. You asked me for help in identifying your superfluous child. I'm afraid I permitted myself to be piqued by the implication that I am some sort of universal office for the recovery of lost articles. When I wrote to answer your request, I gave you short shrift. Matters that I—quite unforgivably—assumed to be more pressing claimed my attention, and I did nothing whatever to help you identify the lost child. I'm sorry. I have tried to explain matters to Colonel Winters, but he has the fixed notion that you are responsible for her abduction. He has army magicians deployed around your perimeter, so I beg you to be circumspect."

"Wait." Thomas held up his hand to halt Mr. Wrexton. He glared at Winters. "Do you mean to tell me all this pother is about Drina?"

At the very sound of the name, the veiled lady in the barouche wailed and buried her sobs in her handkerchief.

Colonel Winters drew himself to his full height and read from his paper again. "If any person or persons do maliciously wish, will, or desire, invent, practice, or attempt any bodily harm to be done to the king's most royal person or his heirs apparent"—Winters put heavy emphasis on the words *heirs apparent*—"that person shall be adjudged a traitor and tried for high treason."

Just the manner in which Colonel Winters said them aloud seemed to me to put the words *high treason* in capital letters. It made me shudder. If I could have buried my sobs in a handkerchief, I might have done so. As usual, however, I had come out without any such useful object on my person.

"Oh, gather what wits the good Lord gave you, Reggie," Thomas snapped. "You know perfectly well I've never done anything of the sort. In any event, the Duke of York is the king's heir apparent."

Winters dropped his official air and answered Thomas back. "My orders concern Her Royal Highness, the Princess Alexandrina Victoria, the king's only niece. Until the existence of legitimate issue from the Duke of York, she is next after him in line for the throne."

Thomas turned to me and I could see my own horror mirrored in his eyes. "Drina!" said Thomas, just as I smote my forehead and cried, "Laid couching! I should have known!"

"Drina!" The veiled lady fairly bounded out of the carriage in her haste to reach Thomas. "You do have her, you villain!" In her distress, she struck Thomas a flurry of blows about the head and shoulders, but Aunt Elizabeth and I were able to pull her off him before any serious injuries were inflicted.

In the struggle, the lady's veil was pulled aside. I saw that we were trying to restrain a wild-eyed woman in her early forties. She was dressed with great expense, if no more than moderate elegance, and her eyes were red with weeping. I could feel only pity for the agony the woman must have endured. My pity availed me nothing, however. The moment my grip on her wrist faltered, she boxed my ears soundly.

I fell back, blinking tears of pain away, and saw that the children had broken free of the nurses. Arthur, Eleanor, and Edward were racing toward us, but far in the lead was Drina, her skirts and petticoats lifted a ladylike few inches to speed her flight.

"Pray do not cry, Mama," called Drina, as the children joined us in a small stampede. "I am here. Oh, I am here."

Drina cast herself into her mother's arms, and the pair of them sank down on the gravel, weeping with joy to be reunited.

Aunt Elizabeth and I exchanged rueful smiles. I know my own eyes came near to brimming with tears. How could anyone find anything but joy in the touching sight of a mother and a daughter reunited?

When Drina had collected herself, which she did with remarkable speed for one of her tender years, she turned to Colonel Winters. "Lord and Lady Schofield are not at fault," she stated. With eyes flashing, she turned to her mother. "It is the odious Mr. Conroy who is to blame, Mama. He arranged for Mr. Scarlet to abduct me. I was held prisoner in a dreadful place. Mr. Scarlet told me that if I dared speak a word to tell anyone who I truly was, he would do dreadful things to Feodore, and you would die most horridly."

"Mr. Conroy can do no more harm," Drina's mother said. "He is a prisoner in the Tower." After a moment of devoting herself to her handkerchief again, she added, "I am sorry for my folly, for he deceived me cruelly."

At this, Drina looked distinctly pleased. She turned to Colonel Winters to finish her explanation. "Edward came, so I rescued him. His mother and father have shown me nothing but kindness. Pray do not arrest them for treason, for it is all Mr. Conroy's fault. His minion Mr. Scarlet is prisoner here. He tells people he is a wizard, but it is no such thing. You must make him confess his crimes."

"We rescued each other," Edward protested.

"Drina rescued you, and you know it," Eleanor said in her most withering tone.

"Rescued by a princess!" Arthur said, envy in every syllable. "You lucky devil!"

"That will do," I informed them. "Back to the nursery with you. At once!"

Most reluctantly, the sprigs from our family tree withdrew themselves. I might have felt a twinge of pity at their manifest reluctance if I hadn't known perfectly well they would be scrying us the moment they returned to the nursery.

Colonel Winters folded his piece of paper away with a distinct air of relief. "I will summon the magicians. Thomas, I do beg your pardon."

"Don't be silly, Reggie." Thomas clapped Colonel Winters on the shoulder. "You were only doing your duty. And I don't envy you your orders, if you had to carry them out under these circumstances." Thomas glanced meaningfully at Drina's mother.

"She would come," said Colonel Winters glumly. "Mr. and Mrs. Wrexton were firm in your defense, but she insisted."

Drina's mother, or perhaps I should say Her Grace, the Duchess of Kent, had gone back to embracing her daughter and comparing notes with her. "Indeed, when you were stolen from me, Mr. Conroy ordered me to pretend his daughter Victoria was the true princess."

Drina's disdain was beyond words. Her mother nodded in agreement. "Just so. She was enchanted to resemble you, but manners maketh man, and manners maketh princess, too. The king's request that you and I join him in Cheltenham ruined the scheme, even though he had only met you once and long ago. Victoria Conroy could not fool him for an instant, the ill-bred chit."

Drina's eyes shone. "Mr. Conroy must be tried for treason, for indeed, he did most maliciously will bodily harm to be done to one of the king's heirs apparent."

I noted that Thomas was now regarding Drina with considerable respect. Clearly she found no difficulty in quoting verbatim the words of Colonel Winters's writ for Thomas's arrest.

Thomas said, "Wrexton? Between the pair of us, you and I may be able to turn the trick with Mr. Scarlet, but I don't object to help from the military now that Reggie has offered it. Do you?"

"Indeed not." Mr. Wrexton turned to me. "May we entrust the Duchess of Kent and her daughter to your further hospitality? I fear this interrogation may not be fit for ladies to witness."

Aunt Elizabeth gave her husband a distinctly old-fashioned look. "Then I doubt it a fit matter for gentlemen, either, but I think we will muddle through somehow."

Colonel Winters signaled for his magicians, and I led Drina and her mother back indoors, all the while wondering what on earth we were going to feed everyone. I would back our cook against the army any day, but heirs apparent are another matter entirely.

Thomas, Mr. Wrexton, and every wizard detailed to Colonel Winters's command are downstairs even now. For what feels like the hundredth time, I sign off with the same promise: I shall write the moment Mr. Scarlet gives me news to relate.

Sincerely,
Kate

18 May 1828
Haliwar Tower

Dearest Kate,

You will no doubt be astonished by the superscription. You will be even more astonished—and pleased—to learn that not only will we be coming to Skeynes shortly to retrieve our offspring, but you will also be spared a visit from Aunt Charlotte. I am only sorry that I cannot add the news that you will soon be rid of Georgy as well. I cannot say, as yet, precisely when we can leave, as we have a good many papers to go over before the magicians of the Royal College arrive, but rest assured, we shall come the very minute they do. I expect to write in a few days with more exact details.

I am sure you are eager to know how all this has come about. It is, in a way, Aunt Charlotte's doing, though she did not intend any of it in the least. She has declared herself so shaken by recent events that she proposes to leave at once for Bath to take the waters and to repair her shattered nerves.

Yesterday we followed Aunt Charlotte to Stockton. We arrived quite late in the afternoon, so there was not much time to ask after her. Nonetheless, James inquired at several inns, to no effect.

We discovered the reason this morning, when Walker had the happy idea of asking the stableman about hired carriages and recent arrivals. Aunt Charlotte had, it seems, arrived two days before in a hired coach and driven straight to the home of one of her acquaintances, a Mrs. Pentworthy. (I had no notion that Aunt Charlotte *had* any acquaintances in so unfashionable a place as Stockton, but I cannot say that I am astonished. If there is one thing for which Aunt Charlotte has a positive gift, it is collecting acquaintances. I said as much to James, who remarked that the reason Aunt Charlotte has a multitude of acquaintances is that as soon as they begin to know her well enough to become friends, they find some excuse to cut the connection. I am afraid that dear James is still extremely put out with Aunt Charlotte.)

At Mrs. Pentworthy's home, Aunt Charlotte bullied her way into a night's lodging and then had a terrific argument with the coachman over the agreed-upon hire. So put out was the coachman by this penny-pinching behavior that he flatly refused to remain, and returned to Leeds. Aunt Charlotte had spent the next day visiting every coach-for-hire in town, but after the way she treated the man from Leeds, none of them would take her up without receiving payment in advance. This she refused to do, and returned to her friend's lodgings last night in high dudgeon.

We set off at once in the expectation of finding her still at Mrs. Pentworthy's home. When we arrived, we discovered it was no such thing.

"Oh, she'll be so distressed that you didn't come before she left," Mrs. Pentworthy told James when he explained whom we had come to see. "Not that she wasn't terribly distressed already, poor thing. Some family matter, I take it." She looked at James and me with a bright, birdlike inquisitiveness, as if she hoped we would drop a few more crumbs of information for her to snap up.

As I had been quite expecting any crony of Aunt Charlotte's to be as fond of gossip as she, I ignored her hints and said, "She has gone out, then?"

"On some urgent errand," Mrs. Pentworthy said, nodding. "I loaned her my coach and driver."

I saw a gleam of satisfaction in her eyes and knew at once how it was. However closemouthed Aunt Charlotte had been about her business, the coachman must learn her destination, at the least, and might well overhear something of even more interest. Whatever he discovered, Mrs. Pentworthy would learn in good time once he returned.

"When do you expect her return?" James asked.

"Oh, not before evening," Mrs. Pentworthy assured us. "I heard her tell the coachman she wished to visit Haliwar Tower, and that is a good way up the river."

"Thank you for your kindness," I told her. She pressed us to stay, but James invented a business engagement and extracted us before she could tie us down with teacups and conversation.

Once we were safely away, James's expression turned grim. "Cecelia, I do not wish to say anything invidious about your aunt, but—"

"It is quite all right," I assured him. "You cannot say anything that I have not said myself already at least a dozen times."

James snorted. "I believe I could manage one or two things."

"Well, perhaps, if you use the sort of vulgar language that is permitted to gentlemen but not to ladies," I allowed. "But I think that is taking unfair advantage."

He laughed, as I meant him to, and I went on, "I have been thinking, James, and really, this is the best thing that could have happened."

James looked at me as if I had run mad. "It is?"

"Yes, for it gives us just the excuse we need to visit Haliwar Tower again without arousing suspicion," I said. "Aunt Charlotte is sure to arrive before us, and if she is not in a passion when she gets there, I am sure the Webbs will put her into one very shortly. And after a few minutes spent dealing with Aunt Charlotte in a passion, they will not be at all surprised that we came to fetch her away."

"What a wonderful idea," James said in the tones of someone who thinks it quite the opposite. "So instead of the

Webbs dealing with your aunt, you wish us to do so? How will that help? We'll have our hands full of your aunt on this visit, and the Webbs aren't likely to allow us another."

"You haven't seen Aunt Charlotte in one of her tremendous takings," I said. "I think it quite likely that she will work herself into a sick headache by the time she is calmed down. I am sure she will need to lie quietly for a little before she is composed enough to make the return journey. In fact, I shall insist upon it."

"What about the transformation spell?" James asked. "Haliwar is built around a stone circle, and I have no desire to watch you turn into a terrier."

I noticed that he said nothing about Aunt Charlotte, who is certainly as much of a magician as I am, but I chose not to remark on it. Instead, I said, "Nothing happened the last time we were there, and the Webbs *live* in the tower. If they are the ones who have been using the ley lines—and I don't see who else it could be—they must have a protective spell on the tower to keep the transformation from affecting wizards. If you insist, though, I will find some excuse to ask for a room in one of the wings."

"I see," James said. "I shall leave it in your capable hands."

We set off for Haliwar without delay and made good time on the road. I spent most of the trip casting every magical ward and protection spell I could remember on James and me, just in case. The last spell, just before we arrived at the tower, was the advanced ley-line detection spell that Mr. Skelly had demonstrated just before he was turned into a terrier. I confess to being motivated primarily by curiosity, rather than forethought. The last time we were at Haliwar, my ley-detecting spells went fuzzy and blurred the moment I passed into the courtyard, and I wanted to see if Mr. Skelly's spell would be likewise affected.

It was, but this time I could see why. When we drove through the gate into the courtyard of Haliwar Tower, I felt the ley line spreading out, like a stream flowing into a pond. The whole courtyard was awash in ley power, much more strongly than it had been on our previous visit. The power spread out from Haliwar Tower to the outer wall, and the ley line poured in and mingled with it until I could not tell which was which.

I did not have much time for magical contemplation, however, as we were immediately confronted by the spectacle of Aunt Charlotte haranguing the Webbs. An old-fashioned brougham, which I took to be Mrs. Pentworthy's coach, stood nearby. Its coachman made no pretense of indifference; indeed, it was a good thing his horses were placid cobs, so little attention did he pay them.

James and I descended from the coach, and James told our coachman loudly to walk the horses outside the gate, as we did not expect to be long. We could all hear quite easily what Aunt Charlotte was saying—"And I'll have no more of this roundaboution! Where is my nephew-by-marriage? Where is His Grace?"

"Gone off about his own business, I should think," James said in a carrying voice.

Everyone turned in surprise; they had all been so caught up with Aunt Charlotte that they had not noticed our arrival. Aunt Charlotte paled, then reddened. Before she could start in on us, I said as affably as I could, "Dear Aunt Charlotte! Are you still searching for the Duke of Waltham? What a pity your letters missed us. We might have saved you a good deal of time and effort."

Aunt Charlotte's eyes narrowed. "You know where he is?

"No," I replied, "but we were here when he took himself off, and I do assure you, Aunt, that the Webbs know no more than we of his current whereabouts."

An expression of consternation crossed Aunt Charlotte's face, but she rallied quickly. "And how is it that you are so certain of that?" she demanded.

I smiled sweetly. "We were here when he left. Did you not know? The Webbs were kind enough to invite us all to a house party."

"And you *came*?" Aunt Charlotte's tone of horror drew a frown from James, but she went on, oblivious. "At *this* time of year? To an obscure manor house in the north country to visit a pair of . . . of . . ." Words failed her, or perhaps some remnant of good behavior held her back (though I admit that with Aunt Charlotte, this is altogether unlikely), and she flapped a hand in the direction of the Webbs.

"Do forgive Aunt Charlotte," I said even more sweetly to the Webbs. "She is very excitable, and I fear that she is inclined to be old-fashioned in her notions."

"Old-fashioned?" Aunt Charlotte was nearly incoherent with rage, but at least now she was raging at me, rather than at the Webbs. Mr. Webb looked slightly stunned; I think he had not yet adjusted to the turn of events. His sister was more awake on that head. She was watching me closely, as if trying to fathom what I was about.

Abruptly, Aunt Charlotte stopped. With visible effort, she pulled herself together. In a voice still shaking with suppressed anger, she said, "I despair of you, Cecelia. To forgo the Season is bad enough, but to bury yourself in the north, in places that are not even watering holes, is foolish beyond measure. Especially when your behavior is so outlandish! Do not think the news of it will not reach London. You will not keep your position in Society long if you associate with Cits and foreigners in such free and easy fashion!"

"Aunt Charlotte—," I said, but by this time she was impossible to stop.

"I have heard all about it!" she raged. "Riding those infernal machines and poking into heathen ruins; taking strange dogs and foreign men into your very household! If James were not with you, you would be ruined, married or not!"

"But James *has* been with me," I said calmly. "You are seriously overset, Aunt Charlotte, or you would think better of what you are saying."

"Perhaps your aunt would like to lie down in a quiet chamber for a little?" Adella Webb suggested, a little too smoothly.

"Adella!" Her brother's horrified whisper carried much

farther than he intended. She gave him a look that I could not interpret and made a little gesture, and his eyes widened. Then he nodded and said, "Yes, er, if you would like to rest a little, Miss Rushton, I am sure—"

"I do not require rest!" Aunt Charlotte screeched. "I require my nephew-by-marriage the Duke of Waltham!"

"He isn't here, Aunt," I said firmly. "He hasn't been here for weeks. When you have had a chance to rest, you will—"

I stopped in midsentence. The pool of ley energy in the courtyard, which had been calm and still, was stirring. In the distance, I heard the long whistle of the steam engine.

Aunt Charlotte had started complaining again, which effectively covered my lapse in speech. I looked around. The stirring became an eddy, then a whirlpool, and I realized it was centered on Mr. Webb. "James!" I shrieked, not altogether coherently. "Stop him!"

Fortunately, James knows quite well when to act first and ask questions later. He saw where I was looking, took three steps forward, and milled Mr. Ramsey Webb down.

The swirling ley energy paused. Aunt Charlotte cried out, just as if she had never before seen one gentleman strike another (I stretch the point slightly, I admit; it is not, perhaps, strictly correct to refer to my brother Oliver and his friends as "gentlemen." But then, I do not think it is strictly correct to apply the term to Ramsey Webb, either).

"Idiot!" snarled Adella Webb. I could not readily tell whom she was addressing—James or her brother. She made a gesture, and the swirl of ley energy shifted and recentered itself on her. It began spinning once more, pulling away from the courtyard walls into a tight funnel that surrounded her and her alone.

Mr. Webb regained his feet and lunged at James. Aunt Charlotte shrieked again, in counterpoint with the approaching whistle of the train. "Aunt Charlotte, ward yourself!" I shouted, and activated every warding spell I had cast on James and me.

I was barely in time. The ley energy swept out from Adella Webb and nearly knocked me off my feet. It did knock James off his (or perhaps it was Mr. Webb's lucky punch). I staggered. Adella threw open the main door of Haliwar Tower. "Inside!" she cried to her brother.

I thought she meant the pair of them to dodge inside and bar the door, and I scrambled to my feet in hopes of preventing them. As I did, Ramsey Webb grabbed James's coat and swung him through the open door. Or at least, that is what he tried to do. James is not a small man, and Mr. Webb is neither oversized nor well-muscled. If James had been properly on his feet, I do not think Mr. Webb could have budged him. As it was, James lurched toward the door but caught himself on the threshold.

Adella Webb made an angry, exasperated noise and plunged forward. She rammed into James, shoving him through the doorway and into the tower—and her momentum carried her inside along with him.

For a long instant, nothing seemed to happen. Then I felt the ley energy shift—and Adella Webb shrank in on herself. A moment later, a pug dog stood where she had been.

"Adella!" Ramsey Webb cried in horror. As he lunged forward, the ley energy shifted again—and began to stretch away from the entrance to the courtyard. I knew what that must mean: The steam engine that pulled the coal train had reached the ley line, and was towing it along the railway as it passed.

Ramsey Webb seemed unaware of the shift in the ley energy. He ran toward the tower, pulling at the power as he went. I think he was trying to restore the spell that had protected everyone inside from the transformation spell, but perhaps he was trying to restore his sister directly.

The ley energy stretched, and stretched further, as the steam engine pulled on one end and Ramsey Webb pulled on the other. And then, just as he reached the doorway, the ley line snapped like a child's bootlace that has been drawn too tightly.

"Snapped" is of course not entirely accurate when one is speaking of a river of magical power, but it is as near as I can come. Magic surged into the courtyard as what was left of that end of overstretched ley line pulled back. It surged through Ramsey Webb and into Haliwar Tower, and then back out again. The tower shook, as it had during that last night James and I spent there, and slowly began to collapse.

"James!" I cried, but he had already swept up the pug

dog and charged out the door. He nearly tripped over a rather foolish-looking boxer—who had been Ramsey Webb a moment before.

Aunt Charlotte stood staring, for once quite unable to say anything, as the servants poured out of the house in a panic and the central tower slowly disintegrated. I could feel the magic draining away, and I half expected one or both of the Webbs to resume their natural forms at any moment, but it was no such thing. They both remained dogs.

James looked from the pug to the boxer and back. Then he turned to me and raised an eyebrow inquiringly.

"He was drawing on the ley lines to break the spell on his sister," I said, thinking it out as I spoke. "And the train went by and distorted the ley line at just the wrong moment and caused a backlash." I looked at the dogs. "I don't think the transformation spell is part of the ley line network anymore. I think it's all right here, on the two of them. And it's going to be nearly impossible to take off again, if all the power I felt a minute ago went into reinforcing it."

This left us to deal with the Webbs' servants and the two coachmen. As soon as she recovered her voice, Aunt Charlotte declared herself to be quite overcome and utterly unable to travel. Mrs. Pentworthy's coachman agreed with unseemly enthusiasm that she ought to remain at Haliwar while he returned to his mistress, and we saw him off with a message for Walker and James's valet (who had remained in Stockton). Our own coachman we sent on to Darlington with a message for Herr Schellen and Mr. Skelly (who we

presumed had regained his natural form when Adella transformed into the pug dog).

Then we set about soothing the servants enough to
arrange rooms for James, myself, and Aunt Charlotte, for of
course we could not leave Haliwar with its master and mistress in such straits. Fortunately, Mr. Webb's study and Miss
Webb's workroom are both in the undamaged wings, and
once they understood the situation, the servants were only
too happy to have us search through the papers for a means
of disenchanting their employers.

We found a good deal of interest, and James sent off
an express letter to Lord Wellington. Mr. Skelly and Herr
Schellen arrived yesterday, with the news that the stone circle
at Goosepool has collapsed (and with your latest letter).
They are currently examining the ley energy that remains in
and around Haliwar, and the state of the other ley lines in
the immediate vicinity. A week as a terrier has vastly improved Mr. Skelly's manners; I will be interested to discover
what effect their transformation has on the Webbs, once
we determine how to return them to their normal forms. It
is almost a pity that it is too late to apply the spell to Aunt
Charlotte.

James remains extremely put out with her, as he is convinced that it was her injudicious remarks about "strange
dogs and foreign men" that caused Mr. Webb to attempt
whatever enchantment he was beginning when James
struck him. For of course, Mr. Webb would surely connect
the "strange dog" with the enchanted sheepdog, and the

"foreign men" with Herr Magus Schellen, and leap to the conclusion that we had discovered his enchantments. Though James cannot deny that we would not have discovered as much as we have without the unexpected confrontation (and its even more unexpected results), he still scowls and looks black whenever it is mentioned. I believe he is offended by the inelegance of it all.

For myself, I am simply glad that it is all over, or nearly so. As soon as Lord Wellington sends some wizards to replace us and take charge of the Webbs, we will be on our way to reclaim the children. I do not expect to remain here above another fortnight; I shall write the very moment I know the exact date of our departure.

I am astonished to learn Drina's identity; the child must have a will of iron to have kept so great a secret for so long, threat to her mother or no. It augurs well for her possible future as queen, I think.

Yours,
Cecy

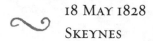

18 MAY 1828
SKEYNES

(Enchanted by T.S. out of sheer habit)

Dear Cecy,

Thank goodness it wasn't you who went through the doorway! Canine life is not without interest, but I hate to think of you in such trim. How fortunate James has never displayed any aptitude for performing magic. It says a great deal that Aunt Charlotte was too shaken to make a sermon out of it, for a clearer case of reaping and sowing I cannot imagine.

I hope it will gratify you to learn that the case against the Webbs will benefit from a witness willing to testify against them at every turn. After many promises, I am at last able to deliver news of the interrogation of Mr. Scarlet.

Mr. Scarlet is not his real name. He was born Adolphus Medway. His mother was one of the servants in the Webb household, as were many of his relations. I find it difficult to think of him as anything but Mr. Scarlet now, so forgive me for confining myself to that name. As Mr. Scarlet was hand in glove with the Webbs in the matter of the stone circles and the network of ley lines, he has offered all matter of testimony condemning them of crimes as black as his own.

What produced this miraculous volte-face, you may wonder? The moment Colonel Winters read out the charges listed on the writ of arrest (with the tactful omission of Thomas's name, of course), Mr. Scarlet mended his manners. Gone was his disdainful air.

"If I swing, I won't swing alone," Mr. Scarlet declared. "There's that blackmailing swine Francis Conroy, for a start, and John Conroy himself over him. More than that, there's a pair up north you should know about, real beauties both—the Webbs." With that, he proceeded to regale us with a litany of his villainous deeds faster than Colonel Winters's men could write it down.

It was crowded in the cellar, and it was with some relief I found myself called away from the throng to deal with a question of kitchen logistics posed by our cook. I would not have left, I promise you, before the burning issues of Mr. Scarlet's guilt had been resolved. No asparagus receipt in the world could have lured me away before I had my curiosity satisfied on the salient points.

From Thomas, I have the full story.

Scarlet was born mere Adolphus Medway, servant to Scalby Webb, a cousin of the pair you know so well. Scalby Webb was sent to university to refine his knowledge of magic, and Scarlet went along with his master. Webb had little interest in magic, as he was intent on keeping to himself and drinking all the claret he could come by, but his servant missed no opportunity to listen at keyholes and pick up what titbits of learning he could.

In Webb's second term at university, he took a fever. Scarlet nursed his master, and claims to have caught a mild form of the indisposition himself. When Webb died, Adolphus Medway traded places with him. So completely had Webb kept to himself, Scarlet was able to turn the trick and assume Webb's station in life and place at university.

Scarlet studied magic diligently and mastered a good deal in his limited time at university. He was adept at aping Webb's scrawl, and Webb never wrote home except to plead for money, so no one was the wiser until the Webbs came to visit their cousin in his rooms.

Scarlet was blackmailed into their service. As an agent of
the Webbs, Scarlet was sent on all manner of errands to do
with their schemes for power and financial gain. They were
intent on concealing their misdeeds as long as possible.
When they learned that Lord Wellington sent for James,
they were sure that some papers of interest to them had accompanied the summons. Hence Scarlet took it upon himself to investigate Tangleford. There is a stone circle there,
as you know perfectly well, and once he had added it to the
ley network, he was able to penetrate your defenses almost
at will. It was never part of his plan to be discovered in his
misdeeds, so Scarlet fled as soon as he detected your spell-
casting to counter him.

Scarlet had no idea he would ever have anything to do
with Tangleford Hall again. It gave him a nasty shock, therefore, when Arthur espied him at the Bull and Mouth.
Double the shock, indeed, as he was returning from Leeds,
having made his report to the Webbs with all speed. As he
was not in disguise, Arthur recognized him. After that encounter, Scarlet made no bones about shifting his appearance more frequently even than usual.

Scarlet was recruited into Conroy's treasonous scheme
when Conroy's cousin Francis tracked him down in London. Francis Conroy had been at university during Scalby
Webb's first term at university. They shared the same tutor,
in fact. Thus, Francis Conroy noticed when Scarlet made
the switch. (More than the tutor did, it seems.) He held his

peace at the time, but kept his eye on Scarlet thereafter. When the Conroys contrived their dastardly plan, Scarlet's talent for shifting appearances made him a valuable accomplice. Francis Conroy blackmailed Scarlet into colluding with the scheme.

Scarlet claims he was given no choice but to play along. Disguised as a physician, he was smuggled into the palace by one of the ladies-in-waiting Conroy had corrupted. Scarlet cast the glamour that made Victoria Conroy resemble the princess. Francis Conroy had plans for Drina thereafter, but he reckoned without Scarlet's initiative. Scarlet spirited Drina away to his pied-à-terre in Stroud. By the time Francis Conroy, using the unimaginative alias of Mr. Jones, found the house in Stroud, Scarlet was long gone.

As an agent of the Webbs, Scarlet had been charged with frightening Daniel into backing the Webbs financially. Daniel foiled the Webbs by running away. They believed he could be brought to heel by threats to Georgy, and so once her whereabouts was known, Scarlet was ordered to arrange her abduction. Scarlet felt that a well-delivered threat would be just as effective and far less trouble, so he did not actually bother to carry out that order.

I wish I could describe Georgy's expression when she learned that, far from plotting her demise, Daniel had been trying to protect her all along. Her eyes went wide, her jaw dropped, and by the time she recovered enough to close her mouth, her lower lip was already trembling. She took herself off then, thanks be to a merciful providence, for a coal cellar thronged with wizards and soldiers was obviously no place for her finer feelings to take wing.

Had Scarlet simply evicted Edward the moment he detected his presence in the cart and left him to his own devices on the road, he could have had Drina safely in his hands almost indefinitely. Instead, he chose to add Edward to his collection of misdeeds. I suppose I owe him some thanks for abandoning both the children without a struggle.

"Couldn't tie my own shoes with the magic the chit left me," Scarlet explained. "Anything that came from the ley lines, she lapped up without even noticing. My own magic still worked, else I'd never have been able to cast the glamour on the Conroy brat. But any ley magic I tried on her fell flat. I followed you at a distance when you came to fetch the brats. I was glad to be rid of her, to tell the truth. I knew I could collect her from you whenever I needed to, provided I was willing to go without ley magic the whole time I had her."

As confident of his ability to draw on the ley network as he was of his ability to fool the Webbs into permitting him to do so, Scarlet made a new plan. He believed, as Conroy had, that Drina and her mother would be too frightened of endangering one another to speak to the authorities.

As long as Scarlet was privy to the ley powers, he had the ability to come and go almost at will, no matter the strength or sophistication of the magical barriers he faced. Rather than forgo that power, Scarlet intended to leave Drina with us until the time suited him to come and collect her like an unclaimed letter. Word of Conroy's arrest had not reached him at the time Scarlet set out to invade Skeynes and seize Drina. If Scarlet had known that the Conroy scheme was discovered, he would never have run the risk of crossing the boundary spell we cast, nor of being linked to Drina's abduction.

Scarlet went on for an hour or more after I left to see about the asparagus. Thomas assures me that there will be testimony aplenty to dish all his accomplices, most particularly the Webbs, and enough circumstantial evidence to establish Scarlet's account as one to be trusted.

Once I left the cellar, my first consideration was the comfort of our exalted guests. My second was the unrest in the nursery caused by the impending loss of Drina. A poor third, I confess, was Georgy's opinion of all this.

No, fear not. She has not written another poem. (Or if she has, Georgy has sufficient good sense—just—not to tell me about it.) No, the new burden of her song is that she has sadly misjudged her poor darling Daniel. I need hardly tell you how tiresome I find this refrain. For all we know, Poor Darling Daniel has had to fly the country to avoid his debtors.

But I must not complain. As you have had Aunt Charlotte to deal with, yours is by far the more odious role. It gives me great pleasure, I must confess, to learn that she more than met her match at Haliwar.

The Duchess of Kent, not surprisingly, intends to whisk her daughter back to Kensington Palace under military escort first thing tomorrow morning. The children seem to be taking Drina's departure in as good part as they can be expected. The loss of their playmate is redeemed, but only just, by the romance of her situation.

Edward is taking this the hardest of any of the children. My heart would be wrung by the look in his eyes if I did not know perfectly well that the next bullfrog to cross his path will set his spirits entirely to rights.

I am only thankful that Arthur and Eleanor have been so effectively distracted by the Wrextons, who are administering the most thorough magical examinations imaginable. They make Lady Sylvia and her tea tray seem quite antiquated in comparison.

I am sure the Wrextons will write you a full account of the twins before they breathe a word of their results to me or to Thomas. Rest assured I shall relate to you any crumbs of information that fall in the interim, on this or any other topic.

Drat. I distinctly heard the parlor maid swear just now. If Edward has found another snake, when I have specifically forbidden him any more experiments in natural history whilst the Duchess of Kent is in residence, I shall make Thomas roar at him immediately.

Until the next domestic disaster then, I remain,

Yours,
Kate

19 May 1828
Skeynes

Dear Cecy,

Peace has descended on our household at last. I am delighted to report that Mr. Scarlet was dragged off in irons yesterday, with soldiers and wizards at the ready in case his recent good behavior wears off.

The Duchess of Kent and her military entourage took Drina home today. I cannot pretend that the departure of the duchess was anything but a relief, but Drina is a different matter.

The children said good-bye to the princess in the relative privacy of the little parlor. (I suggested the nursery, but apparently that was considered beneath the dignity owed Drina's station. The little parlor made a compromise acceptable to all parties.) The Duchess of Kent watched us all attentively throughout for any signs of familiarity. The children could not have behaved better.

Drina was gracious and unaffected about the whole ritual. She took leave of her former playmates with the same dignity she has displayed throughout her stay. How a woman as haughty as the Duchess of Kent could have subjected herself so utterly to the will of a cad like Conroy, I cannot imagine. Colonel Winters told me the man entered the household as her late husband's equerry. He insinuated himself into her good graces until she trusted him with everything, and he repaid her by substituting his daughter for hers.

Drina accepted as her due rather surprisingly graceful curtseys from Eleanor and Diana, and an equally elegant bow from Arthur. Edward's attempt at a bow was interrupted when he thought he saw a bug on the carpet at Drina's feet, but a swift nudge from Arthur recalled him to his senses in time to straighten up before the duchess made any slighting remarks. (Not that Edward would care a jot for any remark an adult could make if he had discovered a truly distinctive bug, mind.)

Diana presented Drina with a rather wilted nosegay she had gathered herself—rather wilted, but still very pretty. Drina kissed both the babies farewell. I cannot speak for anyone else's opinion of that gesture, but I found myself unaccountably moved by it. If ever she should manage to grow into her formidable name, Alexandrina Victoria will make an admirable Royal Highness.

We waved Drina and her mother (not to mention the escort arranged by Colonel Winters) off with cheers. The children were pleased with the grandeur of the soldiers in their red coats. I was pleased to see the back of them. With no soldiers on the premises other than the toy ones guarding the Map, the household felt almost empty. I reveled in the fact that our only remaining houseguests were the Wrextons. (I admit it. I count Georgy and your children as permanent fixtures in the household now.) Life is so much simpler without the military presence.

Mr. Wrexton feels sure that Scarlet's inability to perform magic on Drina stems from the realm itself. Any use of ley power against Drina merely fizzles to nothing. If true, this would explain why Drina had no opinion of Scarlet's magical abilities. It also implies that my spell did less to subdue Scarlet during his struggle with Thomas than Drina's mere presence did.

Aunt Elizabeth has a further refinement to the theory. She hopes to prove that the ley power Drina sapped from Scarlet explains the precocious use of magic the twins display. Until Drina arrived, the toy soldiers were just toys, the Map a mere map.

The Wrextons accompanied Thomas and me this morning as we rode out along the boundary, as Thomas wished to renew his protective spells. I could not help but enjoy myself in such company, and the expertise of both the Wrextons was very welcome in the matter of revising and improving his choice of enchantments. With good weather for the ride, the day approached perfection.

We recast the protection spells and rode through the gates on our way back to the house just in time to see an elegant carriage drawn by four matched bays fairly thundering up to our doors ahead of us.

Thomas rose in his stirrups for a better look at the equipage. "From the look of the daubs on the doors, that's Daniel's turnout."

Thomas, Mr. Wrexton, Aunt Elizabeth, and I gazed at one another speculatively.

"Has Georgy said anything about this to you?" Thomas asked me.

"Not a word," I replied. "She hasn't asked you to frank any letters for her, has she?" At Thomas's denial, I said, "That settles it, then. Georgy would never simply post a letter herself. Indeed, I am not entirely certain she knows how."

"If Georgy hasn't sent for him, Daniel came of his own volition." Aunt Elizabeth looked pensive. "How very enterprising of him."

"Hardly characteristic," said Mr. Wrexton in his driest tone.

Thomas was all impatience. "There's only one way to find out who sent for whom." We urged our horses to keep pace with his as he added, "Georgy can set up housekeeping where she pleases, with her husband or without him, for all I care. But she isn't staying under my roof one more night."

"Thomas," I reminded him, "it is my duty as her sister to make certain Georgy is safe."

"Rubbish." Thomas looked quite fierce. "That is a duty Daniel took on when he married her, and it's high time he remembered as much."

As I was in entire agreement, I did not dispute the point. We made haste—but by the time we had dismounted beside the carriage, its occupant had already gone indoors.

Belton was his usual calm self, and enlightened us as smoothly as if he had been practicing for half an hour. "His Grace, the Duke of Waltham, has arrived to call upon the Duchess of Waltham. They are in the tapestry room."

"All very well so far as it goes, Belton," said Thomas, "but he's not to leave this house without her. Is that clear?"

Belton did not turn a hair. He never does. But I could not help protesting, "Thomas, really—it's not as if you can force them to be reconciled."

"Oh, can't I?" Thomas had that light in his eye that means roaring is not so very far off. "A man deserves peace and quiet and refuge from his family when he is in his own home. His guests can settle their domestic troubles elsewhere."

"Thomas!" Such a statement, in the presence of our houseguests, was so shockingly rude I could not keep silent.

With an airy wave, Thomas dismissed the Wrextons. "They know I don't mean them." He marched through the entry hall, intent on reaching the tapestry room as soon as possible. Hard on his heels, we followed.

At the double doors to the tapestry room, I attempted to speak reason. "You can't simply burst in on them."

"I can do as I please. They can leave if they don't like it." On this note, Thomas threw open the doors.

But the scene we discovered was one of utter domestic tranquility. Daniel was as dashing as it is possible for him to look, given his resemblance to an egg, and Georgy presented a charming picture of repentance as she nestled in his arms.

"Oh, Kate!" Georgy beamed upon us all. "You will never guess what Daniel has done, no never! Not if you tried for a hundred years! A thousand!"

"If he will take you back, fall on your knees and thank God for it," Thomas said. "I might myself."

"He has agreed to testify against the Webbs," Mr. Wrexton surmised. "A very sound notion."

The expression on Daniel's face was easily as fatuous as the one Georgy wore. "Dashed good idea. I think I shall. You wouldn't credit it, the way those two deviled me."

"What *has* His Grace done, then?" Aunt Elizabeth asked Georgy calmly.

"You haven't even tried to guess!" Georgy took pity on us. "Oh, very well, then. He has burned every copy of that dreadful book. Bought them back and burned them!"

"Wouldn't that run to rather a lot of money?" I asked.

"Oh, money's no object now," Daniel assured us all. "Had a bit of luck on the Change. One thing I learned from those ghastly Webbs was how to tell a good investment from a bad one, and the Stockton and Darlington Railway has made my fortune. Best bit of wagering I ever undertook. You wouldn't credit how much more the shares are worth now than they were when I bought 'em."

"Daniel!" So transported by the prospect of Daniel's renewed fortune was Georgy, she could not keep herself from embracing him before us all. This did not seem to discomfit His Grace in the slightest. "Sweet Georgy!" he exclaimed, embracing her in return.

"Sorry to intrude, old man," said Thomas. He marched us out of the tapestry room, closed the doors, and leaned against them. "Lord, what a disgusting spectacle."

"There, there," I said. "They will be gone soon. It's so dreadfully dull and safe and soothing here, after all."

At this reminder of Georgy's true opinion of us, Thomas brightened perceptibly. "It is, isn't it?" To the Wrextons, he said, "It's a mercy you've come to liven us up a bit."

"Isn't it?" agreed Aunt Elizabeth. "And if we hurry, we will just have time to tidy up before luncheon, too."

Daniel and Georgy joined us for a blessedly humdrum meal, which I am delighted to report was entirely dull, safe, and soothing. Thomas does not have his heart's desire just yet, for Daniel intends to spend the night here. But Daniel will take Georgy with him when he leaves tomorrow, and whatever fortune should befall them once they cross our threshold will be no concern of ours, or, at least, not much.

You will be here before long. The children rejoice at the thought.

A safe journey and a swift one to you and James. We look forward to seeing you soon.

Love,
Kate

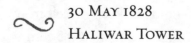

30 MAY 1828
HALIWAR TOWER

My dear Thomas,

Wellington's wizards have arrived at last, so Cecelia and I are free to go as soon as we have finished turning matters here over to them. Expect us to retrieve our assorted off-spring approximately one week after you receive this letter.

I suppose you will not wish to wait for our arrival to learn what has been happening here. If Wrexton is still with you, I am certain he will also be eager for news, though I believe Old Hookey's people mean to ask for his opinion as soon as may be.

The situation, in its briefest form, is this: Mr. and Miss Webb remain dogs for the moment. Miss Charlotte Rushton removes to Bath on the instant, or so she has been saying for the past week; apparently, she feels a need for stronger restoratives than those provided at Cheltenham Spa, where she had previously been staying. Her shattered nerves seem quite up to the task of terrorizing the Webbs' servants, however, and as she appears to derive considerable enjoyment from doing so, I expect she will remain as long as we do. Never fear; I shall not bring her to Skeynes. Haliwar is large enough that we meet only rarely, but not even the anticipation of seeing the look on your face would induce me to share a coach with her for three days.

Cecelia, Skelly, and I have spent the last week sorting out the Webbs' study and workrooms. The fellow was a demon for records, and his sister kept meticulous notes on her magical experiments. Between that and the maps Wrexton brought up with him, I fancy we have pieced together most of the matters that have been puzzling everyone.

I believe I have mentioned before the fact that the

Webbs inherited Haliwar from their great-uncle. What we have discovered is that the great-uncle was the last in a line of magicians and wizards dating back to Cromwell's time, who had been charged with the job of overseeing the ley line network that Cromwell had established to keep his vision of Parliament intact. Haliwar was the keystone and centerpiece of the network. Lyndhurst, who is heading the newly arrived delegation of wizards, thinks that Cromwell's spell is the reason there have been so many difficulties over the Parliamentary reform bills these past fifteen years and more, but his theories remain unproven.

What we do know is that Ramsey and Adella Webb knew all about the ley line network and determined to exploit it in every way they could. It is a good thing they thought mainly in terms of money; I shudder to think what might have happened if they had attempted serious political manipulation. Their plan was twofold—to repair and expand the ley line network so as to increase their influence, and to use the network as a stepping-stone to wealth.

Their first attempt at moneymaking was an abortive try at peddling Parliamentary influence. Fortunately, no one believed them capable of doing any such thing, and they had just sense enough not to reveal the manner in which they intended to exert their influence.

When the Stockton and Darlington Railway looked like becoming a success without them, the Webbs turned to a different scheme. They proposed the competing southern railway project, and discovered that they could use the ley network to influence members of Parliament not only to approve their bill of incorporation, but to invest in it, as well. Once their railway was approved, I believe they intended to manipulate both the railway and Parliament to promote their fortunes further. One can see where it would have led. In the end, they'd have tried to run the entire country for their own benefit.

Unfortunately for them, things began to go sour when the steam engines started running regularly on the Stockton and Darlington. The engines disrupted the ley lines and looked like putting a premature end to their plans. So they started using the ley lines to disrupt the engines.

That brought Herr Schellen onto the scene. Judging from her notes, it was Adella Webb who contrived the transformation spell, using the ley lines and the stone circles as the focus. Skelly has a long list of reasons why this was an incredibly foolish thing for them to do; I shall get him to write them up and include them separately for Wrexton's edification. The only one that is directly pertinent is that they still hadn't determined just what the railway was doing to the ley lines, so using the ley lines in an untested spell was unutterably foolish.

The Webbs didn't see it that way, of course. Their spell looked like an unqualified success. As soon as they were certain Herr Schellen had been transformed and was safely out of the way, they sent a manservant (your Mr. Scarlet, I believe, who seems to have been surprisingly busy about more plots than one) to collect his personal effects in secret. Once they were sure that Herr Schellen's landlady thought that he had simply absconded without paying his rent, they went back to business, sending Scarlet south to link additional stone circles to their ley network whilst they tackled assorted potential investors.

Daniel, Duke of Waltham, was high on their list. It's a good thing for him that, like you, he seldom bothered to take his seat in the House of Lords, because the ley network was still tuned to affect Parliament. The Webbs wanted access to a stone circle near that ancestral castle he brags about, as well as to his bankers, and they'd have had it if Daniel had been attending to politics as regularly as he attends to the gaming tables.

The Webbs were also worried about the effect of the steam engines on their ley network, as well they might have been. Lyndhurst is of the opinion that it was the regular interference between the engine and the central ley line that let Herr Schellen's transformation spell leak out into the whole network. Skelly thinks the spell was flawed and "overdistributed" from the beginning. Whatever the reason, it meant the Webbs had to invent a counterspell in order to keep living at Haliwar Tower.

By the time Cecelia and I turned up, the Webbs thought they had things back under control. Schellen was still safely out of the way, and Scarlet was busy linking new stone circles to the southernmost end of their ley network. Daniel was being uncooperative, as usual.

The Webbs apparently didn't know what to make of us.

Their initial impression was that I was interested in investing in a railway project, and they invited us to Haliwar partly in the hope that they could persuade me to join their unlikely southern enterprise, partly to see if my interest would persuade Daniel to invest, and partly to discover what we really wanted. They had very nearly decided that we were useless to them when Daniel vanished and the earthquake occurred.

The earthquake was, as you have no doubt realized by now, not an actual earthquake at all, but a disturbance caused by all the ley power the two of them had been building up around Haliwar in pursuit of their various projects. By then, they were quite sure that one of us was a wizard—I believe they detected some of the spells Cecelia cast while we were in residence—but they settled on me as the likelier candidate! Don't burst your waistcoat buttons laughing. In any case, they were delighted to see the back of us, as they had a good deal of magical repairs to do, in addition to the physical ones, and they didn't want any magicians around to notice and ask questions.

In Webb's place, I should have kept more careful track of my departing visitors, but he had other things on his mind. The gossip that drifted back to him all involved my apparent interest in the Stockton and Darlington, and he assumed he had been correct about my interest in railway investment. Then word reached him of Kate's transformation (I believe this, too, can be set to Scarlet's account), and someone mentioned that Cecelia and I had adopted a sheepdog.

I believe that at that point Webb panicked, or else he would not have sent to Mr. Medway to arrange that singularly transparent attempt to obtain the nonexistent sheepdog from me in Leeds. His sister was more composed. Wellington's men have confiscated the notes on the spell she was designing to deal with Cecelia and me, and are sending it by special messenger to the Royal College. I expect Jacobs and Monksleigh will be delighted; they love dangerous experiments.

At the last, it was the steam train that ruined them. The new engine is at least as powerful as Stephenson promised; it might have been enough to break the ley line all by itself. With Ramsey pulling power from the line at one end and Miss Webb's transformation spell sloshing around between the stone circles, the result was inevitable. All that uncontrolled power blew back through the tower, and instead of transferring the transformation from Miss Webb to her brother, it duplicated the spell. Skelly has been trying to work out the mechanism for the past week, without success. It doesn't help that we have to keep the two dogs well separated, or they spend all their time growling ferociously at each other. I'm sure that he and Lyndhurst will work it all out eventually.

I believe we have also found a solution to the problem of the interference between steam engines and ley lines in general. Shortly after Herr Schellen and Mr. Skelly joined us at Haliwar, the two of them entered into a little debate on matters mechanical and magical, in the course of which I was called upon for an opinion. As I do not share your fascination with magnetism, I was forced to refer to that book you loaned me in London.

The three of us proceeded to examine the behavior of some iron filings on a sheet of paper, with and without magnetic influence. Watching the iron dust jump into little whorls around the end of the magnet gave me the notion that perhaps some similar effect might be used to cause ley lines to bend around and over a steam engine. The engine might then pass through the lines without dragging them out of place, as if it were tunneling under them. Schellen and Skelly leapt on the idea, and I confidently expect them to have an experimental model ready for testing within a fortnight.

My fingers are cramping and I refuse to begin another sheet. Whatever else you burn to know, it can wait until Cecelia and I arrive.

Yours,
James

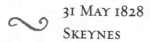 31 MAY 1828
SKEYNES

Dear James,

You may well be on your way south before this letter reaches you. If it goes astray, such is fate. If it reaches you, then just this once you may have it in writing.

I was wrong.

Reggie Winters is not the half-wit I took him for. The

fellow sent me a dozen of port as an apology for having served me with a writ for high treason. I call that handsomely done. As you have always spoken eloquently in his defense, I will share the port with you, provided you don't dally up north until it's all gone.

In truth, you deserve every drop of the stuff. If you hadn't dished the Webbs, the Stockton and Darlington Railway would not have turned out to be such a cracking good investment. Thus, Waltham would never have recouped his fortunes and Georgy might be here still, ghastly thought. Not only that, for the way you've dealt with dreaded Aunt Charlotte, you deserve any amount of port. Come and collect your reward. If it isn't too much trouble, collect your children, too. They're all very well in their way, but they seem to be missing their parents.

Sincerely,
Thomas

June

Dearest Kate,

It was perfectly splendid to see you again; my only regret is that our time at Skeynes was necessarily so brief. Next time, you and Thomas must come to Tangleford, though I cannot promise you anything like the stimulating activity we have all had these past few months. (And a good thing, too!)

The children are still quite full of their visit, most especially their unexpected introduction to a royal princess. I am astonished at all the exciting things you left out of your narratives. I also had no notion that the country around Skeynes was infested with poisonous snakes, nor that they commonly grew to such a great size as Arthur and Eleanor assure me they do. (Arthur has taken it into his head to emulate Edward in keeping a menagerie, and seems to feel that I will be more likely to allow livestock in the nursery if he regales me with tales of the *much worse* things his *much younger* cousin is permitted to do. Eleanor, of course, supports him loyally, though she is far more interested in the new greyhound pup James procured on the drive home.)

Fortunately, I expect their interest in snakes and frogs to be short-lived. The new magic tutor, whom Mr. Wrexton was kind enough to recommend, arrives next week, which should occupy the twins most thoroughly. (And I am most grateful to Thomas for taking them aside and explaining all the bloodcurdling things that would certainly befall anyone foolish enough to attempt to scry through all the protective spells surrounding the royal family, else I am quite sure we would have found Reggie Winters and his men awaiting us at Tangleford, charges of treason and spying in hand. Arthur is quite incorrigible, and Drina made a profound impression on him. And James trusts far too much in the efficacy of a simple, stern parental prohibition, despite several instances in which a prohibition was of no preventative use whatsoever.)

The Wrextons are still in London, but they return to the north next week. Mr. Wrexton has come up with some ideas for reversing the transformation spell that still afflicts the Webbs, and with their artificial ley line net in disarray, the collection of wizards there should have no difficulty in keeping them restrained. James tells me that Lord Wellington is still pondering whether to charge them officially with treason or whether to turn them over to the Royal College of Wizards for the summary judgment of their peers.

He—Lord Wellington, that is—is also considering setting up some more formal office to handle the apprehension and punishment of magical malefactors. It is all very well, James says, to claim that wizards are the only persons truly capable of dealing with magicians and other wizards, but without a department to investigate suspicious incidents and pursue unusual happenings, it is too often mere chance that brings such persons to justice. Since the heir to the throne was very nearly kidnapped and replaced by Conroy and the rest, and since Parliament has been tampered with all unrecognized these many years, and since both these things were the work of rogue magicians, it seems very likely that the duke will carry his point with both Parliament and the king.

I am not certain, but something James said made me think that Lord Wellington intends to appoint Thomas as the first chief of his wizard catchers. He has, after all, demonstrated a certain ability in that regard, and I believe the position is not intended to require much in the way of tact and diplomacy. I think it best if you do not disclose this to Thomas, as it may be only my imagination; I mention it to you only to give you warning enough to prepare for Thomas's inevitable reaction, should it come to pass.

The Royal College has made considerable progress in cleaning up the remains of the Webbs' ley line network. Aunt Elizabeth tells me that there is considerable debate over the advisability of likewise taking down the older network, the ancient one that Cromwell and his wizards made partial use of for their own. She thinks it unlikely that the effort will be made: First, because a magical spell that binds the country together is no bad thing; second, because now that the Royal College is aware of it, the ley lines will be constantly monitored to make certain that no one is tampering with the spell, so it cannot become a new danger; third, because nearly everyone wants to study the network, which they will not be able to do if they destroy it; and fourth and last, because no one has been able to propose a method of dismantling it that is at all likely to work.

The ancient ley line network is, you see, far more intricate and far more stable than anyone had anticipated. Those spell casters knew their work well—Cromwell's network required constant watching and adjusting to last a mere two hundred years, but the old network has been in place for several thousand years, at least, without requiring any additional attention. Mr. Skelly has become so absorbed by the investigation that he rarely even remembers to make critical remarks about England.

James is off to London next week to make a final report to the duke in person; after that, I look forward to a peaceful and uneventful summer, enlivened perhaps by the occasional frog. Even a new and interesting magical tutor is unlikely to *completely* deter my twins, after all.

Your contented,
Cecy